THE LOST LADY OF THE DARKWOODS

A L ROJO

THE
LOST
LADY
OF THE
DARKWOODS

 A catalogue record for this work is available from the National Library of Australia

https://www.nla.gov.au/collections

Title:	The Lost Lady of the Darkwoods
Series:	Shifters of Azanir
Volume:	Book I
Author:	Rojo, A L
ISBNs:	978-0-6488690-4-7 (paperback)
	978-0-6488690-6-1 (ebook-epub)
	978-0-6488690-5-4 (ebook-Kindle)
Subjects:	FICTION: Romance/Paranormal/Shifters; Fantasy/Romance; Romance/Fantasy; Fantasy/General

Cover concept by A L Rojo
Cover design and interior formatting by Katelyn at Design by Kage

A L ROJO

SHIFTERS OF AZANIR
BOOK ONE

ALSO BY A L ROJO

The Pack of Farrowline Series

The Heart of Farrowline
The Power of Farrowline
The Strength of Farrowline
The Pride of Farrowline

AUTHOR NOTE

The Lost Lady of the Darkwoods contains themes of abuse, violence, trauma, explicit language and adult content. This novel is intended for adult readers.

Please head to www.alrojo.com.au for all content warnings and information on all of my novels.

TERMS

Azanir - The realm of the Azanite

Azanite - Shifters of Azanir

Zaric - Language of the Azanites

Azar - Nobility and Royals - An Azar is born into this ranking. Only other way to become an Azar is through binding and finding a mate within this ranking.

Thal - Workers/Commoners of Azanir - A Thal is born into this ranking. The only way to elevate a Thal's status is to complete their training in the Drengar Academy or mate with an Azar.

Drengar - Hunters that protect the realm - Drengar are the only ranking in society an Azanite can work towards. The title holds status in Azanir as they are the protectors of the realm.

Medir - Healers - A Medir is born with the power of the Sun Gods to heal. They can be born of any ranking.

Wraiths - Demons that haunt the night. Wraiths hunt the Azanites for their energy which they need to cross into our world and form shape.

PROLOGUE

*M*Y BODY HURTS. *My eyes sting and I cry out for my daddy until my voice feels like I drank down my hot tea too fast like Nanny Meryl tells me not to. My arms won't work and I cry because the lair that is like my daddy's, but strange and bigger, is burning. The fire looks funny. It's blue and doesn't burn my skin like the one that Kennan uses to make me stop following him. My teeth hurt as they hit together and I don't understand anything because fire burns and doesn't make you cold—right?*

I can hear people shouting and screaming and my heart feels broken. I don't want to look anymore but my feet won't move. I'm at the big scary door to the lair and everyone is running out and I look up when a shadow passes over me and clap my hands to my ears when a screeching sound fills the night.

I scream once more for daddy but he isn't there...

I don't feel good and I open my eyes and scream at the many faces that look down at me.

'No. Not again. Please Daddy. Don't.' I look over at Mummy standing near the door but she turns around and walks away. She never helps me. She is angry at me for something and I don't know why. She is always angry at me, no matter how hard I try to be a good youngling.

I'm scared and try to push the blanket over my head like Nanny Meryl taught me to do when I woke up and felt afraid of my scary dreams.

Daddy is talking to the four men around my bed and I scream and cry for them to leave me alone. Daddy tells the man with the purple eyes to give me the needle that makes me sleep.

'Please Daddy, I don't want to go to sleep! It's scary and it hurts.'

I can hear my Nanny Meryl shouting to everyone to leave me. 'She's but five years old. You can't do this.'

When I look over at her, I have no idea why one of Daddy's big, mean Drengar is holding her. My chest hurts and I cry for someone to help me when the scary Medir comes over to my bed and grabs my arm. His touch always hurts me.

His touch always makes me go back to sleep and to the scary dreams.

TEN YEARS AGO...

The darkness presses against my body.

All I can hear is the pounding of my heart which adds to my fear. I know that if one of the Drengar walk past, they'll be able to hear it too and ruin all the progress I've made.

Back against the cold, stone wall, on a level of the lair I've never been on, I try and fail to draw in enough air into my lungs.

A wave a dizziness rushes my system, forcing me to screw my eyes shut to block out the world. The darkness of the corridor is not helping. It's forcing the beast to the surface of my mind. Her instincts are to find the comfort of our room. The night is no friend to someone like me and why I'm in my father's lair, surrounded by fierce, battle-hardened Drengar.

The Drengar are males born with the skill to defend our realm from the night demons that threaten our existence. They're patrolling the grounds and yet, I still feel the urgency to get somewhere safe. Which is the most confusing aspect of this entire decision.

There's a part of me that believes staying here, in this world, in my father's lair, to be the best place for my survival. However there's another, louder part— the part of my soul that has always marked me as strange and different, the one that haunts my dreams and has me waking most nights screaming at the things I see. The part I keep hidden after learning very young that I shouldn't share what I see. *That's* the part that shouts for me to run.

To leave and never, ever come back.

I'm hurt. I'm confused, and I'm frightened.

No...I'm terrified.

Terrified of what I'm doing and terrified to get caught.

Peeking around the corner, I stay glued to the wall and quickly glance up and down the deserted corridor.

Doubt eats at me but I've made it too far in the plan to give up now. This isn't the first time I've cursed the dreams that give me just enough to frighten me but not enough to tell me anything real.

There's no one in sight, so I move.

Slowly at first, I keep to the cold wall. My hand running along the uneven surface until I get to the next bend.

Beast on high alert, I keep my senses open.

I honestly thought I'd be caught by now. I've made it out of my room, down three flights of stairs and to the back door of the lair without seeing a single Drengar. It's odd and weird and does nothing to help me calm my battered nerves. I've grown up with these halls being guarded constantly.

Stopping when I think I've heard something, I once again plaster myself to the wall and try to manage my raging heartbeat. I can see the door. I know that I only have a few more minutes before the outside guards change, which means, that if I don't move it soon, I'll be stuck here forever.

It's now or never, and never means never. I'll be locked away after this. Or sent to be bound to some male my father will choose for me. A male not fated to me. One that my father will be able to control.

After the conversation I heard between my father and his advisors a week ago, a conversation that had my dreams predicting a terrible future of blood, pain and death, I cannot possibly stay.

I've lived my entire life not knowing why everyone treats me differently. Why my mother detests me and why I'm constantly kept separate to the rest of my family and guarded daily. I always believed it was the dreams, but after learning young to keep my mouth shut, I learnt it had nothing to do with them. Even when I kept what I saw to myself, they never changed their ways. Some dreams are filled with horrors and death, some are of magical places and pleasure.

I was quiet. No one knows I still have them.

I had no answers until that conversation I overheard.

It explained so much and broke my heart at the same time. Everyone has been treating me poorly because of something my father did. It didn't have anything to do with the fact that my beast wasn't strong or that I haven't found my fire, despite my age. I have been treated badly and it wasn't because of my 'weirdness' or my dreams. I discovered so much listening to that conversation. The unfairness kept me in my rooms, praying to the Sun Gods.

I'd rather die than stay here, which is probably going to happen tonight when I get through those doors and out into the night. There are dangers outside these walls, as well as within.

I have my escape planned out. My maid Meryl promised that the humans she has paid to help me are good people.

That's how stupid I am.

The human man that Meryl instructed me to find told her that he'd wait until the moon hits the highest point of the sky before setting sail to the human lands across the wide expanse of ocean. A world forbidden to me. The idea of crossing the Veil between the worlds has me quiver.

A shadow passes down the end of the hall and I hold my breath and push harder against the wall fearing that this is it.

Breathing heavily, I wait, my ears straining as I become hyper-focused on my surroundings. Fear chills my blood when two large, imposing males appear and disappear just as quickly.

Stomach churning, I have no control over my emotions or the beast in my blood who pushes painfully at my skin, causing me to fall to the hard, stone ground on one knee.

Pain shoots through my body at the impact. Gripping my abdomen, I bite the inside of my mouth to stop my cry of agony and taste blood. The damn beast is not making it easy for me to escape. You'd think that she'd be on my team, but no, she hasn't made this entire night easy and I thank the Sun Gods for the first time in my life that she can't take control.

Blinking back tears, I ignore the water dripping down my face and stare at the distance between me and the large wooden door. The endless void seems to grow as does my doubt that this is the right thing for me to do. I've never stepped foot out of the lair with the sun asleep. Never.

Right now, I long to be in my bed waking to one of my terror nightmares, feeling a different kind of fear. Not this mind-numbing terror pulsing through my veins right now. A terror that has my lip wobbling and my body vibrating.

With one last shaky breath, I judge the distance from where I stand and the door to my freedom and run. I run and run and push open the heavy wood and never look back.

CHAPTER ONE

*T*HE DARKNESS IS HEAVY *as it presses against my body.*
I sink further and further downward into the icy water. Limbs like lead and my body fighting with itself to take a deep breath, I grieve everything that I've left behind.

I can see the flashes above. A violent storm. I know that this is my end.
That this is how I die.

'Stop it, Raff.'

Rolling my eyes, I keep my focus on my breakfast and not on the lady behind the kitchen counter whipping up a batch of pancakes. It doesn't matter that I'm an adult now, she still reprimands me like the dirty, hungry teen that appeared at her front door nine years ago, all moody and broken, waiting for her to decide to keep me.

'I didn't do anything,' I protest lamely and glare at the smug fiend down the chipped table smirking in my direction.

'You're playing with your food, girl. Stop or tell us what's the matter,' Laney exclaims, leaving no room for argument. Laney is not someone you want to mess with. She's tall for a human female, practically skin and bone, with warm blonde, straw-ish hair that falls in a neat thin, mass down her

1

back. There's an energy about Laney Matters that screams independence and confidence, which I guess is needed in a suburb like Grisham. The docks are not that far from our street and the main city is only a bus trip north. We live in what's known as the 'rough' part of town.

I stop mixing my oats and begin to spoon some reluctantly into my mouth. Despite my constant hunger, I don't have the stomach for it today. I woke up feeling restless and tense. The typically quiet beast in my blood, who I've spent ten painstaking years ignoring, seems to be stirring. The pain in my gut while I stood under the scolding shower after I rolled out of bed an hour ago was enough to have tears fill my vision and me cry out in agony.

She's not happy about something and that thought has my mind a million miles from the cosy, run-down house. I haven't felt her in so long that there are days that I forget that she's there, that I'm not like the others eating around me right now.

Laney's strays.

We're a mis-matched group of abandoned souls, all brought together and loved by the woman now demanding Van stop teasing me.

The shit-stirrer still smirking down the table drops the look and opens and closes his mouth in shock at being caught eyeing me like we're teenagers again getting each other into trouble.

'Busted,' Danny whispers from beside me. The boy is relatively new to the house and I grin at the way his mouth shuts when Van throws the young kid the evil eye. I have to give it to my best friend, he's a pain in my arse most days, and I'd never give him a compliment willingly, so as to not over-inflate an already inflated ego, but he gives a very convincing glare.

Poor Danny doesn't know what to do and I jump in to save the new kid.

'Van just can't keep his eyes off me, Laney. It's not his fault that he finds me irresistible,' I tease, keeping my voice serious and unaffected by the chuckles that fill the house. Danny isn't the only new soul. While I grew up with Van, the two young children sitting across from me, Tiffany and Toby, are still trying to find their place amongst the chaos.

Not that it'll take them long to settle in. Laney's purpose in life is to spread love and provide a safe-haven for lost souls— her words, not mine.

Which is exactly what I was when Van found me behind his school digging in the trash bins looking for food. A very lost, lonely and frightened soul, learning how to live in this strange human world.

I had to learn the rules of this society quickly. The language was the hardest part to pick up.

The humans at my father's lair spoke this tongue but only Drengar and male Azar were permitted to learn. An 'Azar' is the title given to the ruling class of Azanir—my birth realm. It's kind of like calling someone a noble, in human terms. I learnt that comparison in my human history lessons. The Drengar, our hunters, learn because they're out in the world, keeping it safe from the wraiths, so it's a necessity for their role.

Meaning, I had no idea how to say hello when I first got here.

I think everyone thought I was unable to speak in the beginning. Laney hired a speech therapist in the first year I was with her. A very kind, older lady with grey hair that she always rolled at the back of her head. It didn't take me long to pick it up with her help.

I owe everything to Laney.

I'm twenty four years old and she still hasn't kicked me out. When I first showed up all dirty and skinny on her doorstep with Van begging her to let me stay, I was sceptical and suspicious of the entire situation. I hid food under my bed for months and Laney didn't bat an eyelid at my behaviour. Even when I started to feel more comfortable and began to hang sheets over the large window in my bedroom, and horde blankets and pillows on my bed to create a little lair to rest in and feel safe, she never made it seem like what I was doing was odd.

In all fairness, at first, I didn't realise that humans slept in open rooms, with the moonlight beaming in through glass, unprotected by the evils of the night, until I moved into Laney's house. Despite living away from Azanir, I'm still frightened to be out in the dark.

When I made it to the docks, I always found shelter in fear of wraiths, demons of the night, that hunt my kind for their energy and fire.

It seems conditioning and having fear shoved down your throat from the moment you're born does have an effect.

I was always weird, even as a youngling, and I guess I always will be. I ran from a world because I didn't have a place and thought that things would be easier for me here. I was wrong.

Van and my found family gave me hell for months when I first moved in about the way I covered the walls in my room and slept surrounded by soft things.

'Yeah, our Raff is irresistible. Like a moth to a flame, with one touch, you're dead.' Van makes a show of running his hand over his throat before faking his untimely death.

A shiver runs over my body. He's not far from the truth. If only he knew who sat at the table with him right now, playing with her oats. It's a thought I've contemplated for the nine years I've been sitting at this table. Ten years, if I include the one year I lived on the streets. It's a long time to keep a secret.

A dangerous secret.

Chapter Two

Laney reprimands Van like the mother figure she is.

'Sorry, Laney,' Van concedes with a wink in my direction when he catches me staring.

I've no power over the smile that breaks across my face. Van's a troublemaker and a massive pain in my arse but I love him beyond words. He's tall with lean muscles. He works at a gym as a trainer. His dark, blonde hair is all messy and falls over his ears and eyes. Laney's always on his back to get a haircut but apparently, 'chicks dig it,' which makes no sense.

Van's also really smart despite the fact that he never finished school.

'His temper got in the way of his future', the head teacher at our local high school told Laney the day he was kicked out.

It was also the day I tried to quit too, but neither Laney, Van nor my other foster brothers would let me. I had opened up a great deal once I started human schooling.

It was much better than the tutors I had back in Azanir. My early years were a lonely experience.

I loved learning about the history of this world and I fell in love with their music. Everything changed the day I found myself in a program learning how to play the piano and violin and anything else I could get my hands on. There was no music in my father's lair. Only at feasts or special occasions would they hire the human minstrels to come and perform. I was never really allowed at those gatherings. It was always 'unsafe' for me to be around the Azar—the nobility.

I didn't want to listen at first when they tried to stop me from leaving school with Van though. I was adamant that I wasn't going to stay if he wasn't there. Eventually they all wore me down and I conceded and ended up finishing. Van's my best friend and loyalty's a character flaw of my beast.

'Just eat your breakfast,' Laney tsks. 'We all have a busy week ahead of us with the wedding and all. Van, you said that you'd mow the lawns after work and Danny, you can help after school. Raff, you need to be at the church this afternoon for the rehearsal, so don't forget. I know you have that presentation at work you've been trying to finish so make sure you organise your time today.'

Dread feels like bricks in my stomach. Originally, I thought this morning's meltdown in the shower was because I have a big presentation on Friday which could lead to a major promotion. Meaning a pay rise that'll not only help me, but Laney and the others. However, I don't think that's the problem. I feel like something is wrong. That something big and momentous is coming.

'You have a funny name, Raff,' Tiffany mumbles from across the table and I chuckle at the way her stoic, silent brother gasps and throws her a mighty death stare. Tiffany pales and shuts her mouth and I can taste the fear leaking from the pair of newbies.

Laney finds the entire thing funny as she moves from the kitchen to the table with a pile of sweet smelling pancakes balancing precariously on a chipped serving dish.

Van eliminates the tension from the young kids by agreeing in his smart-arse kind of way. His brown eyes sparkling as he looks to me to evaluate my reaction.

I don't take offense to him checking, I've been known to get grumpy quickly. In all fairness, it's sometimes not in my control how much my moods flip-flop around. They should try living with a beast in their body—even a quiet one like mine is loud enough.

'I can't tell you how many times I've told our Raffy that she can change it.'

I continue to force the oats down my throat, uncaring of the conversation. Raff is not my full name. It's a nickname one of my maids used to called me back in my past life. However, no one around this table will ever find that out—not if I have anything to say about it anyway.

Contemplating the repercussions of my secret and what they'd all do if they found out who I actually was, I feel the muscles in my left arm tense and ripple. I hide my gasp and hurriedly place my arm in my lap, my heart rate spikes. I've never felt my beast like that before and end up trying to control my breathing.

Laney sits and says, 'now, let's stop giving Raff a hard time and finish our breakfast.'

'Who's givin' our Raffy a hard time?' a new voice says as the back door is opened. It's enough to help me find my composure.

Laney lights up at the appearance of two of her favourite strays and the woman trailing behind the pair of bulky men with her focus on the device in her hand. I swear every time I see Carly these days, it's with that damn phone.

Scott and Brent, my foster brothers, are wide shouldered, bad-mouthed and love to be the loudest people in a room. But like Van, I love them beyond words. Even when they make me do things I do *not* want to do. Laney ushers them all closer to the table and hops up to get more plates and food for our new arrivals.

'I think...I think it was me that...that was giving her a hard time,' Tiffany stutters in a voice that has Laney look up sharply from the plates she is organising. Van frowns over at the young girl. Her terror tastes horrible in my mouth.

Before I can tell her that she is safe, Scott steps up to the table. The chair he pulls out scrapes along the floor, making Tiffany wince and I don't think that I'm the only one to notice the way her brother shuffles closer to her side as if ready to spring into action and defend his sister if things get violent.

It makes me mad and I have no control over the low rumble that happens in the back of my throat. Tiffany's wide, frantic eyes look to me in both question and horror and I dip my head and shove a spoon of oats into my mouth to shut my beast up.

She's so unsettled today, and I bite the inside of my mouth to keep her rage in check. I just hate the fear such a small, defenceless little human girl has. She is nine. Nine! She refuses to sleep anywhere but next to her brother each night and from the report Laney shared with me the day before they were removed from their last foster home, I know exactly why.

It makes me murderous. I ran from my home and my family, from my father and the Drengar who are all cold, rigid males. They have powers these humans could only dream about and yet, they'd never, *ever*, hurt a youngling or a female the way some human men and woman do.

Instilling fear is not a gauge for power and strength. It's a weakness of people who believe themselves mightier than what they truly are.

Something I've learnt some humans need to learn.

The oats turn to ash in my mouth and I quickly swallow away the evidence of my rage.

Scott and the others either ignore the involuntary sound that I just growled or didn't hear it because no one bats an eyelid in my direction or acknowledges Tiffany's pale face.

Taking the seat beside the girl, Scott makes a show of pulling out a chair for his fiancé and helps Carly sit while she texts.

Brent grabs the plate Laney quietly brings over and begins to fill it high with pancakes and eggs. He sits down beside Van.

'Well, continue,' Brent declares like he's asking someone to pass the butter. His eyes are set on Tiffany and his smile is one not many can refuse. Brent is all beard and rough features. His arms are covered in tattoos and the leather patchwork vest he wears screams authority.

I scowl. Van laughs loudly. Laney sighs and Tiffany pales even more.

'Wh...what do you mean?'

The poor kid.

'I mean, continue giving Raff a hard time.'

Now I know they heard the noise I accidently just made. Scott grins wide before he winks at me and even Carly looks up with a small frown as if confused by what she has just heard. Laney just stays out of it.

'We could start with that bed of hers,' Scott offers while helping Carly fill her plate. 'All those pillows and the weird obsession she has with everything being soft.'

Damn fools all laugh at me. Even Danny cracks a smile.

'Or her room in general. All those blankets hanging over the windows and walls to make it dark,' Van interjects, a little too enthusiastically for my liking.

'Or the way she makes those funny noises and will never be outside at night, like never go out or leave the house,' Brent continues.

'How about that time in the beginning when she cut her hand pretty bad and she shouted at Van and then sat out on the back grass baking in the sun with nothing but her underwear and bra, and that night it looked like her hand was almost completely fixed.' Scott laughs. I cringe. Laney chuckles. Brent seems uncomfortable. Van just grins like he's remembering how I got that stupid cut and how it *was* all his fault. I want to open my mouth and tell them all that I wasn't sunbathing but stay quiet.

'What about the height. She's freakishly tall for a chick.'

'But has killer legs,' Danny chimes in and then shuts his mouth when Brent, Scott and Van glare warningly at him. The poor kid is beetroot red and my small chuckle matches Laney's. It's the only thing that eliminates the charged tension.

Of course it's Van who starts back up again with, 'what about the weird grey eyes? If you really stare at them, they seem to glow,' like he has no idea how to read a room.

I internally flinch. There are moments in my life that I have no idea how the people around me haven't asked me who I really am.

'How about the fact that everyone in this damn neighbourhood is afraid of her because of that one time Van got beat-up by the Stanley foster kids, and then she went all feral and started a fire in their front lawn after kicking the four boys arse.'

Danny sits in rapture, listening to Scott's story that turns into a full blown argument and tease session as Van defends the fact that he was not 'beat-up', while I try to suppress the memory of that damn day.

The fire was not my fault. I didn't even know I could do it. I had never been able to before and was one of the reasons I was treated so badly back in my father's lair.

Laney was not impressed that day though. It took me months to pay off the fine and the bill for the property damage by doing odd jobs around the neighbourhood.

Tiffany's small, timid giggle makes the entire table relax and I find myself unable to care about the teasing knowing that she's not afraid anymore.

Laney comes back to her seat and hands Brent a plate of food while she tells us all to move on from this conversation and leave me alone.

'Thank you,' I manage to say just as I take a gulp of water to wash away the yukky after-ash taste in my mouth.

'Yes, let's move on. Raff, we need you at the church at five,' Carly exclaims as I groan loudly. The laughter around the table is both annoying and uplifting. 'You said you'd be okay to play at the wedding. Do you not want to do it anymore? It's next Saturday. I don't know what I'll do if you can't play. Daddy has told all his business associates that you're playing after Scott sung your praises for months when Mummy was trying to find musicians.'

On and on she goes as I'm reminded for the billionth time since Scott proposed last year that she's getting married.

I've no power over the way I look over at Van, who does the exact same thing back. He rolls his eyes and I bite my lip to keep from smiling. It's not that we don't like Carly, she's nice and sweet to Laney, but there's an air about her. An energy that rubs me the wrong way. She has long blonde hair that you can tell costs a fortune to get that shiny. Her features are feminine and soft, kinda like she paid for that chin and the nose. And she is rich. She reminds me of too many females I grew up around.

We still have no idea how Scott even got a chance to speak to her, let alone date and now marry her. I think her dad is some kind of CEO...I have no fucking idea, and is it bad to say I don't really care?

I mean, Scott's happy, Laney likes her and she doesn't turn her nose up at our small, run-down house. Or at the fact that our fence is half broken and there have been three gunshots in the last hour since we started breakfast, so I don't hate her. It's just another character flaw of mine—loyalty and distrust. Scott is mine to protect and I just don't know her well enough.

'No,' Scott grumbles. 'Raff will play for us. Won't ya, Raffy?'

I don't miss the subtle warning in my foster brothers tone or the 'don't make my already stressed fiancé even more stressed' look he throws me.

'Of course, Raffy is excited,' Laney chimes.

Yeah—playing for hundreds of people during the most important day of Scott's life with a beast under my skin who's making it very hard for me to concentrate right now and could do fuck knows what on the day of the event to make it hard for me, like she did the last time I had a super important performance a few years ago— yeah, super excited...

I just nod and mumble my agreeance.

CHAPTER THREE

'FUCKING! FUCKIN'! SHIT! THIS day sucks.' I groan and bang my head on the cheap desk.

Laney used to find it hilarious that some of the first words I spoke were cuss words. My high school on the other hand, did not.

Van and I thought for years that she had no idea that he'd sneak into my room late at night and help me to learn all the naughtiest words that he knew—

which were a lot. I'm not ashamed to admit that it took me a while to realise that he was teaching me something that'd get me in trouble.

Damn Van.

'Bad day?'

I don't bother to look up at the man who has just walked into my crappy office. Firstly, because I knew he was coming the moment he stepped off the elevator at the other end of the floor, and also because he warned me yesterday that he was going to drop in today and buy me lunch.

The smell of lemon bodywash and harsh tones of musk aftershave fill my nostrils as he moves around my seat to lean over my shoulder to see what me has cursing the universe.

'Why is the screen flashing white and blue like that?'

My next groan is deep and loud. Miles just laughs like I'm the funniest person he's ever spoken to, but that's Miles, I guess. Always laughing. Always positive. Always a little too eager and pushy.

Miles is the reason I got a job here. We met four years ago in a bar just after I bombed an audition for one of the most prestigious musical colleges in the country. We drank, we flirted, we had fun and then he offered to help me get a job at the fancy advertising firm he worked for.

I started working here at the reception desk, booking meetings for the executives and doing computer admin. Now, I'm a junior team member working under a nice older lady. After next week, if all goes well with the meeting, I could be promoted and be making some good money. With more mouths to feed, Laney needs the cash. The funding she gets barely covers school items for the kids and I need to start thinking about my future.

But nothing's going to happen in my meeting if this damn screen doesn't stop flashing at me.

Miles leans over and taps away at the keyboard to my left, mumbling to himself about how I'm the only one he knows who could break a computer software system created by leading experts in the country.

'Honestly, Raff, this office has state of the art technology. How did you do this?'

Looking up, I tuck my hands under my chin and lay against the table, my focus on the flashing screen. 'I don't know,' I whine. 'I didn't do anything. I was just about to save all my work because I have to leave to get to the church and the piece of shit computer started doing this.' Rage ripples through my body, blurring my vision and has me clench my eyes shut to help calm myself down.

This fucking day!

I should've gone back to bed after the shower incident this morning. I should've thrown the mountain of blankets everyone was teasing me about at breakfast over my head and ignored the day. Laney would've given me a hard time and Van would've probably taken the day off work to sit in my pitch-black room with all its pillows and blankets on my double bed and watch bad TV with me.

'We need to get this to the IT department.' Miles stands tall and after checking his expensive watch, grabs the phone from his back pocket, mumbling about how late in the afternoon it is, and starts texting away. I just sit and watch him.

Miles calls someone and begins to speak to a guy name Dwight about what my screen is doing and I comply when he instructed me on which buttons to turn on—all of them I've already pressed. He smirks when he asks me if I tried to turn the computer off and on and I throw him a mighty glare.

'I'm not incompetent,' I mutter and huff when he tells me that someone will come pick up the computer. I look out the long window to my right and the bright sunshine outside and wish for the hundredth time today to be outdoors. My energy is lapsing and I need a boost so bad that my skin starts to itch. That's the one thing about living in the human world that I'll never get used to. They spend too much time indoors. Too much time out of the sun and not under its warmth and power.

'They'll be here in an hour.'

'I'm never going to get this done.' The realisation hits hard enough to have my heart rate spike and my palms go all sweaty. Flight or fight is not the bodily response I need right now. The beast becomes unbearable when my adrenaline spikes.

'You'll be fine for your presentation on Monday.' His words make me a little less homicidal. 'However, if you don't move your butt right now, you won't survive what your brother's going to do if you don't get to that church for the rehearsal. Come, I'll buy you lunch on the way.'

That makes me laugh and pulls me out of my overpowering thoughts of how hot I am and how a bead of sweat is dripping down my back.

'Fuck, you're right. Scott will actually kill me if I'm late. He's become extra over-the-top and it has everything to do with Carly and her family. I don't know why I said yes to playing. I felt pressured.' Sighing, I lean under the table to grab the heavy wooden case protecting the expensive instrument inside. An instrument I normally only play in the privacy of my own room. For myself.

'You worried that it'll happen again?' His tone draws me from my thoughts and plunges me back into the small well of nerves in my stomach. I don't know why I told Miles about the incident that had me pack away my instrument and refuse to play for anyone ever again. I guess it was the night I discovered my love for expensive scotch and Miles had to basically carry me home. Which was also the night Scott, Brent and Van met Miles for the first time. Saying it didn't go well is an understatement.

'It was pretty dramatic. I fainted on stage in front of all those people and totally ruined my chances of getting into Joffrey's Academy of Music.'

It was the only time in my life that I actually felt my skin bend and stretch painfully. Before I passed out under the pain, I truly thought I was going to do something I'd never done before. Something that I was always told growing up that I'd be unable to achieve. To let my beast take over and shift my form is not a gift I have. Maybe that's why she is so angry today. Maybe she wants out.

Miles's heavy hand falls on my shoulder. 'It was five years ago, Raf. You're a different person now.' I don't know what my face is screaming but it's enough to have Miles cackle in laughter. 'I'll take you to lunch and then to the church. Get your things.'

Now eating my bottom lip, I quickly work through my options. Weighing the pro and cons of catching the train and bus to the upper north side of the city where the rich live or taking Miles with me to the rehearsal.

'Scott and Brent will be there.'

I don't understand the soft look on his face or why he finds that funny again. Scott and Brent aren't the biggest fans of Miles. Frankly, they're downright rude and hostile to the man who they believe 'only wants to get in my pants', which I find disturbing on so many levels. Mostly because Miles is my friend, maybe my only friend outside of my foster family.

He's one of the only human males that I've ever found kinda attractive. I guess he's handsome. He's tall, with light brown hair which is always styled in a perfect crew cut. His nose and jaw are very symmetrical and he's really nice and supportive and always brings me coffee and food, which is the best way to win me and my beast over. However, the bitch under my skin refuses to let me get close to any man. Every time I feel an inclination of lust or sexual interest, she shuts it down rapidly.

Bitch.

'Scott and Brent don't intimidate me, Raff. They're just being good big brothers. Come, I'll text I.T to get this done for tomorrow. If Scott doesn't try and maim me that is.'

I agree, but deep down I know there's a high chance that might just happen and I'll end up having to protect him...again.

CHAPTER FOUR

ESPITE HOW OVERBEARING MILES can be sometimes, I like the way he lets me be...me. I've been half out the car window soaking up the sun's energy since we left the café and he hasn't said a thing. Nor does he raise an eyebrow when I jump out of the car when we finally pull up in front of the big church and pull my work heels off. Placing my wooden case down, I stand, barefoot, on the pristine, crisp green lawn within the church grounds.

Arms wide, I soak in the warmth of the blazing sun. Every ray of light feels amazing and I lavish in the heat that seeps into my pores and through my body. Bringing with it the joy of its energy and power.

I sigh in pure pleasure and feel my muscles relax for the first time all day.

I stand like that undisturbed until I think I hear a click like my photo has just been taken and I twirl around to Miles's telling me that we should go inside. I put my shoes reluctantly on and follow him up the impressive stairs of the building.

I feel good. Really good. Until the inside of the church comes into view and we both stop in our tracks.

It takes me way too long to register everything I'm seeing. 'This is...'

'Over the top?' Miles offers as I seem to have lost the words for what I'm seeing.

Standing side by side at the open door to the church, I take in the explosion of lace and flowers and decorations and fight the need to avert my eyes from the overstimulation.

'That's an understatement. How are they allowed to do this when the wedding is a week away?'

Miles shrugs as I try to process. There are people everywhere. An arch at the start of the aisle, a red carpet, half made flower arrangements at the end of every long pew and then some monstrosity of a stand at the very front, near the altar. I can't bring myself to look at the musicians area that has been created at the left front corner. In my opinion, it's all one big mistake and completely distracts from the beauty that is the old building. It has a gorgeous domed, exposed beamed roof with stained glass windows around the entire structure.

'Excuse me.' The very firm voice has me shift my focus from the ceiling to the woman now in front of us. She's short and wearing a very pink pantsuit and has the tightest bun at the back of her head that I'm not sure how she can function. Her eyes skim unchecked over my outfit and she eyes me like I'm some kind of troll. 'You can't be here. This is a *private* event. The church is closed.'

'Aren't churches open to the public?'

'Not this one. Not for two weeks.'

I have no idea how they can do this. I knew Carly's family were rich and important but rich enough to shut down a church...

Every word she speaks grates on my nerves. It's condescending and I follow her gaze and look down at my outfit. My black pants and loose sleeve, ruff trimmed, green blouse are from a mainstream department store but they don't look too bad. I look to Miles for the answer, and bless him, he shakes his head at me as if understanding what I'm asking by my raised eyebrows.

She doesn't seem at all offended by the sight of Miles though. Her purse lips morph into a flirtatious smirk. 'Stephanie Hill.' Her manicured hand comes out to offer Miles a handshake while I stand forgotten. Obviously his designer suit doesn't insult her.

'Miles Bradford. We're invited. Raff here is the music.' Miles offers his hand while placing the other against my lower back as if providing some kind of comfort. However, I can't seem to care that much about what Stephanie thinks. She has nothing on the evil female I thought was my mother for thirteen years. She can look at me with all the judgement in the world because nothing can compare to the fire in my stepmothers gaze.

Stepmother? Is that the right term? What do you call the female that your father is mated to that he cheated on and produced a child—me—behind her back? Let's stick with stepmother. It seems fitting. I read a fairy-tale once with an evil stepmother character and couldn't help but visualise her. I'm self-aware enough to know that I have some deep-seated issues around the female I thought was my mother and her lack of love for me as a youngling. Up until the day I discovered the truth, I truly thought that I was the issue. That I was in some way 'bad'. Learning it wasn't me but the circumstances of my birth that caused the hatred, made the entire situation worse though.

So, when this woman nods after throwing me a look that screams, 'how could your department store clothes get this designer guy' and then tells us to 'follow', I don't bat an eyelid. Her heels click against the stone floor as she storms away.

Miles whispers, 'you look lovely Raff. She's just jealous that she doesn't look like you.'

I cringe and hide it as best I can. Sometimes I see what Scott and Brent mean when they tell me that Miles is a little much.

I don't know if I should be offended that she makes a point of moving away from the expensive looking decorations and around the side of the pews like my poor outfit might ruin the luxury of the place.

Scott and Carly appear from a door with a greying priest just as we reach the front. All three seem to be having an amazing afternoon. There are a lot more people around the front of the pews, all young and pretty and excited.

Clutching the case I refuse to let Miles carry for me, I ignore the not so subtle glances my way and return Scott's smile when he sees me. Poor Carly doesn't seem like she really wants to be coming over and talking to us right now but she does and we share an awkward hug.

'I thought you'd miss the rehearsal,' is all she says and I quickly check my watch to realise I'm about five minutes later than the time Scott told me to be here, which is half an hour before the actual rehearsal starts.

When I don't offer an apology, Miles steps in with a quick greeting that's returned by Carly and frowned at by Scott. I never notice how large my foster brothers are until situations like this. We all grew up on the streets, until we were taken in by Laney, so they're all muscle heavy dudes with an air of violence about them. The streets harden you.

Miles does his best to not look too uncomfortable when Scott says, 'I didn't expect to see you here, Miles.'

'I offered Raff a ride.' He points in my direction as I try to tell Scott to back off my with eyes. But he isn't listening.

'Thanks. I'll take her home.'

I could slap him.

'It's fine, he can watch. He'll be here next Saturday, won't you Miles?'

'He will?' Scott and I say together. I had no idea that he was invited. Carly has only met him a handful of times and Scott doesn't even try to hide his dislike of the man.

'Of course, he's your date, isn't he?'

The question leaves me dumbstruck and confused. 'I don't have a date.' I never RSVP'd for a plus one. *Did I?* I still sometimes get confused when filling things out and understanding forms. The invitation to this wedding was definitely a confusing mess of questions about diet and restrictions and times and dress code.

'What do you mean you don't have a date?' Carly asks like it's an afront to nature that I'd be a female without a date to a wedding.

Is it wrong to slap the bride five days before her wedding? Probably...actually...nah, probably not the best idea.

'I mean, I don't have a date. I didn't know I needed one.' I look to Scott for some support but he's being no help and I swear that the sides of his lips are twitching. Now, I know I can slap the groom and get away with it!

Van appears beside me the moment Miles turns to me and says, 'I could be your date, Raff.'

Van's laughter fills the church and Scott grumbles a, 'not gonna happen,' just as I open my mouth and stutter, 'I...uhhhh...I...'

Who knew I'd be saved by Carly who unexpectedly says, 'Oh!' as if she didn't just throw me under the bus. She's completely clueless of the awkwardness she has created.

It's not that I don't like Miles. The problem is that I'm already anxious about playing and the reception is at night. I don't like going out at night and I'm not sure I'll be able to ignore the pull in my soul to get inside. I don't know how all that is going to work and I didn't even think about inviting him. Also, this'll be my first human wedding and I don't know the protocol so I didn't want to invite someone who wasn't actually invited and who Scott doesn't like.

It's fair to say a lot was going through my head when I sat down to RSVP to this damn wedding.

Turning, Carly waves towards a very stern looking woman speaking to two very nervous younger ladies up the aisle. 'Mother, come and meet Scott's foster sister, Raff. She's our violinist.'

Mrs Carly's Mother—*I really should remember what Carly's surname is*— waves back and heads towards us and frankly if the world opened under my feet to swallow me whole, I probably wouldn't try to run away and just let it take me. Anything would be better than being here right now.

Carly's mum looks exactly like Carly. Her blonde hair is obviously dyed and her face has definitely had work because she looks like she could be her sister. Not that I judge. You do you—I always say. What I can judge her for is the way she runs her blue eyes over my outfit and then forces a smile before focusing on Carly. 'Wow, you're so tall for a woman. It's a pleasure, *Raff*,' she says with a hint of criticism of my name. 'Carly, the florist needs you before we get started.' Clearly done with me and this conversation, Mrs Carly's Mum turns from us.

'Of course. Just take a seat and I'll let you know when you need to get in position.' Carly isn't looking at us anymore and she finishes her sentence as she hurries off.

'I should get going.' Miles isn't looking at me and I know I've hurt his feelings. He too hurries off after telling me he'll see me tomorrow and I just can't find the emotions to feel bad when Scott tells us that I'll be playing in twenty minutes.

CHAPTER FIVE

'SHUT UP,' I WARN the smirking fool beside me. 'What're you even doing here?'

'Just wanted to come and watch. Ya know? Support my sister from another mister.'

Rolling my eyes, I don't say a word. Van is lucky he's from 'another mister' as he so eloquently put it.

'I don't need support,' I reply. 'I'm not going to fall apart again.'

I hope.

His snicker doesn't give me much hope or support. 'So, you gonna invite Miles to the wedding?'

'Fuckin' hell,' I mumble. 'I kinda have to now, don't I?' I'm really contemplating just faking that I'm sick on the wedding day. I try to back-plan an illness in my mind instantly.

Maybe if I start coughing next Monday, I can hype it up on Friday and then be all set to stay home on the Saturday.

'You're thinking about how you can get out this, aren't ya?'

'No.' *Damn Van.*

'Yes, ya are. I can see the little wheels ticking over in your brain.' I swat his finger as it curls in the air around my temple and bite back a curse.

Chuckling, Van leans back on the pew and wraps an arm around my shoulders. 'If I have to go to this nightmare of a wedding, you have to come too.'

'And who's your date?'

'Missy Tomos,' he says all proud of himself like Missy Tomos is a prize he's won.

'Fuckin' hell,' I repeat louder. Missy has lived on our street my entire time with Laney. She's a stunning, long legged player, who has a new fling every week. I kinda like her and kinda wanna punch her in the nose, so that should be fun. Add that to the many reasons why I should start complaining of a sore throat now.

'Speaking of nightmares, I heard your one last night. You okay? It's been years since I've heard you speak in your dreams.'

Freezing, I feel the colour drain from my face. I slowly turn my head to look at my foster brother. He's checking-out the ladies who are walking up and down the aisles talking about flowers, completely unaware of how he has made me feel. Closing my eyes, I try to remind myself that I'm safe. That no one is here to force me to sleep.

It took me so long as a youngling to work out what they were doing to me. Why they wanted me to live in my nightmares and why after a particularly bad experience when I was eight, I began to keep what I saw to myself and pretend like I no longer had the dreams. My father and his Medir, Azanites gifted with the healing power of the Sun Gods, eventually stopped coming to my rooms. Until I woke a few weeks before I ran away to a Medir over my bed, my father at the door, and I realised that I must have spoken in my sleep—loud enough for them to hear.

I quickly wipe my face when a stupid tear slips from between my lids. I hate that there's still so much fear.

'Do you reckon you'd want something like this one day?'

Frowning, I try to process what he means. With my mind locked in the pain and horror of my past, I roll my eyes when I realise what he's talking about.

Yeah right...I find the whole idea of binding yourself to another living being for eternity to be the absolute stupidest thing a person can do. I don't understand why anyone would do this willingly.

Sometimes I envy humans though. It's not the first time I've wished that I could belong to one world and not be half human, half beast. I believed that living fully with humans would help me to feel a sense of belonging. Help me to not feel so different and out of place.

However, it seems that I'm cursed to never feel like I belong.

Humans are odd. I do envy that while there is power in their ceremonial wedding, they can easily break it with a simple document once they terminate their marriage in a courtroom.

In the world I was raised, there are strict laws, marriage or a *binding*, is unbreakable. When an Azanite finds their mate, they begin what they call a 'mating dance' where their beasts are said to take over control in order for the binding to be completed and their souls to be united. It is for life. In every sense of the word.

Fastening two souls together is serious stuff and is one of the reasons why I refuse to go back. Females are precious and few. Each one is valued, cherished, and bound as soon as they can, to continue our race. Well, all females...except me. I'm a half breed, an abomination, so I guess I don't count.

'Was that eye roll a resounding no?'

'What do you think?' Trying to not let my face show how absurd this whole show is, I keep my thoughts to myself. Scott and Carly are at the front of the aisle talking with the elderly priest while Carly's mother demands things of the two poor ladies running around behind her with their devices taking notes on flowers and aisle decorations—it's all giving me a headache.

'I think that what Scott has is rare. I think that people like us never get a fairy-tale ending, Raff. Love. Marriage. Money. All of this is not going to happen. We're not born to this kind of privilege.'

It's Van's spike in emotions that draws my attention away from Carly's mother who is now scolding one of the workers about the fact that you cannot mix purple and red flowers.

Words get stuck in my mouth. Words that confess my sins and lies about who I really am.

Van and I are nothing alike.

'Scott found it,' I mumble, taking in the extravagance and opulence of this wedding. Scott looks good in his brand-new trousers and his professional looking button up. He looks happy despite how much shit Van and Brent have given him over the last few months since the engagement.

'Scott got lucky.'

Van's scepticism rubs me the wrong way but before I can say anything Carly starts clapping loudly, her voice piercing through the quiet conversations happening in the church.

'Okay. Okay, everyone.' Carly rubs her hands together and stands at the front of the church acting like a schoolteacher trying to get us all to listen to instructions. It seems a bit excessive because the two bridesmaids, Stephanie included, are sitting on the first pew with their backs straight, hands clasped, waiting like good students. The others stop talking instantly to give the bride their undivided attention.

'Yes, Miss,' Van says under his breath, clearly thinking the same thing I am and I can't help but snicker along with him.

Perfectly manicured brows narrow towards us.

Biting my smile so that I don't get in trouble with the "school maam", I roll my eyes when Scott turns sharply to give us one of his signature glares that screams at us to shut up. It just makes Van laugh louder until Brent appears behind us and whacks him up the back of the head, shutting us both up instantly.

Brent is the eldest. He's hard as nails, rides a motorbike with a bunch of other equally intimidating men and they all wear leather vests. I've heard on the street about who Brent is, but to me, he is my brother. In every way that matters.

Leaning forward, Brent rest his thick arms along the back of the wood pew and asks me how I'm feeling. The case beside my leg seems heavier at the mention of what I'm expected to do.

Shrugging, I whisper, 'fine, I guess. It's not like I haven't played before.'

'No, but you don't like playing in front of people and these ones are extra douche-ie.'

Brent makes me laugh.

'I should be okay.'

'Well, if you feel lightheaded, you're to stop and sit down. We don't need you falling and hitting your head again and ending up in the hospital. Laney nearly had a meltdown last time.'

'I know.'

'We were all worried about you.'

A flutter of emotion forms in my chest and I push it aside. I'm fully aware that I'm not the most loving and affectionate person around. I'm stand-offish, emotionally stunted, and a little too grunty, but I do love my found family.

I listen to Carly explain how next Saturday is going to work and ignore the way my skin crawls when I hear her mention my name and explain the cue that will indicate for me to start playing. That's when ten sets of eyes swing my way. Three of them narrow. Two roll, Stephanie being one of them, and one looks for a little too long at my face and then at my chest.

Creep.

Fighting with my lips to not pull back to show the weird older business dude at the front of the church my teeth, I don't hear my name and the way Carly is telling me to get in position until Brent nudges me.

Crap.

CHAPTER SIX

D *ARKNESS HAS A WEIGHT. A heaviness to it that makes it hard to breath. My heart beats too hard and all I can hear is my heavy breathing in the darkness. I know that I'm in danger. I know that I need to find my way out of here and that I'm completely alone.*

Trapped.

Every hair on my body stands on end as I wave my arms around in front of me, trying to figure out where I am.

A noise has me stop and strain to understand what could be out there stalking me.

The minutes tick by as I stand, waiting. My panic rising with each passing moment until a tapping noise has me swing around and squint, trying to see through the darkness.

One breath. Two.

And then I scream at the sight of razor sharp teeth and distorted face of the monster that jumps out of nowhere, its mouth open and pointed right at my face.

I'm spinning, unable to get my thoughts in order...

I fall backwards. My back lands on a plush mattress, covered in the most exquisite fur blankets just as a hard body collapses with me. His warmth and scent surround me. I feel every groove of his muscles as his bare chest presses

33

against my exposed breasts. Our panting is heavy in our passion. I cry in ecstasy as he pushes deeper in me, changing the tempo. I lift my hand to his back and smile at the rough, animalistic noise he growls in pleasure.

I can't see his face but my body and mind know him. He nudges my neck to the side, trailing kisses down to my nipple. Grabbing his face, unable to not touch him, I lift his mouth up to mine...

Spinning, the world changes and I'm running through the dense forest, the sound of footsteps heavy behind me. I know I have to run.

To keep going.

Fear grips me as I stumble, falling heavily to the hard, forest littered floor. A cry of pain escapes my lips when I hit the ground and I scream for help as a monster made of darkness jumps out and envelops me...

I wake with a silent scream on my lips.

Gulping down air, I grip my chest and pull my knees up so that I can hug myself against the shivers racking my body.

Sobbing, I rock myself back and forth on my small bed, in a self-soothing technique I learnt at a young age.

I don't know what part of the dream I'm crying about in particular. The horrors of monsters and darkness, or that I was taken from a dream with a male who called to my soul. Who touched me with longing and ignited a fire deep in my core that is still hot embers in my body.

I end up rocking myself for what feels like hours atop my mass of blankets.

Slapping Van's hand out of my bowl of hot chips, I snigger like a child and poke my tongue out at him when Brent absently knocks him up the back of the head in reprimand.

Brent doesn't miss a beat. He's talking with three of his buddies about motorcycles and other things that they wouldn't speak of if we weren't in their part of town.

Van rubs the spot and throws me a wink as he devours the one he stole in a single bite. He has a massive plate of potato wedges and a burger larger than mine in front of him.

'You always do that. I told you to order fries.' I lean over to steal a few wedges which he playfully shouts about, but still lets me have. 'I haven't eaten all day.' My moan is loud and unladylike as I take a big bite of my fried chicken burger. It took IT at work most of this week to fix my computer so I've been working through lunch every day this week to get ahead of all the hours I've missed.

My hunger was the only reason why I said yes to coming to dinner tonight. That, and Laney has taken the younger kids to Carly's house for a dinner with her family. Van, Brent and I weren't invited. Not that I really care. I'm exhausted from my lack of sleep last night after the nightmare and then my full workday today trying to get my presentation finalised. My beast hasn't stopped making me jittery and anxious and I'm about to pull my hair out. Besides, *Jordan's Diner* is the best diner this side of the docks.

Phone pinging, I pull it from my pocket and then place it right back in when I see the message from Miles asking if I want to have dinner with him tomorrow night. He's been pretty insistent over the last week to get me to come over to his apartment. I've never been and don't really want to start. I haven't seen him at work either.

'Miles?' Van grins, with a mouthful of food.

'Eww, don't talk with your mouth full. And yes,' I scold.

'What's he want? Dinner? Movie? Impregnate you with his first male heir?'

'Ewwwwa!' I emphasis while Van laughs loudly. 'Why do you all have such an issue with Miles?'

'He's a little creepy, Raff.'

'He's my friend, Van,' I warn. I'm a very loyal beast and while Van may be a little correct, I don't like him speaking badly about Miles.

I'm giving him a piece of my mind when our waiter comes to the table, stopping our conversation. 'Here we go. Chocolate thickshake for you, Raff,' Moira, the stocky, middle aged server, says as she places the drink in front of me. Her orange apron, cream work dress and low bun is sometimes a weird comfort. She always has a nice word or two to say. She always seems to know what I need without me ordering and keeps us all well feed.

'And your soda, Van.' Moira moves aside some of our plates to place down Van's drink. Telling us that she will be back, she has a quick conversation with Brent and some of his guys and moves to the next table.

It's because of Moira and the fact that Jordan's Diner is close to home that I'm here this late in the afternoon. I have about an hour before it gets dark but the pull in my body to get back to my room is starting and my juicy burger is starting to taste like ash in my mouth.

The need to find shelter is like a tug on my instincts. A buzzing under my skin I can only describe as an in-built warning system that I need to find safety for the night.

I've been in the human world for ten years. I've lived on the streets for a year and even in my little makeshift cardboard tent or the small hideaways I'd find around the city, I've never seen a wraith in real life, only in my nightmares. Wraiths are monsters of the night that hunt my kind for our energy. For our fire. In the limited education I was given about them, the night demons are restricted to the moonlight hours, and yet they need the power of the sun to fully form in order to cross over and wreak havoc.

Irony is a bitch.

I don't know if they're here in the human lands but my instincts will always be to seek comfort and shelter when the sun goes down.

Fear was one of the first lessons I was taught as a youngling. To fear the darkness. To fear the night.

'Well, eat up. You're a right grump when you're hungry.'

'Hey!' I grumble but it loses its bite because he's right. My beast needs to be fed to be happy. I still can't help but sneak glances outside though.

'It's not dark yet, the sun is still out. You have time.'

I can't reply to Van's soft tone or the way he knows me so well. I have no idea what I did in my life to deserve the friendship and family I found.

I thought for months as I sat on a ship crossing the Veil between my world and the human world, which is a violent, invisible section of ocean that I feared was going to be my doom, that I was destined to be alone forever.

We sit eating and chatting until we finish dinner and my knee starts bouncing nervously under the table.

'Take her home Van,' Brent says unexpectedly which grabs our attention. It takes me a few moments to understand why he just told us to go. I haven't sensed any danger and no one new has come into the busy diner and with a small smile, I realise it's because my foster brother knows how anxious I'm getting.

Van gets up without complaint, popping the last of his food in his mouth and I follow feeling all light and fluffy that my brothers care for me.

Pushing past Brent and one of his big, burly friends who plasters himself on the booth with his hands up as if making a point that any touching is not his fault, I follow behind Van who shakes hands with a few people around the diner before pushing the door open for me.

CHAPTER SEVEN

WITH VAN'S ARM INTERLOCKED with mine, we laugh and joke as we head up the street towards home. The sky is clear and alight with colour. The streets are still full of people and I find happiness in the tranquillity of the ending day.

There are moments in my life that I feel the extent of what I did by getting on that ship and coming here. I ran to be free and walking with Van towards a home that always feels safe and accepting is when I feel it the most.

'I heard you practicing your violin this morning. I wish you'd play more. Everyone was stunned at the church the other day. It was really pretty.'

'I played four chords before Carly had some bright idea and stopped me.' I laugh.

With his cheeky grin pointed in my direction, he pulls me closer to his side playfully. 'The best four chords I've ever heard.'

Pushing away from him, I tell him to stop being such a suck-ass but keep our arms connected.

Turning down one of the alleys that cuts out ten minutes from our walk, I'm too busy teasing Van about Missy Tomos being his date that I don't notice the danger until it's too late. The hooded man who cuts us off has us both jump in surprise. Van pulls me roughly behind him and I only go because another three dark figures appear at our backs.

'Give us your money,' first hooded guy says and I stand back-to-back with Van and feel his laughter vibrate through my bones. I find it touching and cute that he feels the need to protect me.

'Original, dickhead.' It's not the first time Van and I have been jumped on our walks, but the idiots normally stop once they figure out who we are, which doesn't seem to be working even after Van states, quite colourfully, 'do you know who we fucking are?'

'Give me your money,' the guy just says again and I tense, picking up on the shroud of fear and adrenaline coming from our four assailants. Those combinations are not good and I squeeze Van's hand to show him that I'm not liking this situation one bit.

I find it really odd that the intense feeling I've been getting from my beast for the past week is now eerily silent.

Scanning the alley, I try to assess the situation. Four guys, all pretty short, all smell like this is their first time holding someone up. I can't see any weapons. That doesn't mean they aren't carrying any.

Attention snagging on the one to my right who hasn't stopped shuffling on his feet, I notice the top of a weird white tattoo on his left wrist, just poking out from under his shirt. It reminds me of something but I can't put my finger on it. Not sure why that has snagged my attention, I wonder if he realises how much danger he's in right now, and I'm not talking about from the bigger man standing protectively behind me.

Smirking when he raises his eyes to catch me staring, I see the way his features fall despite the heavy hood and the darkness covering the majority of his face.

'You sure you want to do this?' I ask softly.

Van and the other guy are still arguing and the tension is building as Van cusses and threatens to beat them all to death with his bare hands if they don't leave us alone.

Guy to my right fidgets and twitches and I watch as he nods emphatically. 'Give us your money,' he says to me and I realise that he's just a kid.

'How old are you?' I chuckle.

'Shut up bitch and give me your money.'

I see red and moving without much thought, I step into his personal space and push him aside. I hate when people call me names. It's offensive and while I don't live in my father's world anymore, it's hard to not feel the privilege of who I am sometimes. Of my bloodline.

The kid flies and comes crashing down on a pile of rubbish against the far wall. I can hear Van and the leader fighting with their fists. Knowing that the younger idiot doesn't stand a chance against my Van, I don't pay much attention to it.

'Don't call me a bitch,' is the last thing I say before red-hot pain shoots through my side and has me scream in agony and rage. My skin erupts and I feel my beast with such intensity that my next scream is not caused by the knife now embedded in my side.

A violent shiver causes my muscles to contract and tense, and for a moment I stop breathing.

The world reddens and my awareness shifts. I'm able to block out the pain, grip the neck of the guy who has just stabbed me, and lift him off his feet. His shout of terror at whatever he sees on my face fuels my fury and I catch the half completed tattoo on his wrist that seems to spark a memory before I disregard the thought and throw him across the alley. I watch as he hits the wall with a crack. It's satisfying and distracting until I hear the distinct pounding of my heart in my ears and the world becomes a blur of noise and darkness.

Touching my side, I feel the warm, sticky liquid and lift it up as if I need to make sure that it's my blood covering my shaking hand. My breathing becomes the only sound in the world as I watch a single drop of thick liquid drip from the side of my finger. There is a small voice in my head that screams to stop it. To not let it fall. That I am in danger. I become fixated with the way it hovers before it falls slowly to slam on the concrete. I watch it splatter.

The shiver under my skin comes back and I suck in a breath before I become aware of the commotion around me in the alley. Of Brent and his friends surrounding the now un-hooded, un-moving attackers.

Van is beside me, shouting something in my ear. All I can do is stare at his moving mouth and wonder why the need to run is now beating against my body.

'Raff, fuck. Sit down. Sit down! Brent, there's blood! Brent! She's been stabbed!' That is when everything comes rushing into focus completely and the beast under my skin disappears.

My whimper is soft as the darkness in my vision takes over.

CHAPTER EIGHT

*P*AIN.

THERE'S SO MUCH pain.

Breathing heavily, the muffled voices around me are washed-out and seem far away despite the shadows looming over me. It's too much and my attempts to contain my scream are useless.

Hands touch my body.

Two, oversized, calloused palms grip my face and while I can't see through the darkness in my vision, I can only smell the male who starts speaking to me.

'Breathe. It will be over soon. I'm so sorry.'

His anguish hurts more than the way my body contorts and contracts.

Allowing his scent to wash over me, I take the respite that his proximity provides me to take a much needed breath before the world shakes violently.

Horror takes over at the realisation that it's me and not the hard ground I'm thrashing against that's moving.

I wake from my haunting dream to an incessant beeping that grates on my senses.

Everything seems brighter and louder as I become aware of my surroundings and understand why my skin is itchy all over. I have things stuck to my body at different points along my chest and arms. I hurt all over and the room I'm in is completely dimmed and quiet. I can feel the darkness and while I can't move much, I know that I'm in a hospital bed exposed to the night that is heavy outside the window to my left.

Darkness threatens to pull me back into oblivion, but not before I see something pass by the window. My stomach rolls and all the colour feels as if it's draining into the bed under me. My heart rate spikes and the beeping becomes erratic as I feel my throat close up.

The world goes black and all I can think is that I'm left exposed and vulnerable with one of the monsters from my endless dreams outside the window.

'You got stabbed, Raff!'

'I'm very aware of that, Miles,' I grumble and indicate to my prone position on the hospital bed. I've been here for nearly five days and have finally got a doctor to assess me again and realise that I'm well enough to go home. Don't get me wrong, I feel like shit. My side is still a stitched up wound and sitting in this damn, dark hospital room away from the sun—away from nature—is not the way I'm going to get better.

'You can't be okay to go to home tomorrow. That's insane!' He sounds pretty angry and I try to sit up to grab the water on the small table without crying out.

'I can heal better at home in my own bed.' I pant and reach for the cup and stop when Miles appears at the bedside. He grabs the paper cup and helps me to take a long swig.

I've been having nightmares since the first time I woke up and saw that monster at the window and I'm ready to go home. Something is wrong. I can't shake the feeling that I need to go home.

Logically, I know my unease is probably due to the heavy-duty drugs I've been on, but I want out. I need out.

It helps that the hospital is very understaffed and having my bed for the next victim was a priority for them too.

I was up and walking a day after the surgery, looking longingly outside through the many hospital windows wishing I was outside under the sun. I'm recovering quickly, maybe too quickly, if they had the care to actually pay attention they would've noticed, but lucky for me, no doctor or nurse has.

'I'm serious that you should come and stay at my apartment with me so that I can look after you. I think it's important that you do. I might have to insist.' I don't know if he's serious and slowly lie back while watching him. This is the second time since I woke up in this shit hospital that he has made that offer. He looks lost in thought as he checks his phone for the tenth time and then mumbles that he might go speak to the doctors about releasing me into his care. He also says something about how everything is confirmed, that makes no sense.

'Miles. Miles wait,' I call out. He ignores me and leaves the room.

Slumping back against the mountain of pillows Laney and Van helped me to acquire, I'm not sure if I'm being weird or if Miles is.

'Knock. Knock.'

Smiling up at the group now standing in the doorway, I feel a great deal better at the sight of my foster brothers and my Laney.

'Was that Miles I just saw heading to the nurses station?' Brent tries to keep the annoyance out of his voice.

'Yes. Play nice.' I laugh and try to sit up. Laney rushes to my side instantly and starts to helps. My poor Laney has had a permanent frown on her face since I woke up in this bed. 'He hasn't done anything to you,' I remind Brent as he slumps heavily into the seat next to my head.

'He's a creep.' Brent shrugs like that's all he needs to dislike someone. Just a feeling. Not that Miles hasn't done anything to him.

Not really listening to the conversation now happening between the boys about how they all feel the same creepiness, I feel the distress from Laney in waves.

Grabbing her hand when she fusses over my hair, I try to tell her again that I'm okay. 'I promise Laney. It'd take more than a stab wound to get rid of me.'

She smiles softly. 'I know, my tough, kind, Raff.' The tears in her eyes don't match her words or energy.

'I'm sorry,' I whisper and watch as the water falls down her face.

'Just get better. That is the only sorry I need.' She sniffles.

'Yes, get better before Saturday please, Carly is frantically trying to find someone to replace you at the church but it's not looking good. The wedding is in two days.' I don't know if Scott understands what he's said or how Brent and Van look sharply over to him as if they are about to tell him to fuck off.

I jump in before an argument erupts because Van has that look on his face. 'Tell her to not worry. I'll be there to play.'

CHAPTER NINE

'LEAN ON ME.'

SHAKING my head, I lean harder on Van even though he's already taking most of my weight.

'Fuck you're heavy,' he swears playfully with that cheeky grin on his face that makes me want to smack him and kiss his cheek at the same time.

The small chuckle that escapes my lips has me clench my muscles in pain. My side hurts. My head hurts. My entire damn body hurts.

I was looking forward to being discharged from the hospital and only just won the argument with Miles to not go home with him. I even got him to not be around on my discharge by asking him to give me space to spend time with just my family. He did remind me that he'd meet me at the church for the wedding tomorrow.

However, it seems that my luck was used up on that escape ship all those years ago because the sun is going down and there is no chance that I can feel it's power on my skin and let it give me the energy to heal quicker.

'Just help me into the house.' I sigh and nod my head when Van asks if I'm okay before we start to take the steps to the front door.

Biting my bottom lip to keep my cries in my throat, I know Van can sense how much pain I'm in. His entire body is tense muscle. 'I shouldn't have provoked that fucker in the alley.' It's been the same line he has been saying since I woke up to him beside my hospital bed.

'Van, please, this isn't your fault.'

'I should've handled it differently.'

I don't reply. Taking the stairs is using a great deal of energy I don't have, so I leave it. There'll be plenty of time to correct him another day. To be honest, I'm glad that it was me who was knifed and not Van. I'm not invincible but my healing rate compared to a human is a hundred times better, and quicker. A knife to the side hurts like a bitch but it wasn't going to kill me or my beast. I just need the sun and nature to quicken the healing process. After a good night's rest, I promise myself I'll get a good soak in the early morning sun before I have to get dressed for the wedding. I'll be fit and ready.

I wait for Van to open the door before I shuffle my way in. I don't want to stress Laney out more than she already is so I stand as straight as my poor, wrapped body will allow me and plaster a smile on my face. With me in the hospital and the wedding, every time I saw her this week she looked more and more worn out than usual.

'Why's it so fuckin' dark?' Van grumbles just as I think the same thing. All the lights are off and the place is silent. I don't bother hanging my coat. I can't move my arms higher than my shoulders anyways. 'Laney said that she'd be home to meet us. Danny and the others were supposed to make you a cake.'

'Oh really?' Heart a little uplifted, I ignore Van's teasing snicker when I begin to eagerly hurry down the hall towards the kitchen-loungeroom area. I can smell chocolate and I fucking love chocolate. Chocolate is one of those human world treasures that I discovered early.

'Maybe they went out.'

'I hope they left the cake,' I reply and step through the archway and stop dead at the sight before me. My beast comes to life instantly and I bare my teeth and growl.

Every instinct in my body comes to attention.

Mind racing, I try to process the danger.

Van comes up behind me, chatting away about how we'll eat and watch re-runs of a baking show we are secretly obsessed with, especially the two elderly ladies who judge each creation with a warm smile and loving 'grandma' words that make you feel all fuzzy inside. A show we publicly renounce and mock and yet have recorded for when everyone is in bed and we sit on my mattress cheering on the bakers.

Van doesn't notice that I've stopped and my hand flies out to grip his arm before he can step in front of me. Throwing me a quick questioning look that I catch in my peripherals, I don't bother explaining as my attention is locked on the terrifying sight before me.

Van opens his mouth, I'm sure to ask what the fuck is wrong with me and shuts it when he follows my line of vision to the loungeroom.

He instantly tenses, ready to fight. I stop him from moving to block me with a firm tug that has him pushed instead to be behind *my* back. His intake of air is the only noise in the entire house and I'm sure he was surprised with how easily I just handled him.

I unconsciously shift my feet into a wider stance. My years of training as a youngling coming back and yet still so insignificant that it'll do nothing for me now. Every muscle in my body tenses as I ready myself.

They found me. After all these years.

My mouth feels like sandpaper. My heart is beating so hard that I fear it will overexert itself and stop pumping all together.

I can't believe my eyes. For a moment, I feel like I may be stuck in one of my nightmares and I squeeze my eyes closed for a second. When I open them, I seem to be able to think clearer.

Brain functioning, I scan the room and process the threat.

Three males.

Three Drengar.

One is standing at the window to my right. His eyes a startling, deep blue. It has been ten years since I've looked upon someone of my kind. I forgot how tall the males are, how large and energy-filled their auras are.

Ten years ago, I was a kid. A female between stages of being a girl and a woman, so I don't think I ever truly noticed things like jawlines and muscle-heavy arms and chests. Now though, even in this situation, my beast shivers under my skin.

They are delicious.

The imposing, larger than life male standing beside the lounge, catches my attention when he steps forward slightly. His black eyes are fixed on my face, as if he's reading my body for my reaction. There's a white scar down his left check. It stops abruptly at his Adam's apple. I don't have the time to really admire the striking beauty of him because my beast pulls my focus to the male sitting cross legged at the dining table across the room.

His chair is slightly off centre so I can't get a good glimpse of him. His features are shrouded in an eerie darkness that I can't seem to see through but his body is on full display. He's covered in black leather, much like the other two and I have a deep feeling in my soul that I know him.

However, I don't have time to work it out because another male steps from the shadows to my left, out of the hall that leads to my room and the second bathroom. Everyone else sleeps on the other side of the house.

Everything stills.

For a moment, I thought this could be a coincidence, that maybe the wraith from the hospital drew these Drengar to my part of the world, but all that flies out the window with my breath.

CHAPTER TEN

MY MIND RACES LIKE my heart.

The warrior strolls into the loungeroom confidently and sure of himself. His familiar eyes are set on my face and I can almost read the subtle disappointment on his stone features.

He tilts his head slightly in a gesture that I know he isn't sure if he should do any longer. 'Lady Serafina DarkwoodsAzar.'

It has been ten years since I've heard my full title and the language of my birthplace, Zaric. It's been a long time since I've seen the male addressing me so formally. A predator who causes fear to pulse through my veins as I stand, unable to respond. He hasn't changed much.

Ten years ago he was one of the youngest Drengar in my father's lair. By the crest on his breast it seems that Viktor LongwingDrengar, a male I heard stories about as a youngling and watched from behind furniture and walls seems to no longer work for my father. *Interesting and yet even more terrifying.*

I ready myself for a battle I know I cannot win. Which doesn't seem to matter. I'll protect my family from my old life until my dying breath.

'Drengar Viktor. Where's my family?' I ask, slipping easily back to Zaric, the language flows from my lips and I thank every Sun God that might be listening for keeping my voice steady. I mimic his head bow in respect even though I don't have to. I am a Lady of the house of the Darkwoods. I am an Azar. It seems like I should play nice until I can work out a way to get them out of here.

Van's sharp intake of air is the only sound in the house as the temperature rises. I squeeze his arm and don't miss the way that four sets of bright eyes flick to our connected bodies.

'Back in their lairs, or on your father's lands, as far as I'm aware.'

I don't know if he's being contrary on purpose and I put every ounce of annoyance into my glare. 'That's not the family I meant and you know it,' I state through gritted teeth.

Viktor raises a single brow that has me more and more irritated. 'They have been sent to sleep.'

My heart skips and then sinks into my feet. Laney and the kids are safe but it means one of these males is a Medir, a healer, and that's petrifying.

Looking around, I try to work out who it could be and end up with my gaze on the one with the scar and black eyes. A shiver racks my body. The ability to mesmerise someone to sleep is a gift only possessed by the very powerful of Medir's. Healing is not necessarily all they can do. They are dangerous.

Years of trauma threatens to suffocate me.

I focus on breathing—in and out.

'We thought you were dead. The lost Lady of the Darkwoods. Daughter of the Lord of the Darkwoods,' Drengar Viktor continues. His words drip with annoyance, anger and something else. Something I can't name because I'm not focused on him anymore. My hackles go up and my lips pull back from my teeth as I voice a warning to the male to my left.

My growl vibrates through my bones and I watch with predatory focus as the blue eyed warrior stops the step he was about to take in mine and Van's direction.

'Back off!' I threaten.

The way the predator's blue eyes move from Van to my face is unsettling. This is my lair and they've come around without invitation. My beast holds the power over this space and I have to remind myself of that quickly and tap into a persona I buried under ten years of reconditioning and healing.

These males are warriors.

They're Drengar. Hunters. Their very purpose is to protect and uphold our race, including traditions and customs.

'You shouldn't have come here,' I state in Zaric, drawing my focus from the blue eyed warrior who seems to be having a hard time controlling his smirk...or snarl. I can't tell which one. There's definitely nothing humorous in the way he's glaring at Van or the twitching thick cord of muscle in his neck. The leathers they all wear cover their arms, cut sharply over their clavicles and are tailored to their well-defined bodies. The uniform of a Drengar.

It doesn't matter what family they're from, the Drengar wear the same outfit. The crest on their breast is the only thing to tell them apart and the same one on each of the three standing in my living room is too terrifying to acknowledge. Their uniform is practically invincible. Hard as the very beasts under their skin. You could try and drive a knife through those leathers but you'd come out with a very bent and distorted blade for your efforts before you'd find your head separated from your body. Or burnt to a crisp.

'*You* shouldn't be *here*,' Drengar Viktor snaps loudly, venom lacing each word. His voice ricochets off the walls and bounces on my skin painfully. I flinch.

'What the fuck! Don't you come into our house and shout at my sister!' Van attempts to step out from behind me. He has no idea what the male has said but his tone is enough to get my foster brother riled up. I grip onto him harder, almost desperate as the three standing males come to attention.

'Van, don't,' I whisper despite myself. The last thing I want is to look weak in front of these males but I'm frightened. I'm petrified about what's going to happen and that my world is once again going to be turned upside down.

I've been through so much to create this new life. Yes, it's not the finest and my job barely pays the bills, but it's mine.

'No,' Van demands, trying to get loose of my hold. His eyes are intense as they glare at me. 'Who the fuck are they? Why are they yellin'? And what language is that?'

Eating my bottom lip, I have no idea what to say. I'm so tired and my side is killing me.

Sighing loudly, I decide to tell the truth and then react on instinct when Blue Eyes moves. I become a blur of action. The room spins and I'm not in control over my body as I appear before the warrior who was radiating aggression towards my Van. The step he just took was a big mistake.

I shove him away and watch with unattached interest as he flies back and hits the wall. Totally under the control of my beast, I go with him and land another blow that has him on the floor on his back. I'm no fool, I know that the only way I could do this is because he wasn't expecting my reaction.

Not giving Blue Eyes a chance to think, I'm there straddling him, uncaring of the others in the room. Uncaring of the commotion happening behind me.

I'm vaguely aware of the scarred warrior moving silently toward my Van, who's shouting and yelling as he tries to get to me. I turn my head to see the male grip his face before Van's eyes roll in the back of his head. I have no time to react because Blue Eyes tries to use his body to flip me.

Cursing colourfully, I shout a warning that Van better be okay. I resist Blue Eyes attempts to get me off him. I know he isn't using all his power which annoys me further. However, my mind cannot process any of that. The fear that a Medir is here in my home and that he's standing in the middle of the loungeroom like a deadly, silent statue, is a frightening realisation that is making it hard for me to think straight. I can hear Van's steady heartbeat and know that he is safe. So, I continue to swing my arms and try to rip out those gorgeous eyes of the male under me with my now sharpened nails.

The rush of blood in my ears and the sound of Blue Eyes breathing as he effortlessly dodges and evades each one of my hits is the only sound I can hear. He doesn't seem fazed by what's happened, he just easily moves side to side, not fighting back. In fact, he's acting like he's playing with a puppy who he doesn't want to hurt.

He smirks that damn grin again and I growl a sound I've never made before and then squeak when he grips my wrists and pulls my arms to my side. He hasn't got a scratch despite my attempts and he rises up, his eyes totally capturing mine as he states, 'enough! Before you hurt yourself,' in my face. His voice makes me shiver.

Chest now pressed against his, I wriggle and squirm to get out of his hold and go back to trying to maim him.

Blue Eyes chuckles and I feel the vibrations through my entire body.

'Let go of me,' I warn through gritted teeth. I'm shaking. I'm so enraged.

How dare he! How dare they all!

'When you calm down, I will,' Blue Eyes states and the condescension of it infuriates me more, but my beast is no longer in the mood to be mad. I can barely feel her anymore. She seems more interested in working through each individual scent of the male I'm straddling and it's beyond distracting. His voice is low and rough.

'You're in my lair. My home. You just sent my family to sleep without consent. You don't get to tell me to calm down!' I've never been so furious in my life. Never had the need to rip someone's throat out. Well, Van sometimes incites this kind of anger, but not this aggressively.

'Whatever you say, Lady.' The word Lady sounds like a mockery. Blue Eyes keeps that fucking look on his face that makes me want to smack him and maybe stroke his beautiful face at the same time.

CHAPTER ELEVEN

'ENOUGH! FELIX, LET HER go.' The dominant, alpha voice that fills the house has my beast completely retreat, leaving me aware of how hot and sweaty I am.

Without my beast in control, I fully realise what I'm doing. I forget how to move. How to speak. All I do is stare like an idiot at the grinning warrior, whose nose is very proportional to his face. Almost supermodel worthy.

I wonder how offended he'd be if I said that to him.

I have no idea if the Drengar know a great deal about human culture but they're ego-filled dominant predators who probably think themselves masters of the universe, so he'd probably be offended.

His strong jawline *is* cut to perfection though.

I realise I should be reacting, not contemplating what his skin tastes like and shake my head. 'Let...me...go!'

I watch mesmerised as his thick, manly eyebrow rises in humour at my inability to complete a sentence properly. There's a boy-ish quality to his handsomeness and it might have something to do with how his dark, blonde hair falls around his face. I curl my hand to resist the urge to fight against his hold so that I can touch it.

'I said enough. Serafina, your humans are safe and well. Look.' Viktor is beside me in an instant, standing tall and imposing over us and I quickly look behind me to observe the way the scarred male is carrying Van effortlessly toward the opposite hall. I can finally focus enough to hear the others in their rooms, their soft breathing and the steady heartbeats are comforting.

In the morning they'll forget what they saw today. Forget what happened here. I want to cry because deep in my soul I know that it'll mean they'll have no idea why I'll be gone because that's where this is headed. These Drengar will take me back to my father.

The male under me smiles wide before he removes his hands from my wrists and pulls back onto his elbows clearly feeling the fight leave me completely.

Viktor's immense power and energy surrounds me and I look from his outstretched, oversized, calloused hand and then slowly up to his face. His features are harsher than Blue Eyes. His brown depths remind me of the colour of the ancient Trymber tree of my home, its bark is dark brown with lines of honey. His eyes scream his power and dominance. Of a life lived fighting and battling. Drengar eyes. Viktor's straight nose and high cheekbones aren't bad to look at either. His black hair looks silky smooth and is tied in a loose bun atop his head with a leather strap. But none of it helps to quench the sorrow forming around my heart.

He doesn't look particularly impressed and I have no fight left in me to protest when he moves his hand in a demanding gesture for me to take it. With no more steam left in me and my beast now quiet once more, goosebumps erupt on my skin. Viktor doesn't move. He just waits for me to take his hand which I begin to do and then suck in a loud breath as pain shoots through my body. With the adrenaline now out of my system, I whimper and clap my hand against my bandaged side instead.

I feel the blood on my skin just as the male under me tenses and sits up. Our chests touching again. Large hands grip my upper arm and I feel his breath on my cheek.

'You're bleeding!' Drengar Felix exclaims, the instant heat he radiates encompasses me.

My head spins and I whimper. Pushing away from him, I groan as I stand, refusing help. I can feel all their eyes as I grip my side and shuffle to the lounge to hold onto something so I don't collapse. I know my stitchers have popped, just not sure how many. I need to lie down.

Closing my eyes, I breathe through the pain. 'I need to sleep. You can all leave now.'

'I didn't touch you. Why are you bleeding?' Drengar Felix seems pissed and completely ignores what I've just said. He's hovering close. 'Let Wilder take a look.'

Looking over at the scary healer who steps back into the room, I swallow and stifle a chuckle. 'No thanks.' There is no way that I'm going to let that dude near me. His eyes are black in colour and his skin is a shade darker than the other very tanned males. The white scar just adds to his eerie persona. The Medir is taller than Viktor and Felix by a foot and his black hair falls to his shoulders.

'My stitches have popped. I'll be okay,' I say through gritted teeth. Tired, I feel like I've run a marathon. Their combined voices are muffled in my ears. I need to go to bed. I need the sun.

'I think it best to sit and let Wilder—'

'No!' I growl, but it has no bite. To be honest, it's breathy and weak. 'Leave, so that I can go to bed and sleep.' That's when I feel him. The male that was sitting quietly at the table. He finally stands and despite the pain and the feeling of complete exhaustion, I find myself transfixed by the way he moves.

His energy, like the size of him, fills the space with a weight that takes the very air from the room.

Transfixed, I get caught in his pale, blue eyes that stand out against his tanned complexion. His square jaw and defined cheekbones make him one of the most attractive males I've ever seen. He's gorgeous. Beautiful. Powerful.

I can almost see the beast under his skin by the way his eyes glow. He looks pissed. 'Your fear of us is unreasonable, female. Clearly, you've been away from our world too long. We're not here to hurt you.'

'How do I know that?' I spit, unsure where my bravado is coming from.

'Because you are the Lady of the Darkwoods. A member of the elite Azar of our people and because we're not common men who would hurt a female. This human world has affected how you think.' I almost forgot how much contempt our race has towards humans, which does nothing to calm me down. These males have no idea who I truly am. Not even Drengar Viktor. My father spent my entire life keeping me hidden. I was even kept from my brothers and from making friends because I'm not fully Azanite. I'm a half human, half beast. An embarrassment. An abomination.

I'm too busy in my own head that I almost miss what he's saying. 'Our mission as the Drengar is to protect at all costs. Something that you should know but have obviously forgotten after you ran away.' He says the words as if an accusation. Like I'm a child who had done a childish thing. 'And something I'll overlook and not take offense to.' Each word he says hits a spot in my soul. The trauma and distrust of my childhood will never let me trust any of them. There were Drengar in that room watching the Medir put me to sleep against my will. For years.

Protect my arse. I'll never trust them. No matter how good looking they are.

'Excuse me if I don't jump to believe a word that comes out of your mouth.'

He takes a single step toward me, invading my space and I swallow down my fear. He says nothing as his head tilts, studying me.

'What do you want?' I ask quietly, my eyes locked with his. At first, I thought his eyes were pale blue but there's a ring of grey around his black iris that has me transfixed.

'What do you think?' he replies and I don't need to answer. I know what they're here for.

Me.

All I can think is what pretty eyes he has before the room spins and I collapse.

CHAPTER TWELVE

I BLINK AWAY THE *blurriness in my vision to better understand why I'm so cold.*

I appear to be in a carpeted, grey hallway. I hear tapping in the distance. I'm in an office building.

There are three elevator doors to my left and a wall to my right with the strangest, massive logo filling the black wallpaper. There's a numbing breeze coming from somewhere that I could do without.

Nothing seems to make sense. I have no memory of getting here and have no fucking idea where here is, but the voice in my head is screaming at me to get the fuck out. I see lots of black, closed doors. The one down the end has my attention though.

Confused, I squint and try to peer down the long corridor with the flashing neon light pulsing eerily down the far end like some kind of horror movie. It's dark and this is how the dumb girl in the movie always gets murdered.

I hear what sounds like whimpering and while my heart is pounding in my chest and my hands feel sweaty, I feel an unmistakable pull to find out what or who is down the creepy hall and on the other side of the door.

Cursing under my breath at my damn curious instinct, I turn around and make sure that I'm alone and that there are no masked murderers with chainsaws that might jump out and try to chop me into hundreds of pieces.

My bare feet seem too loud against the floor and I hold my breath when I look to my right. A chill runs up my spine and it has nothing to do with the cold.

It takes my mind a moment to catch up with what I'm seeing. One of the doors is open and the brightest, warmest light I have ever seen is radiating from the crack.

With a shaking hand, I tentatively touch the surface of the door and gently push it open and frown at the way the light disappears to reveal a very mundane, stereotypical skyscraper office space. The city is familiar somehow.

Floor to ceiling windows show the darkness and the bright lights of the still-awake city down below.

The desk nearly takes up the entire space in front of the glass and I take a small step inside. Pulled in by something unnameable.

I search the dark space. There is a lounge and a back door to the right. A kitchenette and a massive office table close to the door.

It is the office desk that has my attention though. Scanning the surface as I get closer, I take in the computer, the keyboard, papers and stationary. Nothing seems odd except the black cloth that is covering something in the middle of the desk. Something I know requires my attention.

Moving quietly, I know in my gut that I shouldn't be here. That danger is close.

Hand almost refusing to obey my command, I reach out and collect the middle of the cloth and pull it off gently.

It's a book. A book that shines like the gold it appears to be made of. A book with inscriptions and patterns on the front. It is thick and heavy looking and seems to call to me to read.

A noise behind me has me gasp and spin around.

I scream at the monstrous figure standing against the glass. It lunges for me and I fall backward. Before I hit the table, I'm sucked into a vortex of darkness.

My eyes fly open. I gasp and know instantly that I'm in danger. Struggling to sit, I grip the blankets under me and try to remember where I am and how I got into bed.

My dream plays in my mind, keeping me on high alert and for a moment I don't know what to make of it and what it could mean, if anything.

I become more aware of my surroundings. My gaze flicks to the male standing at my normally covered window looking out into the darkness like he's ready for battle and I shiver. Too many dreams rush back, blurring the lines in my mind. I'm not ready for the fact that my personal space has been invaded by four oversized and intimidating males.

I have no idea what time it is or how long I was out, but by the way my side burns when I slowly sit up, I know that they all respected that I didn't want their Medir to touch me. My thoughts draw to the scarred male sitting against my door, like his weight can stop anyone from entering. His eyes are closed. However, there's no denying that he's very aware of what's happening in the room and as if my thoughts have woken him, he slowly opens his eyes and stares back.

Quickly looking away, my gaze collides with Blue Eyes. I don't return the smart-arse grin on his face as he plays with what looks like an engraved dagger from his position sitting against the wall under the window.

Drengar Viktor is directly across from where I sit. He's watching me and I find it both unsettling and comforting to know that he's here. Despite everything, at least he's a familiar-ish kind of face and even though they all have the same crest on their uniforms, knowing the stories of Viktor LongwingDrengar keeps me from completely losing it at having these strange males in my room.

Before I can ask them all what they want and if they'd kindly fuck the hell off, Blue Eyes stops flipping the dagger and jumps up suddenly.

All eyes, including mine, go to the window.

There isn't a single sound except my heavy breathing which I'm sure the others can hear very well. In fact, I swear, the scary fucking Medir, glares at me to shut up like I have any power over it.

Ears straining to hear what they can obviously pick up easily, I watch in raptured horror as Viktor walks to the window while removing the long sword, *I didn't even realise he was wearing*, from his back. How I survived on my own for ten years becomes the only thing I can contemplate. That, and how badly my death is going to be because there's only one thing that'd make a Drengar look so grim and ready for battle. Only one thing that could have a Medir rise to his full height from the ground and crack his knuckles as if preparing his hands for a fight.

Wraiths.

Fear for my family wraps around my chest and I pray that the demons stay outside where they belong.

All four males seem to grow in size. Three at the window and one at the door, blocking my chances to escape or to run and make sure Laney, Van and the others are okay.

'How many do you feel?' Drengar Viktor asks Blue Eyes and for a moment I stare, stunned at the way the younger warrior closes his eyes.

There's a heartbeat of silence before he opens them and mouths a number that has the dominant predator at the window finally glance from the darkness. I try really hard to work out how many he has just said but come up with nothing. I want to scream for him to speak up for the rest of us to hear.

All I catch is the way Viktor's left brow twitches slightly. My temper flares to life and not being known as a patient female, I grumble, 'well, how many are there?' The voice in my head screams at me to shut the fuck up and not poke the dominant predators.

They completely ignore me.

'There's a great deal here we need to consider, Alastair.' Drengar Viktor sounds grim. I have no control over the way I absorb the name of the male who I can't help but want to stare at like a stalker.

Alastair.

The name conjures up memories and dreams that I can't seem to hold on to. They slip from my mind.

I'm being dumb which makes me even more frustrated.

I shuffle from out of the stack of blankets, unable to keep still. Throwing my legs painfully over the side of the mattress, I try to catch my breath. I'm an idiot to have attacked Drengar Felix with a fresh stab wound.

'I know,' Alastair growls and my eyes slip to him and then to the statue-like Medir at the door.

'We need to get out of here, or they'll come at the house and there are too many humans here for us to protect.'

I can't help but agree with him and am about to tell them all that they should probably go and take the wraiths with them, until a noise outside has me squeal the most embarrassing sound that has ever come out of my mouth.

A sharp bang fills my room and I'm off the bed in an instant. The darkness outside seems to get denser and I feel my insides fall to the floor.

'Wraith Scouts,' Felix states, all boyish smirk now gone to be replaced by the look of a hunter.

'Viktor, what are the options?' Alastair asks, while pulling weapons from under his uniform. It's amazing how many pockets he has.

Each one of them starts mimicking his actions.

'There's a human cemetery four blocks over. That's probably our place to wait this out. I saw a few mausoleums that we can find shelter in. There are too many to fight right now and this house is impossible to secure. We also have the female who we need to bring with us. She'll complicate things. Her beast won't want to be outside at night, but we need to.'

My hands instinctively go to my hips even though it hurts—*I can't help it*. They aren't paying attention to me anyways.

'We move quickly, staying in the streetlights,' Drengar Viktor continues. He doesn't seem at all fazed even though every word he says is terrifying. *They plan to go out there—with all the wraiths?*

I wonder for a second who Alastair is to hold so much power over the others as they all seem to be waiting for his instructions. 'Move out,'

Alastair declares and I finally notice the four bags in the corner near the door. This entire situation is starting to give me a headache and it only pounds harder when all four males grab their bags and put their weapons in easily accessible parts of their uniform before all their eyes fall to me...waiting.

'Uh...what?' I look down at the baggy trackpants and the loose, very old t-shirt of Van's to make sure there are no holes showing my boobs or something. Confirming that, while I look terrible, I'm decent, I ask again, 'what? Why are you looking at me like that? Shouldn't you all leave now before the wraiths come?'

Blue Eyes grins before throwing Alistair a humorous look that he doesn't return. I swear Drengar Viktor rolls his eyes even though I can't imagine any Drengar with their big-arsehole personalities to do something so mundane as an eye roll.

'Lady DarkwoodsAzar, you're coming with us,' Alistair states, leaving no room for a response. I have an overwhelming need to flip him off. Too bad. Hot as sin but an arse...*just my luck.*

I open and close my mouth before saying, 'no.' Preparing myself from what I know is coming and keeping a wary eye on the Medir, I clench my fists. He is who I have to be cautious of. The scary healer hasn't looked at me since moving to his bag...thank the Sun Gods.

However, they don't say anything. Drengar Viktor takes a dagger from Blue Eyes and fixes it into his belt before he lifts a bag and throws it on his back. He turns slowly, has some kind of eye conversation with Alistair, and stalks towards me.

My body screams to back up, to cower away from the mighty male who towers over me. The width of him covers the room from my sight and my heart quickens. There's nothing on his face to hint at his emotions and the beast under my skin stays quiet, unfazed by the fact that we could be squashed with a single swipe of his hand.

Refusing to back down, I tilt my head back painfully so that I can still keep eye contact even though I'm about to lose the contents of my stomach in fear.

It's hard. Alistair was right before, I don't think I'd ever have been afraid of these males before I ran away…well, the Medir, yes, but not the Drengar. I was a lady of a powerful house. My father is the Lord of the Darkwoods. We're Azar. He's a male only answerable to the King of Azanir, and even then, my father's Drengar were great in number and strength. Living in the human world, repressing who I am, *has* made me soft. Has made me forget how to be the daughter of a mighty Lord.

Inner voice shouting out words of encouragement for me to find my backbone and stand up for myself evaporates as Drengar Viktor stares and stares. His brown, honey-lined eyes narrow and I want to touch his silky hair. My thoughts scatter when he says in his deep, timber voice, 'you have two options. You stay here and you die and bring death to your humans, or you come with us.'

I speak without thinking. 'The wraiths are here because of you. They'll leave when you do.'

I watch as his brow rises in the most patronising way. 'Oh Lady, the wraiths aren't here for us. It was *you* and *your* blood that brought them here. You and your blood that brought *us* here.' His gaze flicks briefly to my side before capturing me again in their depths.

Confused and not believing a damn word that comes out of his mouth, I refuse to be intimidated or manipulated. 'Leave.'

'Viktor.' I barely hear Alistair. My entire focus is on the predator in front of me so when something slams against the window, I squeal and jump. Flight or fight reflexes on overdrive, my body automatically moves towards the Drengar. Viktor grips my upper arm while turning to see what the noise was with a chilling growl that I feel in my soul.

Too busy staring at the now cracked window, I'm so terrified at the fact that I think the darkness outside is now thicker that I don't really register when he says that my time is up and lifts me up and over his shoulder.

I scream and shout and try to ignore the raging pain from my wound. Arms and leg flaying around, my yelling turns into a plea when the black eyed male stalks towards me.

The Medir is the last thing I see before I black out.

CHAPTER THIRTEEN

*B*REATHING HEAVILY, I COME *undone wrapped in the arms of a male who smells like lemon and oakmoss. Like pleasure and power.*

Large hands sprawled against my stomach, the tips of his fingers play with my hardened nipples, I blink my eyes open. I notice the light washing through the room from the open glass balcony doors. Sheer curtains blow in the breeze and the bed under me is rounded and covered in the most exquisite blankets I have ever felt.

Grabbing one of my thighs to lift my leg up and backwards to sit against his hip, the hard length waits at my ready entrance before he pushes into me. Hard and thick. I cry out under the intensity of his touch.

Spinning, I'm thrown roughly onto the grey, stone floor. Pain erupts up my spine but I have no time to think about it. I need to get up. I need to get to the door before they lock me in. The world is a haze of colours and I finally get to my feet to only hear the squeaking of a heavy door and the slam as it clicks into a lock.

I scream even though no one is there to save me.

Eyes snapping open, I'm met with darkness and a shadow looming over me. I attack without thinking. My dream bleeds into reality and I have no idea what's real and what's fantasy as I claw and punch and fight against the hard body of the male who grabs me.

I don't want to be locked away. I don't want to be afraid anymore.

My mind is too fuzzy.

Too groggy from the nightmare.

The voices bouncing around don't register. Instinct screams at me to be free. To protect myself at all costs.

The small spark of awareness that flicks in and out grows until a voice cuts through the haze and I can hear my name despite how weird it sounds in my mind. *'Lady Serafina. Stop! Calm down. Now!'*

The 'now' breaks through my panic and I blink at the male I'm crushed against. I'm off my feet, his arms caging me to his body. Our faces inches apart.

Chest heaving, heart pounding, my arms collapse against his shoulders. Eyes wide, I take in the black eyes and the unusual scar that runs down his face. I become fixated on the way it snakes down his neck and then moves sharply across his throat and stops abruptly. His hair is the same colour as his eyes. His skin like chocolate, begging to be licked.

My beast finally wakes and draws in his scent.

I almost scream again at the familiarity of it.

A wave of exhaustion hits and darkness invades my vision. I know that if he wasn't holding me, I'd fall to my knees.

'Let me go,' I whisper, my voice quivering. The darkness of the weird place we're in, coupled with the fact that I'm this close to a Medir, makes it hard to keep my composure. I want to cry and I hate crying in front of people. I haven't let someone see me shed a tear since a night a long time ago when my tears and pleading meant nothing to the ones who were supposed to keep me safe.

I watch Wilder frown slightly. I study his square jaw and his hair. It falls to his shoulders. He's not as 'pretty' as Felix or as handsome as Alistair and Drengar Viktor. There's an energy around him though that I think would intrigue me if I wasn't so frightened of him.

'Lady Serafina, you're safe. You have nothing to fear from us.' Viktor's voice comes from behind and startles me.

Head snapping to my right, I study the male standing so close he's almost touching. His honey lined eyes are soft and I find comfort in them until I come to my senses.

'Only if I do what you tell me to do?' I sound like a child but I'm pissed. They forced me to sleep. They took me away from my home. I'm being manhandled.

Frowning, Viktor seems to want to say something before his brow furrows. 'Wilder will let you go if you promise to calm down. The last thing we need is for you to hurt yourself. We have enough to worry about while we're in here.'

With limited options, I nod once.

I scramble away when Wilder lets me. In less than three steps, my back hits a wall and I slide down until my butt collides with the cold, tiled floor. Still breathing hard, I finally have enough control over myself to absorb my surroundings. Felix and Alistair are standing near what appears to be a solid, stone door.

Afraid of where I am, I screw my eyes shut after I scan the small, square building and see all the plaques naming the dead people buried in the walls. I refuse to look at what I'm leaning against, deciding quickly that ignorance is bliss.

Their words from my bedroom come crashing back and I fight the growing panic. I'm in a fucking mausoleum. A place humans bury their dead. A concept that still baffles me. In Azanir, we burn our dead. Sending them back to the fire. Back to nature.

I become aware of the screeching, nightmarish sounds from outside as the wraiths bang against the stone. The four Drengar just stand like a barrier between me and the door. Each one silent and watchful as the scraping and banging continues.

Knowing I can't take much more, that my poor nerves are completely shot, I lower myself onto my good side and curl up. With everything else on my mind, I haven't had the chance to think about the pain in my body and I look to Wilder, to the Medir who could fix me easily.

A bone deep exhaustion pulls on my soul.

I wish I was in my bed. Surrounded by my blankets and pillows.

Chapter Fourteen

I DON'T KNOW HOW long I lie on that cold stone floor, falling in and out of sleep, unable to move. Unable to care about anything. My life has completely changed in the space of a few hours. A week ago, the only thing I had to care about was my work presentation, which is now a complete mess. And the wedding, which is tomorrow—or today— I have no idea what the time is.

Thoughts snapping to Laney and Scott. To my Van, and Brent, and the kids, has me sniffle and quickly wipe my face. They're going to wake up and have no idea where I went. They'll live their entire lives not knowing what happened to me, and that's just heartbreaking.

If Viktor was right and the wraiths are here because of me, and it was my blood which is the reason that the demons are attacking, how can I possibly go home? I'll be homeless again, having to leave Grisham to find another city to get lost in. I have minimal money in my bank account, not enough to help me start over.

I'm screwed and tired.

So very, very tired...

'Serafina?'

My heavy lids refuse to open. I want to cry and scream and be left alone. *I can't go back. I've lost everything.* All I can hear is feet shuffling and weapons clinking.

Viktor and Felix have a short conversation and I hear Alistair ask a question and then reply even though no one answers him. 'Are you sure?' he says and I know he's crouching down next to me. His energy surrounds me.

'This entire situation is strange. We're here in this damn realm looking for an Azanite betrayer and we just happen to find a female living amongst humans on our journey. It's odd, don't you think?' Felix muses.

'Very.' Alistair's voice bounces off the stone walls.

'Maybe she was sent to us by the Sun Gods.'

'I'm not sure what use a female like Serafina DarkwoodsAzar would be to the ones we hunt, Felix. She'd be no use to the humans we're hunting and she left Azanir at thirteen.'

There's a pause.

'That is an interesting theory, Wilder.'

Pause.

'No, she seems to be more afraid of you. Yes, I know.' There is another pause. 'I don't know her story. I only know what happened after she was presumed lost.' Again I have no idea who Alistair is speaking to.

Viktor is the next to start talking. 'I wasn't there when she ran away. To be honest, we didn't know if that's what she did. A great number of the court of the Darkwoods believed that she was taken. Some thought she was dead due to an accident. The Darkwoods are dangerous, so that was always possible.' Viktor sounds close.

'I remember hearing about the lost Lady of the Darkwoods. Even from all the way in the Riverways. The details were very vague though and I don't remember it being much of a hot topic. Like a passing comment. Which I find strange now that I've met her. Why wouldn't her father and the other Azar have started a massive search for her? What about your father, Alistair? Did he not think it important to find her?' Felix asks.

Lost in the in-between of sleep and awake, I find their words strange and hard to register.

'My father did for a little while,' Alistair replies. 'It's hard when her own father put a stop to the search. We hadn't really heard much of the Lady of the Darkwoods. There were rumours as to why Lord DarkwoodsAzar kept her isolated from his court. Clearly, they were all court gossip.' Alistair pauses and I'm left more confused by my eavesdropping right now.

Who the hell is his father? And people from other courts gossiped about me? I'm sure nothing good was said.

'We all heard the rumour and clearly they were *very* wrong. She doesn't look like she was in a freak accident as a youngling and was left with her face distorted like a wraith.'

What the fuck?

'Please,' Viktor grumbles. 'She's nothing more than an entitled Lady who was given everything she ever needed and yet ran away. My guess is that she did it for attention but her father didn't indulge. She probably didn't expect the whole thing to get this far. She has probably been waiting ten years for us to come and find her. To save her. I doubt she's the one we're looking for.'

Rage builds under my skin but it isn't enough to fight the pull of exhaustion. If I could open my eyes and speak, I'd tell Victor LongwingDrengar to go fuck himself!

There's a heartbeat of weird silence before Felix says, 'I agree with Wilder. She looks genuine in her fear of us. Especially you, friend.' There is a distinct sound of hard fabric being slapped and I can picture Felix clapping the scary healer on the back. I have no idea what's wrong with my hearing though because I didn't hear Wilder speak.

'I don't believe she's the betrayer either. I don't want her to be afraid of us.' Felix sounds like he's pouting and I really want to look. I can't open my damn eyes.

'None of us do, but we'll proceed with caution,' Viktor grumbles.

'Well, it's definitely not what we're looking for in the human realm.'

'No, and we need to get back to our mission. We cannot get distracted by a beautiful face or let it hinder our senses. As Viktor said, we'll be cautious. Let's get her well first.'

Alastair is still crouched beside me and his words take a moment to sink in. *Did Alistair just call me beautiful?* 'I'll take her.' Pause. 'Wilder, I know what I'm doing despite not being the awesome Medir you are.' Pause. Then there are a few chuckles from the others before I'm shuffled and lifted.

Groaning, I still can't open my eyes or speak.

'Grab the door Felix,' Alistair says and I panic thinking that we're going outside where the wraiths are, but then warm light filters through my eyelids and the fresh breeze of morning filters through my senses.

I feel the power of nature almost instantly.

Curled up against a warm, hard chest, I take a true, deep breath. I open my eyes slightly. The pain of the brightness has me blink away water. I hiss with every step Alastair takes and whimper when he finally crouches and places me gently on the grass.

Staring at the stream of clouds, I study the beautiful morning sky. Awash in colour, the sun chases the darkness and my soul seems to relax for the first time since the stabbing.

I hated the hospital, then I spent my entire first night out of that hellhole in a damn mausoleum. It hasn't been the best week, that's for sure.

I'm barely aware of the males around me or the way Alistair apologises about having to lift up my shirt. I can't find my voice to answer. I want to weep under the magnificent feeling seeping through my body, even through my clothes the sun seems to be doing its job. And it is amazing.

I close my eyes as the male's large hands brush against my now sensitive skin. He's gentle and respectful as he lifts the fabric of my oversized t-shirt to expose my abdomen and then makes quick work of ripping off the bandages that were placed over the wound by the over-worked nurse before I left yesterday.

The entire process hurts more than words can describe and yet the moment my bare skin is exposed to the sun fully, I feel its power. I can't care that the males are all asking me how the wound happened. Or demanding that I let Wilder heal me.

None of it matters. All I can focus on is the blissful feeling of the heat on my skin. Of the way my beast finally rises and wakes. I didn't realise how weak I was and how much danger we were both in. She drinks up the warmth and lets it sink into our muscles. The strangest tingling begins in my side and I take a deep breath, drawing in the healing power of nature.

The brain fog disappears and I become a great deal more aware of my surroundings.

Turning my head to the side, I see row after row of ancient looking headstones and monuments. Not even the fact that I'm in a cemetery can turn off this blissful feeling.

Turning to my other side does though...dramatically.

Four large, attractive and deadly looking Drengar stand tall and stone-like watching me with a mix of expressions.

Viktor looks grim. Felix seems amused by something he can see on my face. Alistair's eyes are narrowed like he's grumpy. Wilder isn't looking at my face but at my side, I can't read the look on his face, the only hint to emotion is the way his hands are curled into fists.

I don't know if I was in the right state of mind all night until now and the gravity of my situation hits me...hard.

With my side now completely pain free and my body fully regenerated, thanks to the power of the Sun Gods, I try to formulate a plan in my head. For once, my beast seems to be in agreeance. She doesn't want to go back to Azanir any more than I do.

Brow rising slightly when none of them look away, I wait for them all to realise they're staring and avert their eyes. Which they do eventually. That's when I spring into action.

Chapter Fifteen

Legs pumping even though a moment ago I was barely conscious, I have no time to think about anything except my escape. Tapping into a beast I've tried to ignore for ten years and giving her complete control, the world flies by.

I can hear the docks up ahead and believing I'll be safe-*er* in a more populated area, I don't stop. Don't hesitate.

My chest heaves with the exertion. I'm so unfit, it's pathetic. My fear of being dragged back to my father fuelling my speed.

I weave in and out of the trees surrounding the cemetery and try to work out where to go. Scott's wedding is today but I can't risk going home. It's extremely early so no one will be up yet.

Miles comes to mind and I try to formulate the best plan to get to his house. Each one harder to achieve then the next.

All I can hear is my heavy breathing and the pounding of my feet and then I come to a screeching halt on a short scream when out of nowhere Viktor appears before me. His face hard and unmoving as his eyes glow red.

Fuck!

Pivoting and almost breaking my ankle sliding on the littered leaves under foot, I change direction. Tears fall down my face and even though I can't hear the massive male following me, I don't stop and almost collide into Alistair who growls when I swing a fist and somehow dodge his attempt to grab me with his trunk-like arms.

He too doesn't follow when I run away and I change direction again when Felix appears from the trees slowly.

Heart pounding, I break the tree line and stop dead at the sight of the ancient cemetery and the mausoleum I was locked in last night. Tears falling freely down my face, I hate myself for the way I just allowed these males to herd me back here. The voice in my head screams at me to continue to run but when I finally get the sense to keep moving, thick, muscle heavy arms wrap around my body from behind.

Caged against a warm, hard chest and a male whose scent almost sent me into a panic last night when he grabbed me in a similar way after I attacked him, I roar my frustration and fear.

A dream flashes in my mind and I physically shake my head to expel stupid images that make no sense.

Throat raw from shouting and screeching for Wilder to put me down, I try to kick back at his shins to no avail. I shake and move and contort my body to try and get out of his hold which is just as useless as trying to hurt him.

'Let me go!' I scream— like full on, all out scream.

'Stop. I won't hurt you.' His voice makes me shiver and I hate myself.

'Like fuck you won't. You're holding me against my will, that's hurting me!' I manage to say past my burning throat.

'Strong wraiths can walk the early morning hours before the sun takes its hold. Running into the trees at this hour is unwise.'

'Did you just call me dumb?' I snap and yet there's a part of me that isn't that offended. I should probably have remembered that. I was never allowed out of the lair until the sun was fully up and giving life to the world.

I haven't stopped trying to get away even though it's futile.

'You fear me. More than the others. Why?'

'You...you...you're a Medir,' I whisper, unsure why I've answered and the moment I feel his arms slacken is when I drop and fall to the hard ground with an oomph and scramble away.

Turning, I glare up at the male frowning down at me. Breathing heavy from fighting against his hold, I watch as his brow furrows in uncertainty. It's like...like I've offended him.

Shocked, I open and close my mouth a few times, unsure what to say. I think I finally realise how good looking he is. Like the others, he is tall. Males of our kind are so much taller than a typical human. It's the beast in their blood. Our human-like form is only one side of ourselves even though technically there is no real human left in our bloodlines. The thought would send some very proud Azanites into a tailspin. To have human blood would be an abomination.

Like me. I'm half and half. I'm not fully Azanir and not fully human. I don't fit anywhere.

Wilder has my full attention and for a moment I wonder what he looks like in his other form. Images brew in my mind and I have no idea if it's my imagination or memories of dreams I've had. Wide shoulders, a body thick with muscles and a waist that tapers slightly under his leathers, even his scar adds to the allure of him. His jet-black hair falls loosely around his shoulders, softening his hard, masculine features slightly and for a moment I have a weird sense of reality and dream blurring together in my mind.

I see Wilder in front of me in his black uniform, then his image changes. Before me, he stands in loose pants and a tan linen, long sleeve shirt. Then in short pants with no shirt and a body that has my eyes pop. I've never seen anyone with a fucking eight pack before and it makes me instantly overheat. Before me, Wilder changes and he's a warrior again but this time he's covered in blood from head to toe and I have no idea if it is his or someone else's. My panic chokes me.

Blinking rapidly, I come back to the present and know I must look completely freaked out.

Wilder takes a single step forward, his eyes full of concern and something else...something I can't name or respond to because the others appear around me.

Surrounding me.

They're a wall of muscle. I feel all my options slip away with the breeze that picks up my hair and slaps it across my face.

Felix and Alistair stand either side of me while Wilder moves so that Viktor is directly in my line of vision. He doesn't look very impressed, especially when I get a burst of adrenaline and think I can get away and try to jump up and run again, to only be blocked and knocked down, surprisingly gently, by Felix.

'You done?'

About five responses filter through my brain before I decided on, 'no.'

Alistair and Viktor share a look that has me fold my legs and sit with my arms crossed like a petulant teenager who is refusing to clean her room.

Running his large, man-ly hand through his dark hair, Viktor show a hint of emotion other than grumpy for the first time.

'If you think I'm going to make it easy for you all to kidnap me and take me back to Azanir then you better get ready for the biggest fight of your life.' I manage to infuse as much anger and truth into my words. There's no way that I'm going back to my father.

Never!

There's a heartbeat of silence before Alistair speaks and I refuse to turn and look at him.

'No one is here to kidnap you, Lady Serafina. I believe we have all shown that we're here to protect you after the fight we all had last night with one of the biggest collections of wraith demons I've ever seen.' I turn on that and feel my jaw hit the floor. Alistair looks to the others for clarity if what he's saying is correct. They all nod.

'Yes, I don't think I've ever seen wraiths act like how they did last night. Do you think this has something to do with our mission, or her? It was as if they were going after....' Felix clears his throat and lowers his gaze when Viktor makes a deep noise in the back of his throat that has every hair stand on my body.

'What does...what do you mean?' I stammer, feeling the colour drain from my face as I realise that they're being serious.

'It means that we have a great deal to discuss,' Alistair replies. 'We're not here to kidnap you, Serafina. However, the options that you have seem very slim. If we hadn't showed up last night when we did, I'm afraid that you and your humans would be dead right now. Let's go get something to eat and talk. I feel like this is going to be a hard conversation for you,

Serafina DarkwoodsAzar. It's your choice. We're wasting too much time here.'

His words sink in and sit heavily in my gut.

Is he serious? Did they...save my life? What does he mean by a hard conversation for me?

The others agree with Alistair and his idea of food. Felix, a tad bit noisily. Viktor all but growls at me to follow before they start walking away.

Refusing to get up, I wait and watch them retreat. To start with, I'm furious, then I start checking them all out because hey, I'm a warm blooded female and all four arses look cut and firm and juicy, but then I become really aware of my surroundings. The further away they get, the more I see the darkness in the trees and how the sun is nowhere near high enough for me to be safe out here in the open, in the middle of a fucking cemetery.

Eating my bottom lip, I curse loudly and jump up when my overactive mind sees things in the shadows of the trees.

I stomp towards the males, not believing what I'm doing.

Chapter Sixteen

I DON'T KNOW HOW I convinced these four oversized brutes to follow me to Jordan's Diner. It may have something to do with Felix and how much he was complaining about being hungry while Alistair and Viktor tried to work out a safe place for us to eat. When I mentioned this place, they didn't hate the option, so here we are.

Sitting in my favourite booth, locked between Brute One—aka Viktor, and Brute Two— aka Alistair, I fiddle with the laminated large menu, unsure what to do or say now that we're all seated and looking at each other.

The oversized clock on the wall has me breathe a little easier knowing that it's only five thirty in the morning and that I have a few hours before I need to be ready and at the church.

I haven't uttered a word since we walked in and the handful of customers around the mostly empty diner and the three workers stopped what they're doing to gape at our party.

The only one talking is Felix, who hasn't stopped narrating every thought about all the things he wants to eat and even asks me for my recommendations while completely oblivious to the fact that I haven't responded to his endless questions. 'I'll do pancakes and bacon and maybe a side of waffles, I think.'

Are waffles even a side option?

Felix nods weirdly to Wilder, who's next to the long window across from Brute Two, as if he has just said something.

I'm too busy going over how my morning has been that when Moira appears at the end of the table and says my name, I'm not ready and jump in surprise. Gripping my chest, I can only imagine what I look like from the way Moira is staring at me suspiciously.

She waits. The guys stare. I start fidgeting with the menu.

Shit. 'Sorry, what?'

Smiling a smile I know is very practiced, Moira repeats, 'I didn't think we'd see you today with Scott's wedding and after the attack. We were all really upset to hear what happened to you.'

I nod, unsure what to say.

The energy changes completely around me. Heat fills the booth. Comforting and frightening heat that incites a really odd reaction in my body. My beast blinks and stretches as if waking up from her slumber. She is such a pain in my arse sometimes. I could use her help right now getting away from these males but she seems more interested in the feeling of the warmth radiating against our skin.

'So, who are your friends?' she asks.

Shuffling against the cheap, red vinyl booth seat, I try to come up with a lie and end up just squeaking, 'just old friends,' and pray that the males stop looking at me.

Lucky for me, Moira doesn't seem at all aware of the heat or the intensity of the males. 'Riiiiight,' she draws out, eyeing each male individually and I can only guess what she's thinking.

When her eyes land on Wilder she smiles though and I sit gaping like a fool at the twinkle in the middle aged woman's eye. 'They don't look old. You look mighty young and large and... big.' She's practically eye-fucking the scary Medir who just throws her a smouldering look that has me shiver and maybe sit up straighter. My shoulders brushing Brute One and Brute Two but I can't care.

Did she...is she...flirting? And why does that kinda infuriate me? Also large and big are the same thing...serious!

Now mad at myself for caring so much, I pray to the Sun Gods for assistance.

'What can I get you all?' she asks, now skimming that gaze over Felix like he could be on the menu.

For a moment I'm unsure if they know enough of the human tongue to answer. They've only spoken Zaric with me since meeting them. We have humans in our homelands. There aren't very many occasions that humans and our kind interact though. The exception is the handful of human's that live and work in the lairs. The ones that hold high positions as the lair servants are the only ones permitted to speak our language.

My old life was filled with arrogance and bigotry and elitism that even as a youngling, I found unjust.

Felix, who seems quite pleased with himself, angles his body like he's making sure his entire god-like structure is on full display for her pleasure. 'I'll take the pancakes with a side of bacon. Three strips. Also a waffle. Maybe two.' Felix's accent has me stare. It's strange and has his words dip in certain sections that just adds to his hot-ness.

Moira's brow rises slightly but she is so used to me, Van, Brent and the boys that she understands big appetites. 'Sure, Sugar. Ice-cream or syrup?'

'Both,' Felix grins and coaxes another one from Moira. I thought I liked the woman. Now I wish she'd just go away.

'And for you handsome?' she asks Wilder who flicks his dark gaze to me briefly and I swear I see a ghost of a smile. There is a part of me that wants to bare my teeth and demand he not flirt back. Not that he is, but I'm still pissed and I have no Sun Gods idea why!

'He'll have the same as me,' Felix cuts in.

'Sure thing,' Moira purrs. Like actually purrs.

Slumping back against the booth cushion, my leg starts bouncing in annoyance.

'And you?' she doesn't seem too eager to put on the charm for the male blocking my escape from the booth. Viktor doesn't even look up as he orders a bunch of eggs and bacon and toast with Alistair asking for the same as he hands the menu over without any interest. Their behaviour calms me slightly so that when it's my turn, I just ask for the usual, which she understands.

'Chocolate or strawberry today, Raff?'

The idea of a thickshake peps me up a little. 'Chocolate, please.' It's definitely a chocolate kind of morning.

'We will all have one,' Felix adds just as Moira goes to collect the menus. She finds that very funny before she moves off.

'So, you were attacked?' Viktor didn't miss a beat. I give a small gesture that I let them decipher. 'By whom?'

I refuse to look at Viktor who's now tapping the table, waiting for me to respond to his demanding question. He sounds like Brent or Scott, except he hasn't earnt the privilege of my respect or a response just because he asked. The memories of home come back hard and fast and all my lessons of the Drengar start replaying in my mind.

They're the protectors of the realm. The warriors trained from a young age to learn the art of keeping our kind safe. To keep our people going and protected from the demons who try to extinguish our fire. Warriors who train hard. Their lives are devoted in servitude of their mission. The upside that I could always see was that with all the danger came authority and power that not too many in our world hold.

Being a Drengar is the only position that one can work towards even though Drengar do run in families. Drengar families have younglings that they mould and condition to become hunters and maintain their status.

To be an Azar is to be born into it. You must earn the title of The Drengar. It is earnt. The Drengar are respected. Drengar trump all but Azar.

They're also notorious for being arrogant, quick-to-anger and possessive.

I do my best to not answer Viktor which doesn't do anything because they're all waiting, their expression screaming that they aren't going to drop this. 'I'd rather talk about what you believe we have to discuss and why it'd be hard for me.'

The tension pulses. Felix flicks his gaze to the males around me. His emotions locked away tightly. 'Before we begin, why don't we start with some introductions?' he says. 'Felix SkyfallDrengar. It's a pleasure to be in your company Lady Serafina.' His smile is like an infection you can't fight against. I return it and take the calloused hand he offers over the table. His title doesn't tell me much about where in Azanir he's from.

He calms my nerves and I like Felix instantly. 'It's nice to meet you,' I reply and am shocked at how genuine I feel.

'It seems you know Viktor LongwingDrengar.' Felix smirks.

I nod toward the brute next to me who nods back. 'I saw him around my father's lair growing up.' I shrug, trying to play it cool. Really, I was super obsessed with catching glimpses of him around the place and hid whenever he was in the distance so that I could openly stare.

'I didn't often see you,' he admits quietly and I don't know if he's criticising me or not. 'Your father kept you separate. You were never at court.'

The look on Felix's face is almost comical. 'Why?' Felix asks me, clearly confused. I only shrug again while wiping my sweaty palms on my thighs. The movement caught by every male around me. I'm nervous and they know it. Childhood scars hurts when they are touched.

'It's a little odd that the Lord of the Darkwoods would keep his only daughter away from court.' I have no idea if Felix is waiting for an answer or if he's just musing the idea aloud.

A little done with talking of my father, I take the glass of water Viktor pours and hands me before saying, 'I'm sure the Lord of the Darkwoods can answer your questions when you go back.' I can't help the sarcasm or the way my father's title drips with contempt.

Felix just laughs a sound that has me gape. He smiles as he studies me. His blue eyes sparkling in humour. 'I see your point, Lady. How about I introduce you to this big guy next. This here is Wilder BlazeAzar-Drengar-Medir.' Felix seems super excited to introduce the Medir and I know it's because he wants to see my reaction.

I gulp down the fear that rises in my throat. He has every title of our people. Making him one of the most powerful males in existence.

He's not only of an elite family but the lair of the BlazeAzar's to be exact. I had many lessons of the powerful families that rule my homelands. The BlazeAzar's are a powerful family who live at the very peak of Azanir. It's said to be a harsh environment near the ocean where a massive portal between our world and the world of the demon wraiths sits. Meaning that attacks in the north are many and also means that they produce a great deal of Drengar up there. One of the biggest Drengar academies where males and females are sent to train and study for their Drengar title is in the domain of the BlazeAzar's.

On top of all that he is Medir. Medir's are born with abilities that go beyond the power or beast of an Azanite. It's a mystery really why some are born with extra abilities. There's a Medir academy somewhere in Azanir, its location not widely known. Every healer can heal like a Sun God and are said to have other, intense powers such as being able to place someone into a deep sleep with their minds.

Three titles.

Azar—Ruling Class.

Drengar—Hunter.

Medir—Healer.

I've never heard of three titles and it makes me want to run and hide under my bed.

Wilder's eyes lift from the table and collide with mine as I stare and stare, unable to speak. He inclines his head ever so slightly and if I was standing I'd have to sit down.

'I know, his title is a mouthful.' Felix chuckles and then stops speaking to chuckle again. It's odd how much he does that, like he can hear something I can't.

I don't really know what to do with my body. Felix is watching me and Wilder is now staring out the window, looking all hot and complicated.

We sit in awkward silence.

Viktor goes to say something and is interrupted by Moira and another lady who brings over all our food. The break from all the staring and smiling is just what I needed and I grab at my shake when Viktor politely takes it from Moira and hands it to me.

I shove the straw in my mouth and suck in the freezing goodness in the hope of taking some time to gather my thoughts.

The males dig into their meals instantly and I drink while watching them. My patience running really thin.

I wait rather impatiently for someone to talk and end up blurting, 'and who are you?' to the brute on my left.

Felix laughs and I swear I lose all train of thought. Staring at his gorgeous face, I try to work out why he finds what I just said so funny and why the scary healer is also smiling at the table as if he doesn't want me to know that he has a sense of humour. 'What?'

'My Lady, let me introduce you to Alistair AzanirAzar-Drengar.'

Holy shit!

My world tilts and I grip the table, my thickshake now forgotten. My gaze flicks unconsciously to Wilder to find him staring before I look to the male next to me. To the fucking Prince of our people.

Alistair is eating his food, totally uncaring of the way Felix starts to introduce him further. 'Prince of Azanir. Second Son of the King of Azanir, King Oswald AzanirAzar-Drengar.'

Words scream in my mind and I blurt out, 'fucking hell,' without much thought. I'm screwed. There is no way he'll let me walk out of this diner. It's his duty to bring me home. Our people aren't allowed to live amongst humans. We aren't to interact or reproduce or do anything with humans. Me being here breaks so many of our laws.

Shoulders slumping, I begin to pick at the food on my plate, my appetite vanishing.

Chapter Seventeen

I MANAGE TO EAT a little but don't taste anything.

'You have nothing to fear,' Alistair states, obviously he can sense my emotions. A skill all powerful Azanites have. 'Unless you have somehow betrayed our people or given away our secrets.' There is a weight to every word he says and I have trouble trying to understand them.

'I haven't,' I blurt out. Studying the table, I pick at the laminated top.

'He's right, Lady Serafina,' Felix says, his voice full of warmth. 'You have nothing to fear.'

'Raff,' I whisper. 'My name is Raff. I left Serafina behind when I ran away, ten years ago.'

'And why did you run, Raff?' the young male replies and I finally look up. He seems genuine in his question. There's no accusation. No reprimand, and for a moment I think I might answer him, but then remember myself.

'I'm just a spoilt little youngling who expected my father to follow,' I answer childishly and feel Viktor tense beside me. 'Isn't that what you said this morning, Viktor LongwingDrengar?' I can't drop it and while I know I'm making everyone uncomfortable, I find I don't care.

There's a heartbeat of silence before Felix says, 'You remind me of Kennan.' My stomach drops into my butt and I snap my gaze back to Felix and frown.

I haven't spoken of my brothers in a very long time and I really don't want to start now. Luka and Keenan were much older than me. There is a fourteen year age gap between Keenan and I, and a sixteen year one between Luka.

Our people don't reproduce easily, in fact, it is a major issue and has been for decades now. That, coupled with the steady decline in female younglings being born, is one of the biggest problems to face the kingdom of Azanir. Well, that and the wraiths. This explains why when I was born it was met with shock, apparently, or so my maid used to tell me when she would do my hair and I'd ask her to tell me stories. Obviously, I found out just how much of a shock my birth really was when I was thirteen. Especially to the female I thought was my mother. Would've been a real fucking shock to find out you had a daughter the day she was born.

It's not the first time in my life I find myself thinking of my birth mother and if she ever got to hold me, or if she had a say in how I was taken from her. I know it's useless but I do wonder if she had a choice and if she wanted to keep me. The poor human woman who had a forbidden baby. It's never a good thing when I start thinking about her because it always leads to feelings that I am too messed up to face.

'I think you should all start discussing what you wanted to discuss with me.'

'Right,' Alistair wipes his mouth and throws down the napkin and I can't not watch as it falls to his now empty plate. 'Serafina, we're here in the human realm on a mission to retrieve something that was taken from our homelands by a group of humans. You were not our target. Frankly, your name has been laid to rest a number of years ago. We were tracking the large group of wraiths that attacked last night and they led us to you. A week ago, we found your blood in the ally and knew that you were a lone female which is obviously a startling realisation as it's against our laws for you to be here. We thought you could be a key to what we're searching for.'

I note how the Prince refuses to call me Raff like I asked, but I'm too busy contemplating what he has just said. 'Humans took something from Azanir?'

Human's wouldn't be that dumb. Most of the humans on our homeland were born and raised in the world where the beasts rule. Don't get me wrong, they're treated really well—to a point. Yes, they're seen as lower beings and yes, you wouldn't see an Azanite speak to a human who wasn't of the higher servants and never in their human language—one wouldn't lower themselves to that standard. However, from what I was taught and from the minimal I witnessed, the human towns were well built. People had jobs and homes and money and homelessness didn't seem to exist. Yes, I was sheltered, but the humans never seemed unhappy. My maid taught me they were better off than in the human realms. They had fear of our people, as they should, as an Azanite is a beast under the human façade, but there were rules protecting them as much as our own.

I try to process the fact that these males just stumbled across my existence. 'What did they take?'

All three males look to Alistair and the shift in their energy has me curious and also a little concerned. An Azanite would burn the world down if their wealth was stolen. Stealing is a massive crime. Mostly because our beasts are greedy and have a mild obsession with shiny things. This seems more than that though. Four Drengar, four what appears to be very dominant predators, have been sent on this mission. It must be big and important.

Felix clears his throat and begins to devour his thickshake while Wilder and Alistair have a staring competition. I ask the question again a little louder.

'Our most sacred text,' the prince answers. I look over at Wilder and then away quickly at the intensity of his gaze. 'A great deal has changed in our homelands since your disappearance. The only way to have taken the book is to use the blood of an Azar. A betrayer.'

I just stare at Alistair, not sure if I've heard him correctly.

All the blood is sitting in my feet as a dream replays in my mind. A book. A sacred text. A treasure like that would be stupid to touch. A treasure that I may have seen...maybe?

'That would mean that an Azanite would've help though,' I squeak out, contemplating this a little and rationalising the chaos in my mind. It was just a dream.... only a dream...

'Yes,' Alistair nods and I find myself very uncomfortable with the way they're all watching my reaction.

Then it hits me.

'You think...you think I had something to do with that?' I'm stunned and a little unsure what to do. 'How? I've been gone for ten years and have been keeping my head down.'

Alistair makes a deep noise in the back of his throat and I shut my mouth. I can't believe what I'm hearing.

'We aren't accusing you of anything. We just find it strange that we've run into a lost Lady of Azanir on our mission to retrieve a stolen treasure. You can see how that looks.'

'Do I?' I have no idea what else to say. I eat my bottom lip hoping they don't hear the way my voice catches. My mind screams that I'm being stupid while the other voice in my head growls that I'm an idiot and that of course I know what book they're talking about.

It's been a very long time since I've dreamt something that actually had more meaning than a simple nightmare. *I think...*

'The text was taken by a group of human smugglers who've been causing quite a bit of grief in our lands for a few years now. All small things. Nothing we really concerned ourselves with in the beginning because really they just made trouble for the humans and the Thal families.'

Alistair names the last level of the social system of Azanir. A Thal is a worker. Important in our society but don't hold a great deal of authority.

I fight my eye roll. Of course an Azar or Drengar wouldn't care about a group of human thugs who were harassing humans and less important Azanites. Typical.

'Not until they stole the sacred text in the middle of a wraith attack ten nights ago from one of our Sun Temples in the capital.'

'That doesn't sound easy.'

'No, and the chest it was kept in was spelled to only be opened by the blood of an Azar and well...' Viktor indicates with his hand towards me and I understand. The situation I'm in right now couldn't get any worse. Now I'm being accused of being a traitor and a smuggler.

'You run into an Azar living amongst humans. I get it,' I finish for him. It does look bad and the coincidence is hard to miss.

'Yep,' Felix replies grimly.

'I have nothing to do with this,' I declare, making sure to look each one of them in the eye.

Alistair sighs and I brace myself. I'll need to run if they truly think I did this. 'We believe you.'

It takes my poor, sleep deprived mind a moment to process. Then it dawns on me, 'if you're here for this stolen book, then you aren't here to take me back against my will? It's just a coincidence.'

Viktor sighs dramatically. 'Serafina—'

'Raff,' I cut him off to remind him.

I get a good side eye from that and Viktor continues like he doesn't care what I call myself. 'We don't believe in coincidence and under any other circumstance we would send you back. It is illegal for you to be here.'

I grip the tables edge and bite my tongue. I don't know what it is about Drengar Viktor that makes me want to lash out and talk-back.

'However, we're on a mission of top priority and frankly, we aren't in the business of forcing females to do things they don't want to do. We can taste your fear when our home is mentioned and while we don't understand it, we wouldn't do that.'

His words leave me shocked. 'What does that mean?' I think I know but need confirmation before I start cheering.

'It means, Lady Serafina,' Alistair states and I turn my attention back to him. 'We do not know if the wraiths will return for you tonight or in a few nights or never. In my experience, and with what I saw last night, I don't think they're going to leave you alone. Which means that you're in danger. However, you are a grown female who seems to have a great deal of apprehension and even fear of returning to Azanir. I am offering that you come with us on our mission to retrieve our sacred text and then return with us to our homelands. You will be under our protection and kept safe from the wraiths who now have your scent. We can also keep an eye on you, to make sure that what you say is true.'

So, he doesn't really believe me?

'Don't get me wrong though,' Alistair continues. 'Our mission is dangerous and you will have to follow orders and keep out of the way while we recover the treasure.' He scratches his face and I fixate on the movement. He is handsome beyond anything I have ever seen.

I can't name what draws my attention from him to Wilder though, but it does, and I quickly look away from the black eyes watching me intently.

'And if I say no?' I ask, almost in a whisper. My stomach is in knots.

'Then, we will say our goodbyes and wish you luck in your life and against the wraiths. Our mission trumps anything else.'

My jaw drops. I can't believe it. 'Are...are you serious?'

'Yes.' He nods. 'We will not tell anyone that we saw you.'

I'm gobsmacked. I don't know what to do with myself. I do a quick scan of the males around the table and ask, 'are you telling me the truth?'

They all nod.

Fucking hell.

I quickly go through all my options.

'Okay. Thank you for the offer, but I have a life here and I'm happy.'

There's a pause and I fear for a moment that they were lying to me about letting me go.

'Right, well that is settled.' Alistair's response takes me back a little. I can hear the subtle surprise and contempt. I think I just offended the Prince of Azanir, which doesn't feel like the wisest thing to do. Alistair clears his throat and finishes his thickshake in one gulp. He places it back a little too roughly before he declares, 'we will leave you to your life, Lady Serafina.'

Eating my bottom lip, I watch as Felix frowns and looks to Wilder who studies me briefly before indicating with his head for Felix to go. They both begin to shuffle from the booth.

My beast stands to attention, probably unsure what is happening and why I feel a rush of adrenaline.

Stunned at the emotional reaction I'm having right now, I watch Viktor silently get off the seat and follow when I realise Alistair is waiting for me to let him out. I feel all nervous and self-conscious and maybe a little apprehensive of letting them go.

Alistair pulls a couple of bills from his back pocket and throws them on the table. I feel so tiny with them all standing around me and I wrap an arm around my middle to keep my beast quiet as she has begun to shudder under my skin.

Wilder and Felix are staring oddly at each other and I look to Viktor when he lightly touches my arm. The contact sends a bolt of energy through my body and I suck in a breath. Viktor doesn't seem to notice. The hard look on his face makes it difficult to know what he's thinking. 'What Alistair said was right, Serafina DarkwoodsAzar, the wraiths know you're here. Be careful and stay inside at night.'

I nod, unable to find words.

'Stay well, Lady.' Alistair bows slightly, and he and Viktor head to the doors.

Felix is the next to bow and wish me luck on my own. He hesitates just before he follows the others and I long to know what he was going to say. Moving a little to let Wilder past, I clench my hands at the sight of him leaving and then reprimand myself for being upset that he didn't say anything like the others.

I stand there until the door shuts on one of the most intense and emotionally confusing nights of my life.

CHAPTER EIGHTEEN

S TARING AT MYSELF IN the full length mirror against my bedroom wall, I turn in a slow circle feeling a little lost and unsure of what I'm doing. The navy, midi, A-line dress feels restrictive and scratchy even though a week ago it was my favourite dress from the many Laney picked.

Today though, I feel like my body's too big for my skin and that no matter how many times I pump up my brown, natural curls, they just fall limp down my back as if, they too, are unhappy about what has happened. The only positive is that my side is completely healed and if I really allow myself to think about it, I'd have a meltdown, because while the healing of the sun is powerful, it should still be at least a little tender. Meaning, Drengar Wilder is a great deal more powerful than I feared he was and I was in the same space as him for hours.

Groaning loudly, I give myself a good pep talk and stop looking at the damn dress and stop thinking about the four males.

Slumping on the end of my bed, I put on my black strappy shoes and battle with the turmoil rolling in my chest. I have no idea why I feel so emotional. I don't know how I know that the book I saw in my dream was the one the males were talking about.

I snuck back into my room just as Laney was getting out of bed and pretended that I wasn't out all night with four panty-soaking Drengar in a cemetery. I have about ten missed calls from Miles and about fifteen texts from last night and this morning asking if I'm okay. My head is spinning in regards to the fact that I've seen the book and I can't stop replaying the dream in my mind.

I feel like shit. I look like shit!

The makeup I used to cover the fact that I haven't slept is doing nothing. My normally sun-kissed skin is pale. I hate that I can't close the blinds on the cracked window and hide under my blankets until last night becomes a bearable memory. All I can think about is their offer to protect me.

I know they meant what they said about the wraiths but I have a family and a job and...fuck, I can't sit still.

Pacing, back and forth, I have an overwhelming need to pull my hair out.

The calling of my name has me stop wearing out the carpet and shake off the negative energy. I need to focus. Scott is my priority and it's his wedding. I have to schedule my meltdown for later tonight and be ready for this long day because that's exactly what it's going to be...a freakin' long day.

I've never been in love. I actually don't know what it would feel like. I've read books and watched human movies that try to explain it. To be honest, it just looks like a great deal of work and heartache before one realises that the love of their life was right in front of their eyes. Like a best friend or a brothers friend, which doesn't seem like my path as I look around at the handful of pews on Scott's side of the church. Compared to Carly's side, it's a little bare and leaves me not many options for love.

That's when four faces flash in my mind and I physically shake my head to expel those images quickly. This is not the time for me to be think about the Drengar. Not when I'm standing in the corner of the church with my violin in hand, waiting for the cue for me to start playing the song I chose for this event. I was a little shocked that Carly gave me so much control over the music that will play when she walks down the aisle and I made my choice based on a number of factors. The biggest one is the fact that the Amor Aeternus, *Eternal Love*, is a song played during binding ceremonies in Azanir.

There aren't very many occasions when music is played in my homeland. You only hear singing and instruments when human minstrels are hired, and allowed access to lairs for bindings, funerals and very special celebrations. Azanites don't play instruments.

My maid would play for me though. She was a beautiful flautist and when it was just her and I, she'd let me dance barefoot on the lawns in my private garden. I taught myself how to play this song by memory alone when I was in my late teens by recalling the tune and using my ear to recreate the melody. It probably sounds nothing like the Amor Aeternus, but hey, every time I've played it for humans, there has never been a dry eye in the building and a wedding seems like a fitting time to make people cry.

I'd be crying if I had to bind myself to someone and have to obey them and ask permission to do things.

Feeling a bit awkward standing alone at the front of the church, I do like the view I have of everyone though. I've been people watching since I was escorted to this spot and Van and my 'eye conversations' have been hilarious.

He's sitting next to Laney and Danny in the first row and every time a woman walks in with a ridiculous hat on their head, I eye-scream at him to look and he does some funny shit to try and be subtle. Which he isn't.

Biting my lip, I snort when a particularly hideous hat walks in and Van all but jumps up to get a good look at what has me dying trying to keep my laughter in— which gets him a stern, sharp look from Laney. She doesn't seem too impressed and her mouth is pursed as she speaks to him and I know that Van just got into trouble because he sits with a ghost of a smile on his face.

That's when I realise that I may not have ever felt romantic love but I do know love. Here in the human world. In a place that last night I thought was going to be taken off me, I've found something special. Something unexpected.

No longer making fun of the hats, my focus is on my family. Laney looks beautiful today. She's wearing a gorgeous light blue midi dress that sparkles on the shoulders. The sun spilling into the church from the stained glass windows seems to beam down on her. She's glowing and happy and I have an overwhelming fear that my time with her is limited. Which scares me.

Putting my morbid thoughts down to my crazy, horrifying night, I can't help but watch Van and Danny playing some kind of hand game and Tiff and Toby whisper to each other and watching something on the hand-me-down phone Brent got the twins. My gaze moves to my older foster brothers standing before the altar.

Scott and Brent are looking all fancy in their tuxedos, honestly they both seem uncomfortable standing up with the priest waiting for this to start, but they are hiding it perfectly.

I'd do anything for them.

I'd even stand up here, placing my violin against my collarbone and shoulder and then resting my jaw on the chinrest, despite the last time I performed in front of a crowd and my beast made me pass out.

Indicating with my head when the flustered wedding planner at the back of the room gives me a frantic gesture, I smile to myself about how much fuss they're all making for a day that should be about celebration.

I wonder what they'd do if they knew about wraith demons and what the state of the world would be if there weren't Drengar to protect everyone. Hunters with muscles on top of muscles and faces of pure perfection. Hunters who have weird silent conversations and eyes that shine in ways I haven't seen in ten years. Hunters who...fuck...I snap out of my fantasy of how it'd feel to have all that male-ness against my bare skin and nod to the wedding planner who is signalling me to get ready.

Van and I catch eyes and I fight the roll they want to do when he throws me a devilish smirk as if telling me he's waiting to see if I lose consciousness and ruin Scott's big day.

Laughing to myself, I take a deep, grounding breath and pull the bow against the strings and let the music flow through me. My heart races with the tempo as I remember my childhood listening to this song and seeing my foster brother walk up the aisle to collect his stunning bride from her well-dressed father. It's a sight that has tears form in my eyes and slip down my cheek as I sway to the rhythm that comes so naturally. I just trust muscle memory and my heart to play a song I know the humans in this room wouldn't understand as a declaration of unbreakable bonds and love between two beings. A binding of two souls to one.

Azanites have their flaws but when we love, we love *hard*.

The problem is, when we hate, we are fury incarnate.

Chapter Nineteen

'OH Raffy, sweetheart, you played beautifully.'

Taking Laney's tight hug, I thank her softly and then smack Van on the arm before he can open his mouth and say whatever smart-arse thing he was about to say.

'What?' he cries out, rubbing his arm dramatically. 'That hurt.'

'I didn't touch you,' I grumble and smirk behind Laney's back when she turns to the shit stirrer and tells him that he deserved my whack.

Throwing his hands in the air as if defeated, Van mumbles his annoyance but has the biggest smile on his face because he was definitely going to say something. He grabs me around the shoulders and pulls me into his side in an affectionate hug that has me smile and tell him to get off. That's when Miles comes over with Van's date, Missy, who's wearing a very mini red dress that I'd kill to have the guts to wear. Van quickly lets me go and embraces her in a very inappropriate way that I'm sure is on purpose.

Miles has only eyes for me and while I'm happy to see him, I find it a little uncomfortable how intensely he's staring. My beast huffs and I swear if she was in control, she'd turn her back like a real snob.

'I could listen to you play all day, Raff,' he says sweetly and leans in to kiss my cheek. I feel like a bitch for how I react to him sometimes. 'I was worried when you didn't answer my calls or texts. How are you feeling? You look like you didn't sleep much.'

I try not to take offense and he seems to understand what he's just said because he back-pedals hard. 'I didn't mean you look bad or anything. You look amazing! Really, really amazing. I just worry. Do you need to sit?'

'Good try bud, but maybe stop talking.' Van laughs and slaps Miles on the back before turning with Missy to head over to where Laney is speaking with the newly married couple.

Poor Miles takes the slaps as best he can. Van is lean and deceptively strong. 'Lean muscle,' he calls it.

'It's fine. I feel good actually,' *thanks to the healing power of the sun and maybe a scary Medir.* I shiver at the thought of Drengar Wilder. That male was frightening and yet, mesmerising and clearly very powerful.

An AzarDrengar-Medir.

It makes me quiver to think that I was so close to him. That I was able to function without completely breaking down.

Growing up having my father force me to write down my dreams or sleep with the help of healers left a scar that I know will never heal. It didn't matter that all that stopped after the age of ten. The damage was done. My father would ask, here and there, if I'd dreamt anything and insist that every morning I write in my journal of what I can remember.

I was lying obviously, the dreams and nightmares never stopped. It just took me until the age of ten to work out that I should lie. I had no idea what my father wanted with my nightmares. It was not like I could ever change what I saw from happening when my reality and dreams warped together. I was eight when I realised that those nightmares were sometimes real. I was in the main foyer of the lair when a human man fell over the side of the railing from the top floor. I screamed and screamed, not because he landed at my feet and blood splatted all over my flowing dress, but because I had dreamt it the night before. Moment by moment.

It has only happened to me a couple of times after. Most nightmares I don't remember, which is why I think there was always someone in my rooms writing them down. Always a Medir around to put me back to sleep.

But they weren't healers like Wilder. Medir are not necessarily the most powerful or gifted of Azanites. None I've ever learnt are AzarDrengar as well.

A little lost in the images of the hunter-healer floods my thoughts as I take Miles' arm when he offers it and follow him to the line of cars that will take us to the reception venue.

The rest of the day and night ran exactly as I expected. Lots of meeting new people and standing behind Laney as she proudly greets guests and claimed Scott as her own.

Scott had never looked so happy and while I didn't think I'd have a good time, I end up dancing with all of my foster brothers all night long and loving every minute of it. Even when Miles got on the dancefloor and swung me around, I enjoyed myself.

I laughed and sang along to the music and maybe drank one too many wines with Van's arm draped along my chair. When the evening came to an end and Van kissed his date farewell and I said goodbye to a grim-faced Miles, who reluctantly helped me into the cab with Van and shut the door, I was ready to curl up and sleep for the rest of the weekend.

My drunk mind barely comprehended the darkness around me.

THE LOST LADY OF THE DARKWOODS

CHAPTER TWENTY

HEAD RESTING ON VAN'S shoulder, I shrug when he asks me why he and I weren't gifted a luxury hotel room close to the reception hall we're now driving away from. A long way away from.

I'm actually surprised that we found a cab that would take us to the other side of the tracks.

'Laney did offer for us to sleep in the suite,' I yawn, everything is spinning a little. It feels good.

'I just don't understand why Scott and Carly only got one room for the entire family. I wasn't going to sleep on the foldout lounge with Tiff and Tobey. Brent got one to himself and we got nothing.'

I can't tell if Van is pissed or drunk. 'Who cares, I want to sleep in my bed tonight anyways.'

'Of course you do,' he chuckles and kisses me on the top of my head.

'Thanks for coming home with me.' Night has fully settled on the world. I know I should be feeling something but can't seem to think straight. I'm guessing it's the alcohol. 'I know you and Missy were getting all hot on the dancefloor.' Eyes heavy, I try to stay awake. It feels like I haven't slept in forever.

My head moves with his small shrug. 'I'm planning on getting hotter with her tomorrow.' His words drip with inuendo and I gag loudly in jest which he finds hilarious.

'What about you and Miles? Poor guy looked pretty upset that he wasn't taking you back to his place.'

Frowning, I lift my head and sigh. Looking out the window, I watch the world fly by and wonder what I should do about Miles. The growing darkness outside my window has a shiver shoot through my body. I feel the pull to be inside and yet, I can't remember why I should be afraid. On that thought, I try to remember how many bottles of wine Van and I consumed tonight.

'You going to answer me, Raff? Or are you thinking of marrying Miles?'

'He's a friend,' I reply to the smart arse, my words a little slurred. I was very aware of where Miles expected our night to go tonight. He made it clear a few times that he wanted to take the party back to his place and it was pretty obvious by the way he held me on the dancefloor that he was interested in taking *that* step.

'You know he wants to be more, right?' Van asks and I don't miss the humour in his tone.

'Yes, I'm aware.' *Too aware.* 'I like Miles, a lot. I'm just not interested in him like that. I just don't know how to tell him that without losing him. He's my friend.'

'It's okay to not be into him like that, Raff. You don't have to please everyone. He isn't going to hate you if you say that you want to keep it strictly friend zoned.'

'I know,' I whisper.

'Do you?'

I pull my gaze from the window and stare at my best friend and brother in every way that matters. The thought has me thinking about what Drengar Felix said about my biological brother, Keenan. A male I haven't thought about in such a long time.

Van is watching me closely and I shuffle in my seat at the intensity of it. 'You spend a great deal of time keeping the people around you happy, Raff. It's like you're afraid that if you don't do things for others or look after them, that they may not want you around or something.' He reaches out and pulls my hair over my ear. 'If Miles only wants to be around you to get in your pants than that's his problem and you should tell him to fuck off. Or I can. Or I'm sure Scott and Brent would like to make him go away.'

I shake my head. 'I know they would. Am I being mean to Miles? I don't want to be.'

'I know ya don't. And no, I think you've been giving signals that you just want to be his friend. I think he's just hoping it'll become something more.'

Nodding, I look out the window again to see our house with the crooked metal fence when the cab stops and Van leans over to hand him cash. 'Thanks dude,' he says and makes sure that I have my violin and bag before hopping out the car door and holding it open for me.

I get a weird sense of doom as I shuffle down the seat and hesitate. Frowning, I look up at Van who's standing patiently for me to get out of the car. Not sure what my problem is, or why I feel very hot all of a sudden, I can't feel my beast, or my feet, if I'm being honest, and shrug it off as the alcohol and get out of the cab.

With my hands full with my bag and violin case, I let Van shut the door and bang the top in thanks as the guy pulls away. It's late, really late, and I turn at the odd feeling like I'm being watched.

Hair standing up at the back of my neck, I study the empty, quiet street and see nothing. Mostly the world's just spinning slightly. I don't know how long I stand, scanning the houses and the cars, feeling something is completely off.

'I think I'm really drunk.' I giggle and finally turn back around and freeze.

The fear that hits me has me stagger back and I drop the contents in my arms and scream as my violin case crashes to the hard pavement.

Before me, Van stands, his face a mask of pure horror. His eyes wide and shouting at me to run as he coughs. Blood spurts through his lips but that isn't what has me unable to move. It's the solid, midnight black hand that's sticking out of his torso. The razor sharp claws extend and retract. As if my body is stuck in thick honey, I slowly look to the figure standing behind my brother.

Gasping, I see the wraith and I swear it's smiling at me. The grotesque teeth and distorted face tilts as if enjoying my horror. It's hand is sticking through Van's body. The other slowly drifts to his shoulder and rests there. I watch it in shock and disbelief. It's body is covered in what appears to be black smoke. It looks to be solid and transparent at the same time. Exactly the image of the demons that haunt my nightmares.

I can't...I don't... 'Van!' I stutter and finally snap out of my shock when the biggest surge of adrenaline I have ever felt erupts under my skin and I shout and roar at the same time. The wraith uses the hand he has on Van's shoulder to push him forward and removes the hand impaling him at the same time.

Van collapses headfirst and I lurch forward to catch him. My knees hit the concrete hard as his weight slumps heavily in my arms and I cry and scream and keep his head safe from hitting the pavement.

'Van! Van!' I know that I should be worried about the demon but my brother is dying. There's blood everywhere and I hold Van against my chest and cover his body with my own in a feeble attempt to protect him. 'Van! Please don't leave me.' My voice is barely a whisper. I can hear the shrieking of demons but they sound like distant noises. My entire focus is Van.

The world grows darker and I refuse to look up to meet my death. Pulling Van's face up so that I can see his face, I watch as his eyes dart around in fear. He's pale and clammy and with a shaking hand, I press it against the wound uselessly. His mouth opens and closes and I try to not show him my own terror.

'You'll be okay, Van. I swear. This is all my fault. I'm so sorry. We'll go to the next life together, okay? I'll come with you Van. It'll be an adventure,' I whisper.

My chest burns and I swallow the fire in my throat. I'd rather be on the ground, cradling my Van than trying uselessly to fight a pack of wraiths I know are around me right now. I'll die with Van and I find happiness with that decision.

I follow the way his eyes widen at something behind my shoulder. I grip him to my chest and cover his head with mine at the sight of the demon that hurt him swinging its monstrous hand back to finish us off.

I want to look away, but I can't. I watch that hand pull back as it morphs into a sharp point. I listen to the horrific sound that comes from its wide open mouth and smell the sulfuric stench that wafts from its shimmering, black, smokey body. I stare it down in the only act of defiance I can muster in this situation and hope that Laney and the boys know that I love them.

Regret hits me hard. I should've stayed away from them all. I should have listened to the Drengar.

Time slows as the wraith prepares to attack. My life flashes before my eyes.

I don't register the male that appears from the darkness. His eyes blazing red. His body alight in stunning red and orange flames as he swings his burning sword and cuts down the wraith with a single blow that has it evaporate before my eyes.

I sit, gaping up at the Drengar standing over me. His eyes studying me with so much emotion that I find his gaze overwhelming.

'Wilder.' The word is a plea. A statement. His name slips from my lips like a worship as the tears begin to fall. Relief floods my system.

I sit on the pavement staring up at the male who just saved my life. His muscle heavy arms contract as he lowers his weapon and I watch the fluidity of his movements in awe of his power. Heat surrounds me. Comforts me. I draw in the scent that caresses my skin.

Van whimpers in my arms and I snap my attention back to him and it's like coming out of a trance. 'Van,' I shout as he closes his eyes. Frantic, I look up at Wilder and barely register the other males around him. 'Wilder,' I say his name again and lose all control over my emotions.

Chapter Twenty One

'*L*ADY *SERAFINA, WE NEED to get indoors before more wraiths come,*' Wilder says roughly.

I can't move though. The fact that he saved me doesn't seem to be enough to get me to relinquish my hold on Van and trust someone like him. I don't know if the Drengar will leave my brother here or help me carry him inside. I need to get into the house. I need to get out of the dark. I need to get Van to safety, and I know I'm completely losing it.

Wilder is squatting down on Van's side, opposite me. His thighs as thick as tree trunks and his presence is overwhelming. The night is quiet but I can feel the tension coming from the males standing around us like guards. All I can see is Wilder's large frame blocking the world.

An oversized, calloused hand falls to my shoulder gently and I flinch. 'Serafina, we need to get you indoors.' Viktor's voice is full of authority and when I hear Alistair instruct Wilder to carry me in case I'm injured, I finally find reason.

Wilder is a healer. A powerful AzarDrengar-Medir.

'Heal him,' I demand, leaving no room for argument. The hand on my shoulder slips away. My eyes stay fixed on Wilder. I watch my words sink in. I watch the way his black eyes fall to the still body draped over my lap, the one I have crushed into my chest as I hold him. I see the moment Wilder is about to refuse. I see it in the way those dark depths slowly come back to look me in the eye.

'No!' I say first. My anger sparks. 'Heal him!' My voice wobbles. He can't say no. I won't let him.

'Serafina, we don't heal humans. There are laws.'

I turn my head to the male standing to my right watching my entire world fall apart. 'Fuck your laws,' I half shout at Alistair. 'He's my brother.' My tears are endless. Van isn't moving. He's so still. His breathing is laboured and I just know in my soul that it'll stop soon.

Alistair frowns deeply and takes a small step towards me. I turn my head away and plead with Wilder. A male who frightens me more than a wraith. 'Please. Please!'

Wilder is impossible to read. His gaze flicks to Alistair. To his Prince.

That's when I know what I have to do and it breaks my heart terribly. It crushes me and makes it hard to breath. I look down at the pale face in my lap and move the hair from Van's eyes. I'd give anything for him and so I do... 'This is my fault,' I tell Van, my fingers tracing the lines on his face to hold them to memory. 'I'm sorry, Van.'

I hear Felix curse loudly and the emotion in it is enough for a small argument to erupt between the males as they debate the laws of our people.

'I'll make this right, Van,' I inform my brother and kiss his clammy forehead and sniffle.

Gaze flicking up to meet Wilder's, I hope he can see my hatred of him for denying my plea. Something flicks over his face but I'm already looking to Alistair. I take a deep breath and say, 'I'll go with you to help you find your book.' The male studies me. 'I know where your treasure is,' I declare, hoping that I have this right.

Looking to Van, I feel a sense of relief that I don't have to continue to live in this state of fear of being discovered and taken back to Azanir. It's over. I have been found and I'll go back to my father's lair and confront them all. I had ten years of happiness and freedom. I was greedy to think that this would last a lifetime.

'How? How could you know?' Alistair demands, his tone leaving no room to lie. 'You told us you have nothing to do with this! You lie to get us to help your human.' He's mad and I find I don't give a fuck.

'I've seen it,' I tell him. 'It's gold, isn't it? With intricate patterns on the front cover. Ancient, black wings. Black ink that looks to be melting against the page as if the image is bleeding.' I hear the collective growl and I whimper.

'We never told you what it looked like.' The rage. The power in the voice that fills the world has me flinch.

Fuck.

'You lied to us! You are the traitor!'

Fighting the need to retract my words in fear of the position they'll put me in, I stick to my decision. 'I won't say any more until Drengar Wilder heals Van and then I'll help you get your treasure back.'

A great deal happens over the next few minutes and it's one big blur of activity. Alistair barks at Wilder to collect the 'human' and I'm pulled roughly to my feet by Viktor. His grip on my arm pinches my skin but I don't have the care to ask him to ease up. My eyes stay fixed on Van and I go willingly into the house and fall to my brothers side when Viktor lets me go.

Wilder has placed Van on the lounge and I wipe his face repeatedly for no reason other than to touch him.

The house is dark and quiet. Felix is at the kitchen counter watching Wilder who looks like he's meditating on the other side of the lounge. His eyes are closed and there's an energy around him that seems to glow. Viktor and Alister's anger pounds against my back, making it hard to breath. The situation I've placed myself in is bad...really, really bad.

For Van though. For him, I'd do anything and so I move aside when Viktor demands that I do and watch in rapt horror as the Medir opens his obsidian eyes and erupts in a flame so hot and intense that I have to shield my eyes and throw my arms over my head in fear of being swallowed by the power that radiates through the room.

Legs pulled into my chest, I hold myself and wait. My brain too slow and uneducated enough to fully comprehend the magnitude of the power and force that is Wilder BlazeAzar-Drengar-Medir.

Despite my terror at witnessing something life altering, I can't help but notice how the fire feels along my skin. How the heat wraps a hand around my body in a protective and comforting embrace that has me draw in a breath and moan softly at the ecstasy of it.

Head still buried under my arms, I allow myself to feel the rush of the touch. My core tightens and holds. My now oversensitive skin can almost feel every tentacle of power that seems to caressing my body sensually. My mouth waters and the beast below my skin shivers in arousal and delight.

My reaction is comforting and embarrassing and weird and confusing.

On the floor, hidden from the room, it takes me way too long to get my body under control and realise that the fire and warmth have evaporated.

Slowly, I move my arms and search the room on instinct for any danger. Alistair, Viktor and Felix are watching Wilder who stands behind the lounge, his black eyes staring at me so intensely that I gasp audibly.

Heart kicking up, I force my gaze away and look at my Van. His face has colour, his chest looks whole and his breathing sounds soft and beautiful.

I spring into action and leap up to touch and hug and kiss my brother, uncaring of the tears. Uncaring of the ones watching me.

Van is alive and safe and I whisper my thank you to the male who hasn't stopped observing me.

Wilder nods once as if saying it was no trouble bringing a man back from the brink of death. I have no time to celebrate though because Alistair opens his mouth and my entire life changes forever.

Chapter Twenty Two

Van is sleeping deeply in his bed, all tucked in and peaceful and...alive.

My heart skips a beat at the realisation that he almost died. That the world was so close to losing a man that made the sun shine brighter. That made the days easier to wake up to. That made the hard times and the memories soften.

Crying silent tears in his darkened room, I sniffle my useless apology for what I've done. He'll never know what happened. Felix already explained to me the healing sleep Wilder has placed him under will erase the horrors of the night and while I nodded and thanked the pair before they left me alone to my goodbye, I couldn't help but hate that he'd forget.

Forgetting means that he'll have no idea why I'm gone when he wakes up in the morning.

The tears fall harder. Saying goodbye hurts.

'Thank you, Van.' Studying his handsome face, I realise that I didn't tell him often enough how much he changed my life. He saved me. 'I love you with all my heart and I wish I could stay here with you.' He doesn't stir, just sleeps off the trauma of the night. 'Look after everyone for me.'

Wiping my face, I lean forward and kiss his forehead with so much pain in my chest, it's hard to breath.

'Serafina,' the male's voice has me sit up and take one last look at my brother. 'We're leaving.'

Nodding, I whisper my final farewell and stand off the bed. Defeated and heartsick, I look to the prince in the doorway and sigh at the rage staring at me.

My head hurts terribly and I look down at what Alistair is looking at and frown. My dress is ruined with Van's blood. I'm covered in it. My hands and arms are dried and caked in the red mess.

I swallow a scream.

With shaking hands, I look up when Alistair tells me to follow and without understanding what the look on his face means, I move on wobbly, bare feet.

I find it hard to speak or do anything but trail behind the prince through the crowded loungeroom that doesn't seem big enough for the three large Drengar who are speaking quietly to each other.

Alistair leads me to my bathroom down the hall and I stop at the door and watch him as he pulls open the shower screen and starts the water.

Steam fills the space instantly, and numbly I nod when he tells me to get cleaned up.

Talking doesn't seem to be in my power at the moment though.

'Wilder said you're hurt. Do you need help?' Alistair asks, his pale blue eyes watching me intently. I don't really know what he means and end up standing looking back at him. Mind completely void of all thoughts, I don't know how long I stand like that, watching the male who fills the entire space hesitate before striding towards me and then past me.

'Get cleaned up, we have a long night ahead of us,' and on that he leaves.

Standing under the scolding water with my head rested on the cold tiled wall, I cry the remainder of my tears. I have no idea what Alistair and the others are going to do with me. I could be executed for my 'betrayal' to our people and the worst thing is that the thought of a death by Drengar isn't even what has my heart pound in dread and panic. It's the possibility that they might find out what I can do. Like my father, they might think that my dreams are worth something and keep me asleep, locked in my nightmares for their own, confusing gain.

Taking the time to feel my grief and accept my fate, I remind myself that I'm a fighter. I may have said what I did to save Van but they'll not take my freedom or my dignity.

Pushing off the wall, I finally find reason in the mess of my thoughts. Scrubbing the evidence of my night from my body and making sure the cuts on my legs and arms are clean, I formulate a plan.

Fresh and feeling a little less numb, I stand beside Felix with a small bag of my belongings out the front of my home looking at it longingly.

Standing in the darkness of the night surrounded by two massive Drengar, I don't feel as scared of the creatures that less than two hours ago set my life on a course that I never imagined. The pull in my soul to go back inside is painful, but I find I can ignore it when I concentrate. Felix and Wilder are standing like guards on either side of me. Both quiet and alert and completely ignoring me.

I think about what's going to happen when Van wakes up. What he's going to do when he finds the note I left for them all explaining that my birth family needed my help and that I'll be back. It breaks me. It was a lie, I know. However, a girl can dream and dream I must or else I'll fall into the pit of darkness that has formed in my mind. A darkness I refuse to accept because that would mean I've accepted defeat. I didn't risk it all ten years ago to have it end now.

'Come.' Felix snaps me out of my thoughts.

Not one of the males has looked at me directly and I look back at my home one last time and swallow my tears. I will not cry. I will not break.

Stopping at the sight before me, I get whiplash with how quickly I go from pure despair to stomach clenching humour.

Biting my lip to keep from laughing, I watch the big, scary Medir take my bag and head to the boot of the...what do the humans call it? The 'soccer mum car'.

I can hardly contain my laughter as Felix flicks the passage door handle and the entire thing slides open revealing the seven seater vehicle. There are two captain chairs in the second row that look just like the driver and passenger seats with a space between them to the three seater at the back. Honestly, it's the funniest thing I've ever seen watching the four, scary, powerful Drengar move around the outside of the car arranging the bags in the boot and around the many seats in order to make room for me.

Alistair barks a few orders to the three males. Viktor has a small argument with Felix on where to put one of the bags and Wilder just quietly moves around to the opposite side, opens the sliding automatic door and sits in his single seat like he has not a care in the world.

Laughing softly, I wipe the moisture from my cheeks and hurry when Felix snaps at me to get in before the wraiths come.

That gets my arse moving for sure.

CHAPTER TWENTY THREE

T HE SILENCE IS TORTURE. I'm sitting at the back of the car, on my own, *thank the Sun Gods*, contemplating what's going to happen when we get to the 'dwelling' they discussed earlier.

The conversations have been dull and limited and I allow my exhausted eye lids to droop as the humming of the car's engine lulls me to sleep.

Blinking at the sight before me, I take in the floor to ceiling glass and the beautiful city below. Skyscrapers take up the entire view and while I feel like I've seen this place, I have no idea where I am. We are high up. Like really high, and I press my face against the cool glass to get a better look at the city.

The buildings are covered in signs for big brands and when I press my body harder against the window, I spy a river to the left of the city. It doesn't help to understand where I am though.

I sigh and turn to the office that looks oddly familiar and scream at the wraith standing behind me, it's fingers curled around a golden book. Mouth extending open, the wraith pounces and I barely have time to cover my face before it's upon me.

I snap awake and gasp at the black eyes looking at me.

'Fucking hell,' I squeal. My heart is pounding right out of my chest. My arms are up in a defensive position between my body and Drengar Wilder.

His palms are hot and calloused against the skin of my wrists as he holds them gently and I realise that I may have been flailing around in my sleep.

He doesn't speak, only watches as I get control over my emotions and then he releases me slowly. That's when I realise that the car has stopped. It's still dark and I follow when the Medir indicates with his head for me to come.

Stepping from out of the minivan, I stretch and take the time to absorb my surroundings. We're at a motel. The cream, two storey building wraps around in a semicircle with the carpark in the middle. Brown doors are lined up in perfect order, top and bottom and a questionable, very dark staircase sits snuggly at the far end for customers to get to the top floor.

It's definitely not a place I'd walk alone at night or during the day for that matter. The only reason why I haven't jumped back inside the car is because Felix and Wilder are standing close. Alistair and Viktor are nowhere to be seen. I assume they're over at the reception building with its neon sign declaring there are vacancies.

Felix is having a one sided conversation with Wilder who doesn't seem to be listening as he digs around in a bag looking for only the Sun Gods know what. Wrapping my arms around my body as the instinct to get indoors pulls painfully on my soul, I walk to the other side of the car to stretch out my legs. The main road is all lit up and busy and separates the motel from the gas station, convenience store and what looks to be a bar with rows and rows of motorbikes lined up out the front. It must be around two or three in the morning which blows my mind. Shouldn't these people be asleep? Do they not realise that the night holds dangers?

Wrapping my arms around myself at the subtle shift in the air, I watch a group of badly dressed men walk unsteadily across the road towards the motel. They're laughing and drinking.

One of them trips, to the others amusement, and drops the glass bottle in his hand to the floor. It crashes loudly and I take an involuntary step back towards the car. I didn't realise that I had walked a little too far away from the Drengar. Nor do I understand why I'm so uneasy.

That's when I see it.

A shadow.

A thick, dense shadow staying within the darkness of the buildings. Fixated on it, I watch as it slinks in the darkness, avoiding the light and following the men.

'Lady Serafina?'

I jump. My heart in my throat. I look up at Viktor quickly before turning to the group of humans that are being stalked by something. However, when I look back, the shadow is gone and the men get louder and louder as they get closer to the motel.

'Let's get you inside.'

I don't really want to go but I do for the simple fact that my skin is crawling and I *need* to.

The alcohol still in my system is making it hard to keep my eyes open and I just want to snuggle under some covers and sleep for days.

The wish evaporates when I walk through the open door and actually see the room. I almost start to cry again. There are two double beds. Small and not the right number for the amount of bodies now in the small room. The thirty square metres of ugly carpet, brown textured walls and a tiny,

tiny bathroom in the far corner is depressing. The beds sit beside what looks to be an ancient side table. They look lumpy and uninviting.

I stand awkwardly at the door while the males move in and out of the room, grabbing bags and making themselves as comfortable as they can. I take the opportunity to scan the rest of the place.

There's a small round table that only sits two people under the smudged window directly to the right of the door. It looks just as dirty and old as the side table and could have been a matching set a decade ago. A very tiny, questionable looking kitchenette takes up the left side corner. I really don't think I'd touch anything on the counter that has the handwritten 'complimentary' sign written in bad writing beside it. I see packets of tea and individually wrapped biscuits that I know will be expired. There's a kettle that looks to have had the power cord ripped out and a mini fridge that is louder than the cars on the highway outside.

The males don't look at me or speak until the door is closed and locked behind my back and I'm left staring at four, impossibly huge males who take up the very energy of the room. They all stare and I swallow the apprehension building in my throat.

I watch Viktor remove the large knife from his belt and place it on the side table. Wilder is at the kitchenette counter leaning against it. Alistair is watching me with a wealth of rage in his gaze. Felix seems uncomfortable and grabs one of the creaky chairs from the table and drags it to the middle of the room between the beds. He clonks it down, eyeballs Alistair, and walks back to the remaining chair and sits heavily.

I fight the instinct to turn around and bolt. My beast is quiet. She's a complete and utter waste of space really. I could really use her power and speed. Besides it's night and I'm scared to be out there on my own especially after seeing that shadow. I feel like these arseholes would know that too because they don't seem at all bothered that I'm so close to the door.

'Sit, Lady Serafina.' Alistair indicates to the chair and I hesitate before complying. There's really no point in being difficult. I put myself in this situation.

Very aware that every one of my steps is being tracked, I slump down in the hard seat and wait.

Ridiculously self-conscious, I fiddle with the hem of my oversized tee and wait for the interrogation. Alistair sits on the end of the right bed and Viktor is standing on the other side of the left close to where Wilder is watching me.

'Start talking,' Alistair demands and I sigh heavily.

'What would you like to know?' I manage to say, my voice might have hitched a little at the way Felix begins to take all the weapons off his person and lay them on the table.

'How about you start with why you betrayed our people?' Viktor spits. Those honey lined eyes are narrowed and full of fire.

'I...I didn't,' I stutter and hate myself for it.

'Where is the book?' Alistair growls.

My heart has kicked up a notch and I fiddle with my shirt. 'I...' I don't know what to say. 'I don't know for sure,' is the best I come up with.

'Who took it?' Viktor demands, giving me no time to think and the room becomes unbelievably hot.

'I...I don't know.'

I can't formulate a decent response because Alistair is off his bed and is now leaning over me, half shouting, 'why did you help the human smugglers?'

'I...I didn't.'

'Tell me what you know then! Why did you take our most sacred text? Tell me what the humans want it for and where it is now!' Alistair is all up in my personal space, crowding me. 'Where's the book? You said you know where it is! Tell me!'

I cower back. My body shaking with the energy surrounding me. I want to rage out and smack him. I want to bare my teeth and bite the flesh from his bones.

Instead, I sit, listening to his endless questions of why I'd do such a thing and why I'd lie to them after they saved my life. All questions I have no logical answer for.

'I can't tell you,' I say again and flinch back when he roars. Alistair turns abruptly while running his hand through his hair. All I see when he moves away is Wilder and the thought of him being next up to integrate me gets me talking, and talking fast. 'I can't tell you because I don't know exactly where it is. I know it's being kept in an office building. I can tell you the colour of the carpet and describe the city that I saw from the big glass windows. I can draw it if you give me a piece of paper or something. I can draw all the details. That's all I can tell you,' I implore. 'Please, I need you to believe me. I'll help you find it and accept my punishment for lying to you all, but I can't tell you *how* I know.'

Pulling my legs up onto the chair, I wrap my arms around myself and rest my head on my knees. They want more. My attempts at pleading are useless and I close my eyes to the world when Viktor starts demanding things of me.

That's when I feel him. That's when I peek and see Wilder push off the counter and stride the three steps towards my chair.

My heart kicks up until I fear it will pound right out of my chest.

Darkness sweeps me into its embrace.

I pass out from fear.

CHAPTER TWENTY FOUR

I WAKE WARM AND covered in a pile of blankets. Stretching my limbs, I feel relaxed and rested, something I haven't felt in a very long time. Hungry and having made plans with Van to eat breakfast this morning before Laney and the others get home from staying in the city, I turn to check the clock on my bedside to see what time it is.

Confused and still half asleep, I just stare at the odd bedside table. There is a dagger on the chipped surface and two smartphones. Which is weird.

Rolling on my back, I study the stained roof and suck in a breath as the events of the past two days come into focus.

Fuck.

Heart in my throat, I'm too afraid to move. Too afraid to face the room of Drengar I can sense now that I'm fully awake. I have no idea what happened last night and just lie with my eyes closed pretending that I'm still asleep. The only thing that gets me to stop acting like a youngling is the smell of food that fills the room after the door is opened and closed.

Turning my head on the pillow, I see Felix and Viktor holding paper bags. I can smell pancakes and chocolate. It's mouth-watering and I really, really want to get out of bed and join the four males at the tiny table who are pulling containers from the takeaway bags. They all seem quite casual and relaxed.

I have no idea what they're chatting about when they chuckle over memories that don't sound particularly funny. Alistair throws his head back and laughs loudly at something Felix has just said. Viktor takes a container and a fork and sits on the end of the empty, but clearly slept in, bed to my left. The mattress squeaks as the old springs are tested with his weight. Wilder does the same thing but when he sits on my bed, he does it gently and slowly as if mindful of waking me, which seems absurd. They don't care about me. They're going to kill me once they find out where the book is. I've been marked as a traitor and it's all my fault. To save Van, I've given up my own life. Something I'd do over and over again.

'Come and eat, Lady Serafina. We're leaving within the hour.'

Clearly not as stealthy as I assumed I was being, I sigh heavily and get up. My body aches all over. Not ready to face four mouth-watering-ly attractive and deadly males with morning breath and bad hair, I stumble into the bathroom after grabbing my bag from the floor and slam the door behind me.

Someone has used the shower recently and I get an overwhelming rush of scent that has me grip the small, exposed sink. There is a small bag on the counter and when I take a peek inside, I see the pink toothbrush still in the packet, a hairbrush and a few bands, one of those small tubes of shampoo and conditioner. All things I forgot to grab last night when I was told to pack light.

Stunned, I stand just looking at the bag. Despite the way they yelled and treated me last night, I find their effort and care to get me all this stuff very confusing. I almost soften towards them...almost.

Cursing my behaviour and glaring at my reflection in the mirror, I give myself a great death stare that Van would be proud of and study the puffiness under my grey eyes.

I have a heart shaped face, defined cheekbones and a small nose. My big, round eyes are the same grey colour as my fathers, like dove's wings, Laney told me once. Every time I look in the mirror I'm reminded of him. The tanned skin is all him too and I wonder for the millionth time in my life if I inherited anything from my birth mother.

'What are you doing?' I whisper, knowing full well that the males might hear me. Taking a deep breath, I focus on what I can control— a shower.

I've spent way too long getting ready and not because I care what I look like, I just really don't want to face the males in the room.

I throw on a pair of old jeans that fit like a glove, a plain black tee and run the brush through my brown, wavy hair. I give up on taming the fly-aways and roll up the long, curly length in a simple ponytail. When all is done and I have nothing else to do, I try to find some courage and eventually open the door.

The first thing I notice is the takeaway box on the bed I was sleeping on with a fork placed on top of the white, biodegradable container. The next is the milkshake on the side table. Butterflies and uncertainty erupting in my gut, I head to the bed and sit with my legs crossed. I'm starving and the smell of sweet pancakes and bacon has my entire focus on the food and my stomach and not the fact that four Drengar are packing up the room and loading the car.

Sucking on the straw in the chocolate milkshake, I watch the activity in the room trying to gather as much information on these males as I can.

Which is zero to none. Felix seems like the most relaxed of the four and does a lot of the jobs. Alistair and Viktor just keep throwing ideas of where the book could be and how they've been tracking wraith movements around the country. The most interesting thing I've discovered is that the sacred text will draw the demons of darkness as it is believed to be a book made of pure light—which logically makes no sense. However, not the weirdest piece of my intel gathering. That would be when Viktor started to speak about how the book is closed shut and hasn't been opened in over two thousand years. I had to hold back my rage at hearing that the damn book I've just traded my life for doesn't even fucking open.

Then there's Wilder, the broody, quiet type. Like really, really quiet. I haven't heard him speak aloud which is confusing because I'm sure I heard him talk...haven't I? My brain is all fuzzy.

The others look to him quite a lot though, as if they're listening to him which is very confusing. Frankly, it's just another thing giving me a headache as I try to work out how to survive this mess.

'Here, draw the city where the book is located.'

Jumping in surprise, I was so absorbed in my own thoughts that I didn't notice Felix beside the bed. I quickly look down at the paper and pencil he just threw on the covers before me.

'Um...okay,' I mumble, unsure if my drawing is actually going to be good enough. I have no idea where to even begin. I guess I could try and remember some details. I shouldn't have said I could do this.

'You said you could draw the city. So draw.' Felix doesn't have the same playfulness about him that he had when we first met. My hopes that he could be a potential ally in this situation evaporates like my hunger for the rest of my breakfast.

Putting the milkshake and the rest of my pancakes on the side table, I try to concentrate on what I can remember. Which is always a problem. Details from a dream don't just hang around. They are blurry and a little obscure. That's the reason why I could never really do anything about what I saw, like that human servant that died in front of me by falling from the stairs. I saw certain things in the lead up. Things that brought about a sense of déjà vu but not enough to truly remember or understand in that moment what I was witnessing or do anything to stop or change the outcome.

My dreams becoming reality hasn't happened a great deal. Most of my dreams seem to be in the future so I put them down to just nightmares conjured up by my imagination.

Looking up at the blue eyed, god-like statue staring down at me, I go back to the paper and force my mind to work.

For ten minutes, I sit, cross legged on the bed, tapping the pencil on my knee while trying really hard to remember details. The entire time, Felix stands in all his hot-ness beside me, watching my every move. Totally distracting me with the smell of his scent and the furiously amazing heat of his body.

I try. I really, really do, but the continual, back and forth conversation between Viktor and Alistair about their 'mission' and Felix standing next to me and Wilder now heading to the bathroom and the damn shower turning on and my damn mind now thinking of Wilder being naked while having his shower, even though my damn mind and body are fucking terrified of the attractive and scary healer, I can't take any more. My mind is racing. My senses are on overdrive and my shitty beast decides in this very moment to wake up and look around, causing every hair on my body to stand on end and my body to get all hot and bothered.

Frustration is an understatement to what rushes over me and I reach the end of my patience pretty abruptly, and let's be honest, childishly too. 'I'm not a fucking caged, poor circus animal that can perform on your demand. How am I expected to think with you standing there like that!'

Making a deep noise in the back of my throat that I cannot say was intentional, I jump off the bed with the book and pencil and storm from the hotel room in need of some space and air.

Chapter Twenty Five

S ITTING IN A BOOTH inside the dark and musty biker bar across the road from the motel, I look at the limited words I've carefully jotted down on the paper that are going to be absolutely no freakin' use in the search for the book. All I have is a list.

Glass windows.

Grey carpet.

A river.

Lots of big buildings.

All written in my messy handwriting at the top of the page.

It's shit and all I have. It also won't be enough for the Drengar waiting for me in the hotel room.

Banging my forehead on the table, I wrap my arms around myself and try to think. Eyes scrunched closed, the voice in my head shouts at me to remember, but the other voice in my head is shouting that I'm screwed and that the Drengar are going to see that I'm useless to them and probably execute me today. Which has me spiralling because I don't know if it's normal to have so many voices in your head.

'Rough day?'

I look up sharply. I was so lost in thought that I didn't notice the man who is now standing over me. I watch as he slips into the booth without an invitation. He's a little creepy with his bushy eyebrows and his cut cheekbones. I guess if I was a human female I'd think that he's attractive, but definitely not my kind of thing.

'Something like that,' I reply, moving my paper but he snags it first, irritating me more.

'Glass window. Carpet. River,' he reads aloud. He sets those dirty, brown coloured eyes on me and I think he tries to throw me a flirtatious smile. The beast under my skin bristles, opens one eye a crack and then closes it, completely uninterested and bored, meaning I'm uninterested and bored.

Leaning over to grab the paper from his hand, I frown. I notice the tattoo on his wrist and stop. I can't see the full ink but the fact that it is white has me hesitate. I recoil my hand and try to work out why it sparks a memory.

I come up with nothing.

'Joseph,' he introduces himself by passing me the paper.

Snatching it back, I can't help but say, 'Raff.' Damn Laney raised me right.

'Can I buy you a drink, Raff?' Joseph looks over his shoulder, I assume to call over the bartender.

'No, thank you.' I focus back on my list, done with this weird man. His luscious blonde hair is styled like a movie star. It's weirding me out.

'What's the list for?' The man intertwines his fingers on top of the table.

'Just a list,' I barely say, hoping he'll get the hint. He doesn't, not until I say. 'I'm sorry, but I have a great deal to do.'

'I can take a hint.' Joseph chuckles and I find I hate the sound. 'It was nice to meet you, Raff. I hope to see you around.' The guy gets out of the booth and I can't help but feel a deep sense of unease from what he's just said.

He walks out the door of the bar and I'm left on my own to overthink my situation.

Falling further into the pit of despair forming in my mind, I forget about the creepy dude and focus on what I'm supposed to do about my situation.

The minutes tick by.

I only look up when I scent the male who has just walked in through the heavy door across the room. The smell hits me hard. Unlike the human man before, I feel the Drengar. My beast is no longer asleep. She sits up, watching the male.

Those bright blue eyes land straight on me. Drengar Felix stands taller than any of the handful of men in the bar drinking at this early hour.

All I have in front of me is a soda that the rough bartender with the full beard and long hair handed me with a judgy raised eyebrow. I would've ordered something stronger but I didn't think that it'd help my memory. I'm starting to regret that choice because as Felix heads towards me and my useless list, I kinda wish I was a little plastered.

I watch as he scans the room, eyeballs the three human men at the corner table who've been ogling me since I walked in and then eases himself into the seat across from me. I can only imagine what he would've done if he saw that Joseph guy trying to hit on me before.

Those stunning eyes take in my drink, then move to the paper and then finally land on my face. His expression is hard to decipher, he seems bored, while I'm sure my face has every emotion I'm feeling right now written all over it.

Leaving the pencil and paper between us, I pick up my drink and play with the straw, not wanting to speak first. However, the damn manners Laney forced upon Van, Scott, Brent and I are wreaking havoc on my nerves and I end up sighing, 'sorry.'

My gaze flicks from the dark, bubbly liquid to his face and I watch his left eyebrow rise in question.

'For yelling at you,' I clarify, even though I don't think I need to justify my actions. They're the ones threatening my life and are keeping me...actually...I feel my entire body tense. These males haven't once threatened my life. In fact, they've saved me, twice. They've fed me, kept me safe, provided toiletries even though they think I'm some kind of traitor. It's confusing and I don't like it. I want to hate them.

'I'm not a traitor,' I blurt out. 'And I didn't take your sacred, unopenable text or conspire to work with human smugglers.'

'*Our* text,' Felix says and his voice is deep and sensual.

Frowning in confusion, I look to him for clarification. He studies me intensely before stating, 'it's a sacred text of *our* race, Lady Serafina. Or do you no longer see yourself as Azanite.'

Pushing the soda away, I shrug, unable to voice that I'm an abomination that has no home. I have no idea what they'll all think if they knew the truth. To be a human is one thing. To be half a human and Azanir is illegal— forbidden. And I'm already in enough trouble.

'Did you lie?' Felix questions, his hand coming over to lay over the one I have now playing with the pencil. It's warm and calloused and affectionate.

Blinking up at him, I don't know how to answer. He can't know that I dreamt his book. I might be some forbidden half-breed, but a half-breed who can see things in her dreams, is taking it towards a—cut her head off and throw the abomination in the ocean—kind of hunt. 'I wouldn't blame you if you did. I'm not sure how you knew the book was gold, I guess you could've just made it up in the moment and hoped for the best. You were raised in Azanir.' He makes sure that I'm looking at him when he continues, 'I would've done the same thing for someone I loved, Lady Serafina.'

'I...I can't tell you,' I whisper and watch as he pulls back. Quickly I add, 'but I never betrayed anyone. I've no idea who took the text. I promise. I just...I think I know where it is and I did want to save my brother. He was going to die, Drengar Felix,' my voice trails off and I wipe the stupid tears that have fallen down my cheeks. I hate them. I wait for his reaction. 'It's just not easy to remember.'

We sit in silence for too many heartbeats before he says, 'I believe you, Lady.'

I look up sharply to read his face to make sure he's telling the truth. He really is beautiful and genuine and I could really, really use a friend. 'Raff,' I say quietly, reminding him again that I don't want him to call me Lady. 'Please call me Raff. I'm no lady. I gave up that life ten years ago and I don't want to be reminded of it.'

'One day you will tell me what had you run, Raff. You're safe with us. I hope you know that. While the others can be a little intense, you're a female. A treasure we would never hurt. Surely you know that our females are cherished. Not many are born in a lifetime and we'd never do anything to you. The situation with our race is getting worse. Fewer and fewer younglings are born and even less females,' Felix says absently as he grabs my soda, sniffs it for only the Sun Gods know what and then takes a long swig. I study him, while mulling over what he's just said.

Yes, I remember the state of Azanir and the issues around births and female to male ratios. I was kept separate from society, I didn't live under a rock. The issue was a hot topic even was I was a youngling. It makes me sad to think that they haven't found the reason or the cause to why our race is slowly dropping in numbers. The fact that wraiths cause so much damage and kill regularly doesn't help either.

'I love human soda,' Felix groans in joy and pulls me from my thoughts. 'It's one of my favourite things. That and chocolate and chicken nuggets. Sun Gods, I love chicken nuggets.'

Laughing loudly, I was not expecting him to say that and all the worries of race extinction leave my mind. His face is all lit up and even more stunning. For some reason, it makes me like him instantly. 'Same, Drengar Felix. Same.'

Chapter Twenty Six

'Here! Here! Pull in!'

'By the Sun Gods, Felix, you just ate breakfast,' Viktor growls from the driver's seat.

Felix sits forward in his seat to wrap his arms around the back of Viktor's head rest. 'I know, but I'm starving and this fast-food chain has the best chicken nuggets.' He says fast-food funny and I smile to myself. 'I remember from our last trip to this forsaken human realm.'

Biting my lip, I don't contain my small giggle and get a side eye glance from the Medir in the seat in front of me. It makes me shut my mouth quickly.

'Felix, we'll stop in a few hours when we get to the next town. We can eat then,' Alistair states in his very diplomatic voice. Alistair always seems to be the one keeping this group in check. Like the dad of the group. A really hot dad.

'A few hours,' Felix whines and for a big dude like him to whine, it's super hilarious. 'Wouldn't it be good just to stock up now and then I won't say a single word until we get to the town.'

I watch in amusement as Viktor and Alistair share a look and I don't think Felix is going to get his way, which he clearly knows because he adds, 'Raff loves nuggets too and she will need to eat.'

151

I have no idea why that statement seems to be a catalyst to get Viktor to grumble his annoyance and pull into the drive-thru takeaway joint who really do have the best nuggets.

Felix sits back like he's the champion of the world and throws me a wink that has me laugh, unable to contain it.

We pull up to the line of cars waiting to order at the window and Felix sits like an excited puppy reading the big sign with all the meals. 'Okay, I'll have a twenty-four pack of nuggets and maybe one of those big burger meals. With a soda. Hmmm, and maybe add one of those smaller burgers Vik.'

Viktor's sigh has just made my day and I lean back and watch the show as the big scary males start to list off all the food they want. Except Wilder, he just sits looking out the window as if studying the world.

Today has been weird and surreal.

After the bar, Felix took me back to the room and helped me to grab my things in the small bag I brought with us. He has been really attentive and kind. The others haven't made a fuss about me storming off or not having a drawing to give them. Alistair raised a brow at the short list that I wrote that Felix handed him and after a small eye-conversation between the pair, they stepped outside and everyone has been very cordial toward me since.

Wilder even assisted me into the car by pulling his seat forward so that I could climb in easier.

I missed the rest of the conversation about food orders and am so deep in thought that I didn't realise Felix had asked me what I wanted and then after I didn't reply told Viktor to order me the same as his ginormous meal.

It's surreal watching Viktor speak to the young cashier who's eyes are bulging at the sight of the handsome warrior. I know for a fact it's not because the carload of Drengar haven't just ordered enough food to feed a family of twenty either. I don't blame the guy really. They are mouth-watering.

Handing over a few bills that are probably larger than required, the poor worker goes pale at the wad of cash and watches our car go to the next window where we're told to wait in the waiting bay because of the amount of food we ordered.

No one speaks for ages as we wait for our food and I watch the cars and people as they move around on a lazy Sunday. The takeout place is off the main strip of shops and there are people everywhere.

Bored and unsure what's going to happen tonight when we reach the town the Drengar believe that wraiths are heading towards, I contemplate for the next ten minutes how the wraiths can be so linked to a book—that doesn't even open!

Gaze snagging on a shop front across the road, I sit up straight and blink. Not sure if I'm seeing things, I jump when Wilder touches the hand I have unconsciously placed on the side of his chair. I wasn't aware that I was leaning forward to see out the windscreen properly.

'Raff?'

Ignoring Felix, I'm so caught up with what I think I can see that I jump for the door handle and flick it open. Before I can get out of the car, Wilder snakes a hand around my arm and I swing around and demand he let me go. 'Please! I need to see it.' I don't know what the Medir sees on my face but he drops his hand and I'm off.

I run across the road, dodging cars, only absently aware of the two males following behind me and hurry straight over to the window of the shop and study the picture.

Frantically searching the poster, I see the oversized words declaring some kind of river festival and the dates and time of the event dated two weeks from today. However, that isn't what has my attention. My attention is on the three photos of the city the festival will be held at.

The city.

'Here,' I tap the glass, uncaring if I look like a mad person. 'That's the city, your book is there.'

I've seen the river and the tall buildings. I've dreamt this place...many times, over many years. I just didn't realise until now. A shiver of fear rushes through me and I feel a deep sense of unease.

'Are you sure?' Felix enquires, stepping to my side to take a photo of the poster with the device he pulls from his back pocket. 'The city of Satmark,' he reads from the sign. 'What an unfortunate name. This is the city where the book is?'

'Yes,' I whisper to the glass. I've never heard of this place before. Mind struggling to make sense of how absolutely weird I truly am, I swing around, needing to stop looking at it and stare up at the male towering over me. His silence expected.

Staring, I contemplate the colour of Wilder's eyes and how magnificently dark they are. Of all the gorgeous eyes of the four Drengar, I think his are the most captivating. And then for reasons I can't explain, I have the biggest lightbulb moment. Looking up at Wilder from this angle I can see the long scar on his face and neck better. 'You *can't* speak,' I blurt out like a fucking moron and slap my mouth shout when Felix throws his head back and howls in laughter.

Wilder, just continues to stare, emotions clearly not something that controls the big, scary Medir.

Throwing his arm around my shoulder, Felix pulls me into his side and for once in ten years, I feel small. 'You just figured that out Raff?'

I can't help but melt into the strength and warmth that wraps around my entire body. Caged in Felix's hold, I feel...safe.

Smiling up at him, I make sure that he can see my eye roll. 'I just thought he was the silent, brooding type.' I shrug, much to Felix's amusement.

Wilder makes a noise that has my attention whip back to him but he has turned his back and is now heading to the minivan.

Felix hasn't stopped laughing and begins to follow Wilder with me still attached to him. 'Oh, Raff, if only you could hear our Medir right now.' He shakes his head in amusement and I flick my gaze to the broad back ahead of us and up to the blue eyed god-like male beside me.

I'm so dense sometimes. 'You communicate through your beasts,' I exclaim like I finally understood the punch line to a joke I didn't understand at first. How could I not have realised? I guess ten years *is* a long time. I can be a little kind to myself though. Communicating with the beast is not common. The connection between these males must be strong. Unbreakable. Forged with blood and life debts and only the Sun Gods know what else. Our beasts are loyal but that loyalty doesn't come easy and a connection like that shows a loyalty beyond what humans could understand.

I find myself a little envious.

Chapter Twenty Seven

'WHY IS EVERYONE SO quiet? My beast is starting to get uncomfortable. I don't know if I can contain him for too long.'

I bite back a laugh when Viktor glares through the rear-view mirror at the younger male who hasn't stopped talking for the last half an hour. It hasn't been silent in this car since we left the take-away spot.

'I thought you said you'd stop talking after I fed you?' The Drengar growls and I continue to dip my nuggets into the sauce container.

Alistair huffs as if he knew that Felix was never going to shut up and Viktor ends up mumbling his annoyance for the next ten minutes while Felix yaps away about nonsense of how he thought this trip to the human realm would be just like all the other times and not this exciting. It doesn't take a genius to understand that he means I've made the trip 'more exciting'. Viktor remind Felix that he has only ever been on two missions and that he's barely a fledgling and should be a great deal quieter.

'The top fledging of his year in the academy. Four years in a row,' Felix boasts, his grin wide and directed at me and I wonder again how old he is.

He's obviously trying to impress me, and frankly, I am.

The Drengar academy is no joke and there's no way that the Prince of Azanir, an AzarDrengar-Medir and Viktor LongwingDrengar—a very well-known warrior in Azanir—would bring along a male on this mission if he wasn't just as deadly and powerful as they are.

'For a top fledgling, you should be able to rein in your beast, Felix,' Alistair says casually to the window of his passenger door.

Felix just blabbers on and on about how he and his beast are in perfect harmony until he gets bored that no one is answering him and he flicks his attention to me.

'So Raff, how have you gone undetected so long in the human realm without your beast flipping out? I think I'd go crazy.'

Shrugging, I keep stuffing my face with nuggets and say, 'my beast isn't that loud. She's pretty quiet really. Always has been. Weak and quiet.'

'Even the weakest of Azanites have to shift though. The Thral have to every five days or so, compared to our two day window.' He mentions the lower ranking Azanites in Azanir. The Thal are workers, like commoners in human history. They are skilled and trained to keep our world running. Felix just keeps talking. 'So you must have had to shift at times. Unless you have the discipline of a Drengar,' he laughs, totally unaware that I've stopped eating and am now staring at him.

Alistair turns in his seat as if the thought of me having to shift never occurred to him. The accusation in his gaze has me swallow my mouthful of nuggets. 'That is true. I hope you've never given away our secrets, Lady Serafina. Your presence here in the human realm may be forgiven by my father, the King, if you help us find the sacred text, however, showing humans your true form might not be.'

Brain ticking, I try to work out the danger that I'm in and decide that the truth is much better than what he's now believing. 'I've never shifted,' I say. 'My beast has never taken over. My father had the Medir at his lair examine me a number of times growing up.' I can't help the way my voice shakes and refuse to look at the male to my right who turns to study me. I don't want to look at the Medir. What those so called 'healers' did to me was wicked and traumatising.

'I don't understand,' Alistair states. I hate that I have all their attention. 'Your beast is not weak, Serafina DarkwoodsAzar.'

I just shrug again, unsure what they all expect of me. They can say that all they like but it's the truth. I've never done anything remarkable with my beast.

I don't want to talk about this and look to the floor, hoping that they'll shut up.

'He's right, Raff. We can feel your beast just like you can feel ours. I don't think—'

'Let's leave her alone, Felix,' Alistair cuts him off.

Viktor seems to understand that this is not the kind of conversation I want to be having right now because he says, 'We need to stop to fuel this contraption.' He doesn't sound particularly happy about the idea of having to stop to get petrol and I could hug him for changing the subject.

'Good, I could use a snack,' Felix says eagerly, dropping the topic about my beast and the next few words out of Drengar Viktor's mouth are fucking hilarious. These massive males remind me of my brothers so much that it causes my chest to ache. I think of my Van and how he almost died. I close my eyes and re-live that moment over and over. The wraith behind him. The wraith impaling him. The complete anguish at believing I had lost my foster brother forever. If my beast was stronger, I wouldn't be in this situation. I don't think I'll ever get over what happened. I'll carry the guilt for the remainder of my days.

'Let's stop up here,' Alistair indicates to the large petrol station and rest-stop along the highway.

It's busy and we have to wait for a few minutes until the family in front of us finish up at the pump.

'I'll go in and get some food,' Felix declares as we pull up and Viktor stops the car.

'After you put the fuel into this *thing*. You're the only one who knows how to,' Viktor tells the younger male.

The males all get out of the minivan like clowns in one of those tiny vehicles. Long limbs, giant torsos and muscles that you'd only see on human body builders, I can only imagine how funny it'd be to watch them get out of this family car. It probably explains the look on the poor ladies face on the pump across from the one we've just parked at.

'I'll be back,' Alistair states as he gets out. 'Let's not linger here though. We need to be at the town of Jasper before sun fall and we're a number of hours away. The wraiths will attack there tonight, I'm sure of it.'

Jasper is the name of the town Viktor and Alistair feel is under threat by the wraiths tonight. From what I understand, the group of wraiths that attacked me, twice, have been making their way across the country, wreaking havoc as they go. The Drengar have been chasing them for days and are confident that they're a step ahead of the demons. The plan, or so I can gather, is to follow the demons as they are drawn to the sacred book in the hope they lead us to it, and protect humans and the Azanir secret along the way.

When we got back to the car at the fast-food place early this morning, Alistair and Viktor demanded to know what *I was doing*, Felix rambled on and on about the poster and that sparked a ten minute search for the city of Satmark. We found out it's almost on the other side of the country. A city known for its river and snow. *Best ski resort in the country*. That didn't make anyone happy to hear. Winter is coming and the heat of the sun is lessening with the change of season, but the idea of snow is depressing. Driving that long toward a colder climate isn't appealing.

It also back-ups what the Drengar believe the wraiths are moving towards. Jasper is on the way to Satmark. They all seemed convinced that I'm telling the truth, I hope. They've been formulating a ridiculous plan of a very…very, long road trip to the city and to continue to slow down this horde of wraiths on the way.

Eager and excited to get out of the car, I quickly pack up my takeout wrappers. Felix chuckles for no real reason and I thank him when he turns and flicks the latch on his chair so that it comes forward, allowing me room to jump out.

Stretching, I take in my surroundings. There are so many other cars. Masses of people stand around or walk back and forth from the big building. I see children and pets hanging out of windows, while parents carry bags of food and supplies for their trips. It's crowded and a little chaotic.

Leaning against the front bonnet, I shake my head when Felix asks me if I want anything to eat or drink and have a small suspicion that he'll bring me back something anyway. Felix strides toward the building leaving me with Wilder and Viktor who are both standing beside the car, looking weirdly and silently at the pump.

That's when I see him. The guy from the bar. Joseph is standing on the other side of the area with a group of men. They all look like they belong with the group of guys Brent hangs out with on their bikes. Except these ones don't have long beards and wear leather vests. They wear dark jeans, brown belts and an array of well-made button-ups. It's weird seeing him here and as if he can feel me staring, Joseph looks over and smiles the same flirtatious grin he gave me at the pub. It's an odd coincidence.

I turn away quickly when he raises his hand and waves. He gives me the creeps. I take a few casual steps towards the Drengar who are trying to figure out how to put petrol into the car, feeling a lot safer with them, which says a great deal.

Viktor swings around when I'm close and I get the full force of his annoyance when he asks, 'where's Felix?'

'Uh, he went inside,' I reply quietly, trying desperately to not look towards the Medir who's observing me intently.

Viktor curses in Zaric about how Felix is the only one who knows how to put petrol into the car and goes back to studying the pump. Hesitantly, and not keen to be too close to either of them but not wanting to be alone on the other side of the car with that Joseph guy looking at me, I don't have much choice.

I clear my throat and ask if they need help.

'No,' Viktor says too quickly and then looks up at the Medir who is giving him a very stern kind of look. 'No, thank you, Lady,' he corrects.

A little unsure about what has just happened, I stand awkwardly until Wilder and Viktor have an eye-conversation and then Viktor flicks those honey lined depths toward me. I can see him trying to work through his pride and ego. If I was nicer, I'd go over to the pump and start filling up the car, but I kinda like the way Viktor looks uncomfortable.

I catch Wilder's eye briefly and I may be mistaken but the way his brow rises tells me that he knows that I'm enjoying myself immensely. Which I am.

I wait for Viktor to work through his issues with asking a female for help and hide my smile when the massive Drengar finally says, 'would you please help us with this task, Serafina?'

Nodding, I try to squeeze past Wilder who doesn't move an inch and I end up brushing against his body. I have to remember how to breath and I clear my throat and make sure that *he* can see the look on my face that lets him know that I know exactly what he's doing. I think I imagine the small smile on his face.

Damn the male smells amazing.

Viktor too doesn't seem to understand what personal space means because he's breathing down my neck as I pull out the pump and get to work opening the petrol cap. Viktor watches my every move and I realise that he's trying to learn.

So, I push away my trepidation of being so close to them and start explaining what I'm doing. Viktor nods and asks questions while he waits and watches the dials go up and up.

'And that's it really,' I state, pulling the nozzle out of the car. 'Then you can just swipe your card here or go inside to pay.'

'I'll go inside and do that now,' Viktor says and I nod, a little confused why he's looking at me like he's unsure about something. Maybe it's because we are so close, we're almost touching. Maybe it's because my heart is hammering in my chest at the fact that on either side of me there's a Drengar making it hard to function.

'Thank you, Lady.' Viktor dips his head in respect and after flicking his gaze to Wilder, he walks toward the building.

I can only imagine how hard that would've been for him and turn to place the nozzle back into its correct spot and somehow get all tangled in the long pipe and try to step over it and trip.

Swearing loudly, I try to correct myself and end up falling into strong, muscle heavy arms that catch me without effort.

Blinking up at Wilder's intoxicating face, I open and close my mouth a few times before choking out, 'thank you.' I sound like a fool. A complete and utter fool, but his scent is muddling up my brain. Images flood my mind, confusing me on so many levels. He holds me for too long while I try to remember how to use my legs. He's a fucking Medir, who frightens me more than the idea of the wraiths hitting the town we're going to tonight.

What am I doing?

'You're welcome, Lady.'

My heart jumps into my throat. Staring at his handsome face, I try to process what's just happened and what I'm starting to realise has happened a few times since I met him. I don't know how I didn't realise that he has spoken to me before— in my MIND!

I've never heard a voice that I can describe as sexy. I've read the description and always thought that humans were weird to pay such attention to someone's voice, but now I get it. Now I understand why you'd read it in a romance novel. There's something truly core clenching about the sound of his voice. It's deep, throaty and clear. Full of power and authority.

'That's a little freaky,' I whisper and watch as that perfect face frowns as if he's trying to work out what I mean.

'Yes, I understand that. Using our inner voice to communicate is typically only done through our beasts and to the ones we have bonded with whilst in our true form. I have adapted since my larynx was damaged in a wraith battle many years ago.'

He declares that his 'true form' is the beast and I scoff and finally find my feet and stand on my own. Which makes me want to whimper and step back into his arms. Stupid, damn beast under my skin is awake and takes this opportunity to start paying attention. My inner muscles clench and I shiver in need.

I glare at him instead, at the typical, arrogant response from a male who believes himself powerful and superior. A real Azar response.

'You do not believe our beast form is our true one?'

Affronted, I step backwards and watch as he monitors the action. I snap, in a hurried whisper, 'you better not be reading my mind!'

The most intoxicating laughter fills my mind and I find myself transfixed by the look on his face.

'What did I miss?' I was so fixated on Wilder that I wasn't aware of Felix coming over to us. Wilder was though because he doesn't bat an eyelid. Instead, his gaze lingers for a heartbeat longer before moving over to the younger male.

Chapter Twenty Eight

It's late afternoon when we get to the small town of Jasper. Thinking of where we're headed has me wrap my arms around myself. The temperature has dropped and I'm already freezing my ass off and we're a long way from Satmark and its snow. It's either that which is making me feel like my skin is crawling or the fact that we're at another motel that looks almost similar to the place we were at last night.

Again, two beds. Again, not enough for the five of us, and I sit cross legged on top of the covers on the one closest to the bathroom. It's also the furthest from the door, which is exactly why Viktor told me to get off the first one with a glare like he knew exactly what I've been contemplating for the past hour.

Bastard.

I know that they use their damn beasts to communicate with each other but I'm starting to suspect that they *can* read my mind. Even though I don't actually think that it's a power the Azanites or Drengar have. Well, at least I don't think so.

Flicking aimlessly through the channels on the small television dangling from the roof, I listen to everything the Drengar are discussing as they try to formulate a plan for the night and the suspected wraith attack.

I don't understand half of what they're saying though. It's all tactical talk and unusual names.

My mood has been getting worse all day. I've given them the location of the book, they don't need me anymore, and frankly I miss my family. I miss Van and as the day ticks by I get more and more anxious about what they must be going through having woken or come home this morning from the city to see my note.

Sadness washes over me and I switch off the telly and mope. The note told them that I was safe. That my past had come back and needed my attention. I also said that I'd be back soon. I know they'll be worried though, especially because I don't have my phone with me and that'll eat Laney. She has enough on her plate and has done so much for me that the idea of hurting her, even when I didn't have a choice, breaks me. I know that Van won't remember what happened and I know that he was healed but I'd still wish I had watched him wake up and confirm that he's alive and well.

'I'll get food,' Felix declares. Standing from one of the four chairs near the small kitchenette, he stretches those thick, tree-trunk arms over his head. Viktor and Alistair are bent over an ancient looking map on the table and Wilder is dozing on the other bed. His large frame takes up the entire mattress and honestly I don't know how everyone is supposed to sleep tonight, and then it hits me. The Drengar aren't sleeping tonight. They expect the wraiths to attack this town. They're on a hunt and I'm bloody here with them.

I stand and throw the remote control on the bed and ask Felix if I can come too. If tonight could be my last, I need to stretch my legs and feel the sun.

Watching Felix flirt with the young woman behind the counter who has just taken our order, I find myself hypnotised by his carefree spirit. Tonight he could be facing a horde of demons and yet he's having the time of his life. He seems a great deal more relaxed around humans than most Azanites.

Taking a seat at one of the empty tables near the window, I watch the poor humans go about their afternoon, finishing off the workday and probably heading home to be with their loved ones. Each one blissfully unaware that tonight could be their last.

'Contemplating how to escape?' Viktor asks and while his presence has completely scared the shit out of me, I remain calm on the outside like he didn't just sneak up on me. He must have followed us here.

He pulls the chair across from me out and sits down with a sigh. I refuse to look up or acknowledge his masculine, intoxicating smell. 'Yep, every minute of the day,' I reply as cheerfully as I can muster.

'You wouldn't get far, you know that right?'

It's his tone that has me pull my focus from the group of men who walk across the road. I get a sense that I should remember them.

Glaring in Viktor's direction, I don't let those honey lined eyes distract me from being annoyed and offended, even though all his presence does is make me remember how much of a crush I had on him as a youngling. He was the first male I dreamt of. That I fantasised him holding me and keeping me safe. Until I learnt that I needed to be the one to look after myself. That I shouldn't rely on anyone to do it for me.

'I can look after myself Drengar Viktor and have done for ten years on my own,' I snap, a little petulantly.

'I'm very aware of how you lived for the last ten years, Serafina.'

The audacity of the male has me seeing red, which I worry for a second is actually the colour of my eyes because his own flick the same blazing colour at me before melting into honey.

'What does that mean?' I mutter through clenched teeth.

'It means I'm very curious as to why you traded your life in Azanir for this one.' He indicates to the town outside the window. It's clear what he thinks of this world. My emotions jump from outrage to pity really fast. He doesn't see the beauty in the human world and that is...well, rather sad. Humans live life hard. Yes, they have issues, and they need a lesson in embracing nature and not trying to own it, but they're fun and loving.

'Why are you protecting this town tonight then?' I ask, genuinely curious. 'You believe this horde of demons is hundreds strong. Why put yourself in such a dangerous situation for a race you don't care about?'

Viktor doesn't hesitate, he answers quickly and surely. 'Wraiths pose a threat to our secrecy. If there's a string of attacks that attract the human authorities, our race could be endangered. They must never find out about the existence of wraiths and our kind.'

'Is that honestly the only reason? Not because they're defenceless and good and need our help?' I ask, people watching again. They deserve our help, *don't they?*

'Humans are not our concern,' Viktor replies casually and yet, as I look over and observe him staring at a mother holding hands with a very small child, I know that he has to feel more than just a need to protect our race from exposure. 'You love these humans.' It's a statement more than a question, but I still answer.

'Yes. I find them less complicated than the beasts I grew up around.' I don't know why I said that and bite my lip and keep my focus on the street.

The sun is going down and the pull to find shelter is starting to irritate me. 'They live with such passion and adventure. They love hard and true.'

'I think you've forgotten what it means to be loved by an Azanite, Serafina. You must know that to be loved by a beast is to be loved completely and eternally. Any kind of love. Parent and youngling. Siblings. Lovers.' His words don't match his casual tone. A lady and a man walk past holding hands and I can't help but think of Laney and my brothers.

'I wouldn't know what that feels like. No beast has ever loved me.' I hate the sadness that wraps around every word.

Eyes snapping to the male across the table when his hand covers the one I have playing with a napkin, I stare, dumbfounded by the way he seems to be comforting me.

'I don't know if I can believe that. I watched as your brothers searched for you when they realised that you were gone. I was in the league of Drengar that were sent out by your frantic father. The panic they felt at thinking you were dead was real and fed by their beasts loyalty to you.'

Lost in his strange, lined eyes, I feel everything. Loudly. There is a part of me that believed my birth family wouldn't have noticed or cared about my absence. I don't have many fond memories of any of them. I have two brothers...half-brothers. A father, and a mother, who actually isn't my mother at all. I was only really close to my dad. Yes, we spent time together and he'd take me on small trips around the Darkwoods each morning, but that's all the kindness I remember. My 'mother' kept her distance and in effect, my brothers did too.

Scoffing, I pull my hand away and cross my arms, annoyed at the show of weakness and the fact that I almost felt terrible for what I did by leaving. Almost.

'Besides, the one thing our race doesn't need is to lose any of our females.'

I cackle. 'So, that's it. It had nothing to do with the fact that I left but that you need females in order to keep the Azanir race going.'

'You twist my words in order to feel good about what you did.'

Mouth falling open, I snap it shut with a clunk and grumble my annoyance. 'You don't know me.'

'You'd be surprised. I lived in the Darkwoods from the moment I left the Drengar Academy. I was no more than a juvenile. I knew you. I saw you around the lair, always surrounded by your maids and the Lords elite warriors. Or hiding behind the furniture.'

I feel my cheeks go beetroot red and glare at his smirk which falls from my face when his goes all serious. 'I don't believe that you betrayed our race, Serafina. Tell me how you know what the book looks like and where it is right now.'

I open and close my mouth a few times, unsure what to do or say. 'I can't. You're right though, I never betrayed anyone.'

Searching my face, Viktor stays quiet and I can't help but admire the way his hair falls around his face.

I don't know what Viktor was about to say and can only imagine what it could've been to match the deep frown now on his face. Felix comes over, having clearly finished with his flirting and unloads a tray of boxes and interrupting this ridiculous deep and meaningful conversation I'm having with a male I used to have girlish fantasies about.

'Let's eat. We have a big night tonight,' Felix declares almost excitedly and I take one of the containers and a fork while Wilder and Alistair stride through the doors.

Pending doom doesn't seem at all an appetite killer for these four confusing, complicated Drengar.

Chapter Twenty Nine

NOT SURE IF A *heart can stop by the sheer force of its own pounding, I sit up in bed and look around the dark, freezing hotel room unsure what has happened.*

I look to the bed next to mine and notice it empty. No one is in the room, which I find odd. There isn't a noise to be heard and the darkness spilling in from the covered window means that I should probably lay back down and go to sleep. However, something like a pull on my soul I normally associate with my beast needing to find shelter at this time of day, is telling me to open the front door.

Like a bad omen, the brown door seems to call to me. Its stained wood promising nothing good as I hop off the bed and make my way across the small room.

Hand shaking, I reach out to grab the handle, the bite of the frost surrounding it has me hiss a breath before I jerk it open and come face to face with a shocking scene.

The carpark to the motel is a battlefield in every sense of the word. Four blazing Drengar stand like the perfect warriors they are, fire swords alight, surrounded by the biggest horde of Wraith demons.

Watching in horror as one by one, demons are cut down and evaporate under the heat of the fire the Drengar control, more seem to appear, hungry to suck the heat from each warrior. Hungry for the only power that can make them whole.

Feet glued to the ground, I'm unable to help or move when my attention snags on the wraith sneaking up behind Drengar Felix. The male I've gotten to know as fun-loving and boyish, long gone in the features of the mighty warrior who battles the demons like a beautiful dancer.

I try to open my mouth and shout a warning. Try to understand what I'm seeing as wraiths seem to work together to get the better of the male, yet nothing happens. Frantic, I look around for help and only see a short knife one of the Drengar left on the kitchenette table near the door. Willing myself to move, I begin to cry, thick heavy tears at the fact that there is nothing I can do. My limbs are locked, and staring back at the battlefield, my heart explodes in pain when I watch the sneaking wraith run his hand through Felix's chest.

My scream is soundless.

The others don't seem to realise what has happened. Fighting against the invisible bonds surrounding my body, I stop moving when the wraith turns its head slowly. Its arm lodged through Felix's chest, it looks directly at me. Its distorted face almost seems to be alight with pleasure and if I didn't know any better, it grins.

'Serafina!'

I wake with a jolt that has me sit up, gasping down air. Blinking up at the male frowning down at me, I try to remember where I am. I feel lost. I feel broken and as the dream slips from my mind, I forget why I want to break down and weep.

'Shit,' I whisper, wiping the water on my cheeks frantically, very aware of the four males watching me warily from different points of the room.

'Are you okay, Raff?' Felix looks worried and strokes my back in comforting lines that do seem to calm me down.

'Yes,' I manage to say.

Felix doesn't looked convinced. 'You were shouting in your sleep. You were...' His words trail off and I see the uncertainty on his face.

'You were screaming,' Alistair finishes for the younger male who seems to need a minute. Felix doesn't look well and he sits heavily on the mattress beside me.

'Sorry, just a nightmare.' Panic floods my system. I pray to the Sun Gods I didn't say anything incriminating. Talking while having a nightmare never got me any kindness from beasts like these males and I shut my mouth and pull my legs into my chest.

I don't mean to, and I hate myself for looking over at the Medir to make sure that he isn't close, or maybe it's to make sure he is. I don't know.

Wilder is at the small table near the door, observing me with his obsidian eyes. I shiver. My gaze flying back to Felix who clears his throat.

The curtain has been left open on the window beside the table and I have no idea what time it is. After the meal in the noodle bar, I came back to the hotel with the males, had a shower, and curled up on the bed. I must have fallen asleep watching television.

'Raff, I know that this situation is not ideal and that you're here with four males on your own. But please, I need you to remember that we are the *Drengar*,' he emphasises the word and I have no idea why. 'Trained warriors who are sworn to protect Azanir. We are bound by our beasts, who are unable to hurt an innocent or a female, as well as our honour.' He's speaking to me like I'm not able to understand his words or like I might miss something.

Now when I look around to the males in the room it's in question, not uncertainty. 'Um, I know,' I stammer. My mind is still a bit fuzzy so maybe I'm missing what he's trying to tell me.

Felix grips my hand but not before he hesitates as if afraid to scare me. '*I* would never hurt you, Raff. Nor would I let anyone touch you.'

Now completely lost, I open and close my mouth a few times before saying, 'Drengar Felix, I have no idea what you're talking about.'

'You were talking as well, Serafina. In your sleep.' Viktor steps up to the end of the bed, his body encased in weapons that weren't there when I fell asleep. The colour drains from my face and I can only imagine what they all see to have them all make a collective noise in the back of their throat in outrage.

'I don't...'

'You were screaming Felix's name,' Alistair offers, obviously noticing my despair.

Shit.

'I'd never hurt you, Raff.' Poor Felix looks so dejected and for some reason it makes me deeply uncomfortable.

I sit forward, almost shoving my face in his so that his now downcast eyes have to look up to meet mine. 'I know, Felix. It was a nightmare. I can't really remember what it was about but you didn't hurt me,' which isn't a lie...fully. I swallow the bile that rises in the back of my throat at the image that plays in my head of the wraith that killed him.

Viktor moves in my peripherals and the knife at his belt catches the light in just a way that it temporarily impacts my vision. I think my soul leaves my body.

I jump back. Felix looks like I just broke his heart. I don't have time to care though because I'm too busy trying to tell myself that I've seen the knife before and that's why I dreamt it. That it all happened unconsciously, even though the other voice in my head says no, I haven't seen that knife...damn voices.

There's no time to contemplate what might happen though because Felix snaps his attention to the window and declares, 'Wraith scouts are here,' just before a heavy shadow covers any light from the parking lot.

My heart drops into my butt and I quickly grab Felix just before he rises from the bed. 'Don't go out there, Drengar Felix,' I implore. The others are already moving around the hotel room, preparing themselves for battle.

Felix's blue eyes are alight with excitement for the hunt and no longer hold the hurt from before. They seem to soften as he looks to the death grip I have on his arm.

Raising one hand, he cups the side of my face. The heat of him increasing by the second with the call to battle his beast is now heeding. I can feel the scaly monster under his skin pushing against my cheek as if trying to touch me too.

'You're safe here, Lady Serafina. Just stay inside and under the warm covers.'

'No,' I say, trying and failing to keep him where he is. Felix stands and cracks his neck and I have a clear shot of the room. 'That's not what I meant. You can't go out there. You'll die.'

'Raff, I won't die. I promise.' He grabs my hand and kisses it and I catch Wilder watching me from the other bed. His hands moving over every weapon he has laid out on the mattress and I shut my mouth. Those eyes seem to see way too much.

Felix rises quickly, evading my attempt to grab him again.

'Are we ready?' Alistair asks the room.

Wilder flips the last dagger and places it into his belt, our gazes still locked. I'm stuck to the bed, completely unable to look away. My mind races with my heart. I watch Wilder's left eyebrow rise and for some unnamed reason, I have another lightbulb moment.

'You're a healer. An AzarDrengar-Medir, how was your injury to your voice box unable to be healed?' I ask, very aware that this is not the time to ask why he'd have lost his ability to speak with as much power I assume is under his skin.

Wilder smirks and it's honestly the hottest thing I've ever seen in my life. Hot and confusing...what is wrong with me!

They all head to the door. It's insane how they're casually walking to meet hundreds of wraith demons like they're just going to breakfast.

The heat in the room pulses against my skin, waking my beast.

Knowing I can't stop them from heading to the hunt, I quickly say, 'Drengar Viktor,' and wait for him to look over his shoulder at me. Those honey lined eyes a little curious. 'Could you leave that dagger on the counter in case I need it?'

CHAPTER THIRTY

I'M BEING SILLY AND ridiculous.

I can hear the fighting outside. The shrieking of the Wraith demons is making my skin crawl but the need to open the door and make sure my dream isn't going to come true is eating a hole in my soul.

Standing before the brown door, eating my bottom lip, I look to the dagger and curse myself when I reach over and grab it. I'm surprised at how light it feels even with the large green jewel on the handle and the fact that it's made of solid gold.

Azanites love their gold.

With a shaking hand, I grip the dagger and hesitantly open the motel door and stare at the horrifying scene. The silent prayers I've been reciting in my head have been for nothing because it's exactly as I saw it in my nightmare. Four males. Their blazing weapons. Fire evaporating wraiths.

Useless, I stand, unable to do anything but witness the chaos. There isn't a human in sight, which doesn't surprise me. Just like at my home, the magic of the Drengar keep this battle shielded from them.

I don't know how long I stand there watching, but it feels like hours. Then, as if I'm viewing a movie that I've already seen before, I see the wraiths attack Felix in the same configuration that led to his untimely death in my dreams.

Stunned, I have no control over my raging heart as I look over at the Wilder who is deep in battle with four demons. His gaze flicks to mine for the briefest of seconds and I try to communicate with him that he needs to look to his left. That he needs to help Felix, but a wraith jumps on top of him and takes him to the ground.

The demon coming up behind Felix is close. My heart is pounding. My head hurts beyond words and there is so much adrenaline coursing through my veins that I don't think that I'm fully conscious when I react.

Leaping forward on shaky legs, I run towards the Drengar I'm beginning to recognise is my friend. Who has saved me and made me feel at ease in this crazy situation. A male who was distraught to think that I had dreamt he hurt me enough to have me scream in my sleep.

'No,' I roar, dodging wraiths and burning weapons. I hear my name being shouted into the night. 'Felix, behind you!' I try to scream over the noise of battle, which is useless because he doesn't turn to me.

Coming to a screeching halt, I feel my beast come alive. The fire in my blood has me shaking.

Skin rippling and constricting painfully, I see red. Literally. The world changes colour and I pull my arm back over my shoulder and throw the dagger.

Time slows.

Watching the weapon as it flies past my face, I gape at the blue flame licking its sharpened blade.

My fire.

A fire I've never conjured before in such a way encompasses the weapon. The dagger flips and flips and sails right through the chest of the wraith who had its ugly, now solid arm, at a sharpened tip ready to impale Felix.

Then the wraith just...evaporates.

The dagger hits the floor with a clank that I'm surprised I hear over the fighting.

Instincts blaring, I swing around and shriek at the sight of a wraith standing behind me and then watch as it evaporates instantly.

Shocked, I look over my shoulder and blink in wonder at the Medir who has just thrown a flaming knife of his own from across the carpark and saved my life.

I have no time to think though because all the demons in the carpark throw their heads back and roar as one. The sound is ear shattering.

I fall to the ground and cover my head under the pain of it. I hear the curses that come from the males as if they are effected by the noise as much as I am, and then it stops.

Unsure if this is some kind of demon trap, I slowly drop my hands from my head and look up to see the four Drengar standing around the carpark. Each one with their swords in hand turning slowly and I believe that I might not be the only one who thinks this could be a trick.

A hand grips my upper arm and pulls me to my feet. Looking up at the male holding me, I swallow a very smart-arse retort when Viktor demands to know what I think I'm doing.

'Get her inside, Viktor,' Alistair shouts, and before another word is spoken, I'm hurled backward into the hotel room and back on the bed. Alastair, Wilder and Felix are close behind, keeping a tight formation as they enter one by one and the door is closed by Wilder's boot.

I thought I was scared before but I'd rather run out to a battle with hundreds of wraiths again than sit here with four Drengar staring down at me. Arms folded. Faces like pure stone. Gorgeous stone, but stone.

'You saved me,' Felix declares, his expression the first to change as he blinks at me like I'm some kind of apparition.

'Where did you learn to do that?' Viktor demands, completely ignoring Felix.

'Do what?' I ask.

'Where did you learn to fire transfer?' He doesn't sound too impressed and I have no idea what he's talking about which must be clear because Felix helps me out.

'The dagger, Raff. Where did you learn to transfer your fire to a weapon? That's a skill not even some Drengar can do.'

'You can all do it,' I reply and fight my eye roll when Felix indicates to himself as if saying, *come on, I'm not an average Drengar*. 'I don't know. I've never done that before.' That seems to take a moment to sink in. 'I swear!'

Wilder has one of his weird eye-conversations with Alastair that I'm realising isn't an 'eye-conversation', their beasts are speaking to each other. It's annoying to be left out and I hate that I feel all self-conscious.

'The wraiths are gone,' Alistair throws me a side eye like I might grow two heads and begin to eat them all. 'For now. I was hoping that battle would be enough to slow the demons down so that we might not encounter them again on our travels to Satmark. Let us hope it did just that.'

'Yeah, let's hope for all your sakes because if Raff tells me to stay inside again, I'm staying inside,' Felix states with such finality that Viktor and

Alistair chuckle. Like actually chuckle. Noises other than grumbles and growls just came from their throats and my jaw hits my lap.

'It's strange that what you feared actually nearly happened, hey Raffy,' the younger male says, sitting beside me on the bed with way too much energy. The bed bounces and squeaks at the impact.

I swallow the lump in my throat and shrug a nonchalant gesture that has Felix grin like he knows something I don't know.

The others begin to remove all the weapons from their uniforms and I watch, a little creepily, as Viktor's arms bulge and flex with each one of his movements.

Felix leans forward and whispers in my ear, the sound causes a ripple of pleasure to zap down my spine. 'You saved my life, Raff. Lucky you were there when you were.'

Gaze flicking to his, I stare at the male I feel is teasing me.

I have no idea what his tone is implying. He can't possibly know how I knew...could he?

Chapter Thirty One

S LEEP EVADES ME.

I toss and turn and end up staring at the creamy-greyish roof contemplating my life. Never in a millions years would I've expected that this would be where I ended up. Viktor and Felix are snoring softly in the bed to my left and I shuffle a little to spy the male on the floor next to mine.

I wasn't expecting two black diamond coloured eyes staring back at me and gasp in fright. 'Sorry, I thought you'd be asleep.'

'You haven't stopped moving for an hour, Serafina. How could I possible be asleep?' Wilder sounds amused. His sultry, sleepy tone is hot. I almost throw myself off the side of the bed and on top of him. The only thing that keeps me rooted to the mattress is that I catch the desire my own beast is pumping through my blood and realise it's her and shut her down. It's like that tone of his woke her up and my skin feels all itchy now.

Wilder seems to know exactly what he has done if the damn smug look on his face is anything to go by and I fear that he actually can read my mind.

'Are you reading my mind?' I ask him again and hear him chuckle. Sun Gods, he is divine. AND A MEDIR!

'I can't read your mind. Your body on the other hand is quite easy to understand. Your beast is not as quiet as you think she is.'

That has me frown. I have no idea what he means by that. He heard what I said about my beast in the car not being very strong.

'You're weird,' I say and smile when he laughs in my head.

I've been called many things by females and weird is not one of them. Most of them say quite nice things about me, especially in the mornings.'

'Your arrogance is shocking,' I mumble and play with the stitch on the blanket under me. 'You can speak to me even though we don't share some kind of bond like you obviously have with the other Drengar.' I meant to ask a question but it comes out more as a statement. A statement I'd really like to know the answer to because with my beast awake, I can smell him and my mind is going crazy. Image after image of dreams replay in my head, on repeat, again, and I'm really getting sick of it. Each one is terrifying and confronting.

Wilder just smirks a one sided smirk that has my heart quicken. It's like he is very aware that he's gorgeous and mysterious. A combination I know no female would be able to resist. Human or Azanite.

Drained, I lay with my head on the edge of the mattress, not wanting to stop our conversation.

'You're tired. You should sleep. We head off early tomorrow.' There's genuine concern in his tone, and while I yawn, I know that I won't be able to. *'I could help you get to sleep, if you like?'*

Every muscle in my body tenses and a rush of adrenaline floods my system. His words bounce around in my head, causing me to tremble in fear. Wilder sits up, his brow furrowed at whatever is written on my face. *'Lady—'*

'No!' I interrupt. I back away quickly from the edge and curl up on my side, as far from the male as I can get without getting up and running away.

'*One day you will tell me what happened to you, Serafina DarkwoodsAzar. And I promise to all the Sun Gods, when I find out who hurt you, I'll burn them with a fire they have never felt or seen before.*'

His words are a promise.

A declaration.

I eventually fall asleep, dreaming of a beast rampaging through my father's lair, killing everyone in sight.

The next three days go by without much drama. The most exciting thing to happen is when Viktor and Felix had an argument about stopping for the second time to grab Felix some food—chicken nuggets. The male is obsessed with nuggets and chocolate.

Yesterday, he dragged me to an ice-cream bar in the small town we stayed overnight in and we sat there for two hours while he sampled every single chocolate flavour. It was pretty funny when he spat out the coffee chocolate. I've made a point to keep my distance from Wilder too, which is not as easy as I'd like.

Other than that, I've been bored out of my brain on a road-trip to a city that may or may not be covered in snow to retrieve a stolen gold book that doesn't open.

Really this whole things sounds like a bad television show. One that Van and I would probably watch and deny if asked. The thought of my Van causes a well of emotion to form in my chest. It's getting harder and harder to ignore.

Chapter Thirty Two

*F*IRE. *IT'S EVERYWHERE.*

BUILDINGS burn. People scream. Beasts fall from the sky.

Unable to move, I stare at the chaos, screaming a name over and over again. The name doesn't register, but I know in my soul that I'm calling to the male who haunts my dreams. A male I've given myself to in every possible way. My throat burns from screaming and I wish that my beast would wake up and fight. Wake up and help. My heart feels as if it's breaking in two. Completely ripped apart by the fear of losing him.

Eyes shooting open, I can't think beyond the images in my head. I can hear myself screaming but I can't stop. My tears are endless and I cry from the pain still sitting on my chest. Of the way my heart still feels broken like I lost someone so special to me that the world no longer has colour. Like my entire existence has no meaning.

Sobbing hard, I curl into the body that pulls me into his chest. Solid, secure arms fold around me, caging me in their warmth and comfort. With the dreams hold on my mind still strong, I have no idea how long I sit there and weep into the tender embrace.

I come to my senses slowly and cry for a whole new reason.

'You are safe, Serafina. It was just a dream.'

'No,' I cry, knowing I should push away from him. Knowing I should shut my mouth and not say a single word, that I'm cuddling a Medir. However, I can't move. He feels too good. His scent is too comforting after the heartbreak I just witnessed and I'm not strong enough to survive such emotions without his help right now. 'They're never just dreams.' I'm barely aware of what I'm saying.

'You're all right, Astgeer,' the voice in my head sooths and I close my eyes and listen to the small tune that starts playing in my mind. Wilder hums for me and I cry the last of my tears, listening to his beautiful, deep voice. His thick arms are curled around my body, my face is buried into his solid chest and I breath him in.

Turning slightly, I see the room of males watching me. Alistair is on a chair against the motel door. Felix is under the covers on the opposite bed while Viktor is atop the sheet. They were sleeping feet-to-head like Van and I used to when we'd fall asleep watching television all night. Both males are sitting up, observing me like I'm a wild animal who might start losing her mind.

The concern written on their expressions is enough to break through the turmoil in my mind and I sniffle and pull away from Wilder. His arms drop and I have to bite my tongue to stop myself from asking him to hold me again.

Unable to look at the male sitting beside me, I mumble a quick, 'thank you.'

I take the tissue he offers and try desperately to not lose it again when I look up to see him watching me. Those black eyes. The masculine features and the scar. They make me want to cry again and I have no idea why.

'Are you well, Lady?' Alistair asks from his chair.

Gaze flicking up to his, I see the tension in his shoulders and the way he grips the arms of the chair. The white knuckles are enough to tell me how he's feeling and how loud I was screaming.

'Yes.' I nod, wiping my face. 'I'm sorry,' I whisper, afraid of my own voice. It burns and I can only imagine what it must have felt like to hear me.

'Raff, are you sure?' Felix hops off the bed and hurries to grab me one of the water bottles from the kitchenette. I take it and nod again. It's the extent of my communication skills right now.

'You are plagued with these nightmares. Have you had them your entire life?'

Focus going from the water bottle, I get stuck in dark eyes and finally notice the red around the rims. Wilder's energy rolls through the room. They're all emitting such heightened emotion.

'Yeah,' I whisper.

'I'm sorry to hear that,' Viktor says and I realise that Wilder included everyone in the question he has just asked.

Contemplating how he does that, I'm able to shake off the remnants of the nightmare and get a grip over my emotions a little better. 'It is what it is.' I try and fail to give them all a reassuring smile. I'm sure it just looked like a grimace.

'Well, let's try and get a few more hours of sleep while we can,' Viktor declares after having another one of those eye-conversations with Wilder, who is still sitting very close.

'I don't think I can after that,' Felix grumbles and throws me an apologetic look when I flinch. I hate that I'm interrupting their rest time. These males are always constantly awake and on patrol. They share the duties of monitoring for danger throughout the night and I feel immense guilt at interrupting their sleep. 'I'll take watch, Alistair. You get some shut eye.'

The prince rises slowly and agrees reluctantly. His gaze keeps flicking to me.

The lamp across the room is switched off and the room is plunged back into darkness. I was the first one to drift off early while the Drengar were talking mission business.

Spying the pile of blankets beside the bed, I panic when Wilder gives my arm a small, reassuring squeeze before he goes to get up. I don't know why I do it, and frankly, I don't think I'd ever understand what made me and the beast work together, for a change, to grab the arm of the AzarDrengar-Medir. He swings back around with a frown.

'Please.' The voice in my head screams at me to think about what I'm doing. 'Please, could you lay with me?' My voice is too small. It's too full of terror to be truly mine. If I wasn't so exhausted from the exaggerated display of emotions, I'd kick the shit out of myself, but I'm tired. And I feel battered and bruised.

I expect Wilder to look to the others. It's something they all do, as if they are one unit, and just as I'm about to break the now drawn out, uncomfortable silence that has fallen in the room, he says, *'shuffle over.'*

I bite my bottom lip to keep my grin in check and do as he says. There's not a single sound as Wilder pulls back the covers and nestles in beside me. He is so massive that his entire frame takes up the majority of the mattress. I think in any other situation I'd kick him right back out, but he is warm and safe, and damn her, but my beast makes a terrible embarrassing noise and forces me to curl into his side.

I feel his hesitation at first and then after a few heartbeats, one of his arms rises to curl around my body. I sigh and I think I hear him do the same in my head.

'Thank you,' I whisper into his side. The word doesn't communicate how much I appreciate him holding me right now.

'Sleep, Astgeer,' he commands softly.

I fall into the deepest sleep I've ever experienced in my life with the word Wilder BlazeAzar-Drengar-Medir just called me playing within my mind.

Astgeer.

My beloved.

Chapter Thirty Three

I FEEL LIKE A porcelain doll. For the next three days, the Drengar treat me like I might shatter into a million pieces at any moment.

Felix sits in the back seat of the car with me, feeding me from his bag of snacks. I don't think he has taken a breath in two days, he hasn't stopped talking. Viktor no longer looks to me with annoyance once, he's being nice and its weirding me out. Alistair even asked if I needed him to cut my meat at dinner last night. I think even he realised that it was too far because he quickly back peddled and ended up making me laugh. I don't think I'll ever forget the way they all looked at me with relief, like they were worried I was broken.

Wilder on the other hand has been acting the same. He only speaks to me during the day to say things like, 'watch your step' or 'be careful'. Yet, every night, he silently slips under the covers while I'm drifting off to sleep and holds me.

Last night was different though. When I woke quietly from a nightmare of fire and death, we ended up chatting all night long. Our conversation was funny and a little odd. I harassed him until he told me a story about his home and living as a BlazeAzar. I learnt that he has four brothers, and honestly the idea of there being more of him is just mind-boggling. Is it wrong that the idea of meeting them kept me up longer that night?

Wilder spoke of a home that was filled with love and laughter and parents that he clearly adores.

It made me sad really.

Envious.

The diner we've stopped at is supposed to be the last stop for a few days. Apparently.

I've been placed in the corner of the booth and I'm surrounded by the imposing, overprotective Drengar.

I'm so hungry and moody today that I ignore the males discussing 'mission' business and try to open the freakin' sauce bottle. I didn't sleep properly after my conversation with Wilder.

We finally stopped for lunch after Felix harassed the others for about an hour to get him some food.

Cursing under my breath, I grip the glass bottle and contemplate throwing it across the diner. A very masculine hand appears under my nose and I huff and hand it over to the male sitting across from me and watch as Wilder effortlessly opens the bottle without looking. He's deep in conversation with Alistair and I take it when he hands it over and feel less homicidal.

I dive into my burger and chip meal with excitement, totally in my own world until I look up and stop chewing. Four pairs of colourful eyes are staring and I realise that I was moaning. Noisily and inappropriately.

Trying to shut my very full mouth, I almost choke when Felix laughs and the side of Alistair's mouth moves slightly as if he thought it was funny too.

'You were saying?' Viktor asks the prince, throwing me a weird side-eye and I take the napkin Wilder hands over with a small head nod in thanks.

Fucking embarrassing, and yet, I take another big bite. I couldn't give a shit if they think I'm a pig. I'm emotionally eating and will not stop for anyone.

They finally begin to talk again.

I'm not really listening as they chat about the next part of our road trip until Alistair says, 'I'm concerned.' Burger half devoured, I put it down and start on my fries while I pay attention.

There's a communal grumble of acknowledgement and I slowly dip my hot chip into the mountain of sauce on my place.

'Tomorrow we will cross the state border and then it's a week's drive to the city of Satmark. The landscape will change once we're out of this state. We are headed towards thick forest. You can see here.' He points to certain spots on the map. 'There are small towns for us to stop at. However, they're few and far between. We're looking at days of driving. With little shelter most of the time.'

The map on the table is the same ancient looking one they've been using since I met them. They're all studying it with an eye I don't have.

'We have a few human motels to use but there may be a few nights where we are either in the car or out in the open,' Viktor tells the team and my jaw drops.

'What do you mean by out in the open?' I ask, uncaring of the pretence of not listening. There is no way I can be out at night in some kind of forest, camping or whatever. I've never done something like that. I don't think I'd be able to. My beast might be quieter than the typical Azanite but I physically wouldn't be able to stay outside.

I'm sure they can all hear the panic in my tone.

'We don't know what's going to happen for sure, Serafina,' Alistair says diplomatically.

Everyone shuts up when the waitress comes over with a tray full of drinks. She begins to place down the sodas and coffees. 'What brings y'all out here in the middle of nowhere?' She beams, her badge letting us know her name is Sal. She has a kind round face and an air of gentleness to her. She has on a white apron over the blue and white striped uniform.

Sal isn't joking, this town's in the middle of nowhere. We drove for five hours this morning from another more populated town to this small dot on Alistair's map. The town sits on a flat plain. Mountains fill the horizon on all sides. There is only a gas station across the road, a corner shop next to it and a few streets of houses. Trucks everywhere though. It looks to be a popular rest-stop between the states.

'Family road trip,' Felix answers in his heavy accent. His smooth reply, coupled with the way he looks, gets her full attention.

Felix is the only one who ever speaks to the humans we interact with, unless Viktor is forced to drive through a take-out joint to feed Felix.

'Odd place to go on a trip, you headed to Satmark?' Poor Sal's friendly grin drops when three very intimidating Drengar look sharply in her direction. I just roll my eyes, these males are so suspicious. A nice elderly man asked me a simple question yesterday when we stopped at a grocery store and all four of them appeared at my side instantly, all glare-y and puff-chested. They do that every time we're in a town. I have no idea if they just hate humans or if it's something more.

'How'd you guess?' Felix asks, his tone not so smooth.

'Well, that's the only place to go from here. Unless that's where you came from.' She chuckles to herself, like we are all weird. Which is fair. They are weird.

'Yes, that's where we're headed.'

'Hope y'all are ready for the trip. The road to Satmark is not for amateurs. You may not see another soul for days. They predict the snow will start any day now too.' Her gaze flicks to me. 'You should head over and speak to Larry at the auto shop and make sure your car is ready for the trip. Better to be safe than sorry. Wouldn't want to be stuck on the highway with a broken down car or anything.' She looks around, expecting some kind of reaction from the males at the table, they give her nothing. The kind waitress frowns before letting us know she'll be back with the chocolate cake Felix ordered.

'What is an auto shop?' Alistair asks when she's a safe distance away. He speaks in Zaric so I don't see the point in fearing she might overhear.

'It's a place you take your car to get fixed,' I offer, devouring my chips. If I'm heading towards isolation and potential doom, I refuse to do it with an empty stomach.

'What would we need to fix?' Felix just looks perplexed and I stay focused on eating.

Realising I'm not going to answer, Alistair says, 'Let's just get this mission over with so that we can go home.'

'I second that,' Viktor raises his coffee mug. 'My beast is riding me hard today. I need to give him the reins soon or I won't be able to contain him. These humans would drop down dead if he took over.'

Male laughter caresses my skin and one sensual laugh fills my mind. It has me almost choke on the fry in my mouth. It's a beautiful sound. A sound that I feel all the way in my soul.

Coughing at the unexpected connection, I again, nod my thanks, but this time to Felix who pats my back to help me dislodge the fried piece of goodness cutting off my airways.

I have no idea if the Medir meant to project the noise and I subtly observe him from under my lashes. He's nothing like what his appearance suggests. Yes, he is powerful, more than I'm sure I've witnessed so far, and yes, he has a sense of male arrogance about him that is both irritating and panty-soaking. However, our nightly chats have shown me that he's intelligent and loyal and family focused. I've never been so attracted and so...frightened of another living being in my life, and I've only known the male for a few days.

'Tell me about it. I hate the human world, so many buildings. So much separation from nature. I need to feel the sun on my scales. We have been out of Azanir too long.' Alistair speaks like he's a million miles away.

'I can't wait to go home and see my family. Eat in the dining hall and see how my sister is fairing with her new mate.' Felix smiles into his soda. 'They're planning their binding,' he adds just for me and I nod like a fool who isn't internally freaking out about where this conversation is heading.

Which it does very dramatically. 'The moment we have the book, we're all out of here,' Viktor declares. 'The ship to Azanir taking new humans who've been approved to cross the Veil leaves in a few weeks. We need to be on it.'

New humans can live in Azanir. It's not a process I'm very familiar with but the only way to get there is through the Veil, and for a non-Azanite, it means taking a ship over some very choppy waters.

Looking around, it dawns on me why they're speaking about needing the ship—me. It is the only way I can cross because my beast can't take control to get me there.

I think I'm going to be sick. It's not that I didn't know they'd be planning to take me back but hearing it and thinking it are two different things.

'I need a moment,' I declare, stomach churning. Felix and Viktor don't move off the booth until I say, 'please, I need to use the bathroom.' That gets them to move. I ignore the standing males and hurry to the back corner of the diner, knowing I'm being watched.

Rounding the corner of the corridor, I stop in my tracks at the sight of a big opening in the wall that shows the chef's in the kitchen. However, that isn't what has my heart pound in excitement and anticipation. It's the phone on the ledge.

Sal walks past just as I start contemplating if I should use it and I quickly jump into action. 'Excuse me,' I say in my sweetest voice.

'How can I help you sugar? Not that it looks like you need much help with those gorgeous men around you.' She winks. I flinch.

'Yes.' I try not to look so disturbed. 'Do you think I can use that phone? Just a quick call. It's an emergency.' I don't intend to look through the gap in the wall and see if I can spy the table of Drengar. I can. They're eating and chatting.

A small hand rests on my arm. Sal looks concerned as she follows my gaze. 'Do you need help, love? Are you in some sort of trouble? Should I call the sheriff?'

I get her meaning eventually and quickly reassure her that I'm okay. 'I just, I lost my phone and I need to call my mum. I left home pretty quickly to go on this trip and she'd be worried.'

Sal frowns as if not sure if she should call the police or believe me. 'Of course, a quick call,' she says before heading into the kitchen.

I practically dive towards the phone and dial Laney's number. Praying hard that she answers, I whimper when I hear her voice. 'Hello.'

'Laney,' I whisper, holding back tears.

'Raff, oh my...Raff, where the hell are you? I've been worried sick,' she snaps and I know it's full of love and care. I chuckle despite being in trouble.

'I'm sorry, Laney. Something came up and I had to leave.'

'Something came up!' she shrieks and I can hear a few voices in the background. 'You leave in the middle of the night with a damn note on the counter telling us that you had to go work something out, and now you ring like nothing has happened.'

I hear Van in the background demanding Laney give him the phone. The tears slip silently down my face.

'Laney, I can't talk for long. I just wanted to hear your voice and let you know that I'm okay.'

There is a commotion and then the voice I actually wanted to hear but was too much of a chicken shit to call him, comes on the line. 'Raff, where the fuck are you?'

'Oh Van,' I sniffle. 'How are you?'

'How am I? Raff, I woke up from a fucking hectic night of dreams to you not being home. I went fucking crazy looking for you Raff. We all have.'

I can hear Laney in the background telling Van to relax and then she is back on the line. 'Raffy, tell me what happened. Your brothers have been beside themselves looking for you. Even Miles, Raff. He is so worried. Calls all the time asking if you've contacted us and where I think you might be.'

'I was contacted by some people from my past, Laney. People that know my father and they needed my help. I needed to leave.' I can't deny my foster mother anything so I tell her the bare minimum.

'Your father? Raff, I know you think we don't hear your nightmares, but honey, I've been listening to you scream in your dreams for nine years. People that knew your father don't sound like people I want you to be around. Come home, Raff.' Her tone is full of love and motherly concern and I look over to spy on the males and eat my bottom lip. I would love to drop everything and find a way home but I'm bound by my word to help them find their book. They saved Van's life even when it's forbidden for Azanites to interfere in the lives of humans, even in Azanir itself, a Medir wont treat them.

Meaning, I need to help. I have a debt to pay.

'I can't,' I whisper.

'Why do I feel like you called to say goodbye or something? Don't hang up. Van wants to speak to you and Brent is on his way home. Maybe ring Miles. Talk to one of them. They'll come and pick you up. I'm worried, sweetheart.'

'I'm sorry. I'll try to be home soon.' Which is a lie, I know that now. I could die on this mission. The Drengar could still think I'm a traitor or find out my half breed status and send me back to my father in Azanir to be executed. So many possibilities, and they don't include me getting home and I feel like Laney knows it.

'I'm sorry,' I plea and try to close off the emotion when Laney shouts that she wants to know where I am.

I hang up, cutting her off, and crushing my own heart.

Chapter Thirty Four

I'M VERY AWARE OF the continual glances that come my way and I'm very aware that I'm acting strange. It's just...I can't help it. I haven't been able to stop reliving the conversation I had with Laney. I replay her words and analyse her hurt tone and beat myself up for leaving them with a stupid note.

We passed state lines about four hours ago and the landscape has well and truly changed like Alastair said it would. A light rain has started and the sun is going down slowly on the beautiful forest that fills the landscape. We drive on a quiet, two-way road.

If I wasn't so in my own head, I'd find the environment stunning. The trees are dense and the darkest of greens. Even the trunks are a deep brown. It reminds me of the Darkwoods a little. The lands I grew up were very similar to this.

The Darkwoods are one of the richest resourced lands in Azanir. Medicinal plants were tendered, food plants were maintained and animals of such beauty and power lived freely. However, it's probably one of the most dangerous lands in Azanir. Some animals could kill you with a touch of their poisoned skin. There were plants that could spit acid and holes in the ground that could swallow you whole. And despite all that, and the trauma of my upbringing, there was magic in Azanir that humans could not even fathom.

Beauty. Danger. Power.

'Could you pull over, Viktor, I need to stretch my legs.' The tone of Felix's voice pulls me out of my head and I sit up straighter and watch as Wilder leans over to the young male. Felix doesn't look happy. He looks like he's about to explode and I have no idea what's going on.

'Felix, are you okay?' I ask and am completely ignored, except for the hand Wilder places over the one I have gripping the side of his seat. I shut my mouth taking the hint.

Felix's chest is rising and falling too fast and I bite my lip and swing my gaze to the healer to make sure he is paying attention to what is going on.

'Slow your breathing Felix,' Alistair soothes. The energy in the car is heated and thick. Too thick. I cough as quietly as I can behind my hand.

Felix turns his attention to me and I sit back in the seat at the sight of the beast staring back at me. His eyes are red and bright. I'm sweating. The heat he is emitting into the car is almost painful.

Wilder growls that deep, timbery sound that I've come to know as his beast and Felix returns it. The noise is laced with aggression and I hit the side of the car when Viktor swerves and the vehicle comes to a complete stop.

Alistair appears at Felix's door and pulls it so hard that I fear the thing will come off the tracks. 'Breathe, brother. You have to control him.'

Felix is gripping his knees and has his head between them like what you're told to do when you're on a plane if there is an emergency. I feel completely hopeless and am becoming increasingly aware of how trapped I am at the back of the minivan. Wilder jumps out of the car and I only look over at him because he pulls his chair forward to give me space to get out too. He holds out his hand to me.

I hesitate, not sure which one is worse, going outside into the darkness or staying here with a male who's beast is clearly riding him too hard right now.

I take the hand and melt a little when the massive Drengar pulls me into his side as if totally aware of my discomfort. The rain is light but misty enough to make visibility hard. All around us is thick forest on both sides.

I fight with my body to not wrap around Wilder's middle and end up standing very close to where he placed me and fantasise some pretty crazy ideas of how it would feel to be surrounded by his warmth and strength with maybe less clothes.

The Medir hasn't let go of my hand and guides me to the other side of the minivan where he dumps me right beside the open door. I go to tell him that he can think again next time about handling me in such a way but shut my mouth when those black eyes shoot to me and scream that this is not the time.

Glaring, I contemplate again if he can read my mind and just wrap my arms around my chest and pout.

Viktor is near me and Wilder and Alistair are kneeling beside the car instructing Felix on focusing and clearing his mind.

'I need to go,' Felix says quietly. His beast in his voice, it makes me shiver. Wilder's focus flicks back to me and I get a very arrogant, *'stay,'* in my head.

In seconds, Viktor and Wilder are grabbing the younger male and they are gone into the forest, leaving me a little taken aback.

Alistair just stands at the car door frowning at the spot where they all disappeared. I find I don't like the solemn expression on his face and say, 'Wilder just told me to stay like I'm some kind of puppy.'

That gets his attention. The prince laughs a very beautiful sound that if I had any entrepreneurial bones in my body, I'd record and sell it to human woman and make a bucket of money.

'That's very funny, Lady. Especially if you heard the command he made in my head just before he left you. Clearly forgetting who the prince and commander of this little group is.' Alistair is a very, very attractive male. His eyes are pale blue and he has an air of royalty about him. I think it's the way he holds those wide shoulders in confidence.

All laughter gone, I hold myself tighter. 'Will Felix be okay?'

Face softening, Alistair nods. 'Our beasts aren't very kind when we don't shift. Felix is younger and still learning how to control and find balance. He'll be okay.' It's my turn to nod and I wonder how uncomfortable it must be for all of them to be in this realm. With technology and phones and satellites, they can't risk being seen.

'Come,' he beckons and opens the passenger door for me. 'They'll be a while and there's no point standing in the cold.'

With one last glance to the silent forest, I do as I'm told.

CHAPTER THIRTY FIVE

I MUNCH ON A bag of crisps that Felix handed me when he got back in the car with a sheepish, embarrassed look on his face about an hour ago. He was very apologetic and I honestly have no idea why. He did nothing wrong and it seemed like the others thought the same because not a single word was spoken about it from the moment we started our trip again.

I stayed in the front on Viktor's request so that he could rest in the back seat while Alister drives for the next 'shift'. I offered to drive and got a very stern, 'as if' kind of look that you wouldn't expect someone like Viktor LongwingDrengar to do.

They're probably afraid that I'll drive them off a cliff while they slept or something. Or maybe they think, as a female, I'm not capable. Wouldn't be the first experience I've had like that. Azanir is a place of great beauty, magic and wonder. However, it's sometimes archaic in its ideas around certain things like female and male roles. Yes, there are female Drengar. Not many, or at least there wasn't ten years ago. My maid used to explain that the males of our kind saw a female as a precious gift and with few births, they've become more and more protective over the generations. I never understand why she would say that with a longing like she envied what Azanite females had. I always saw it as a cage, even from a young age, or maybe it was just the way I was raised—secluded and surrounded by humans.

The car is dark and peaceful. The rain isn't too bad and with the warmth of so many Azanites, it's quite toasty in here. With the males sleeping behind us, I offer the oversized bag to the prince and watch as he manoeuvres around to grab some chips without taking his eyes off the road.

'These are my favourite,' he whispers, not wanting to disturb the Drengar sleeping in the back.

I giggle softly, watching the boyish grin play across his face. 'Really?' I look at the bag to see the brand and couldn't agree more. The chilli crisps are probably the worst for you in terms of health rating and I smile to myself and think of my Van. He loves these too.

'Felix is not the only one who can appreciate things in this realm.'

We sit in silence, munching for a bit. 'Do you know why humans and Azanites are forbidden to fall in love?' I ask quietly, unsure why the question falls from my lips.

I say fall in love knowing it's a human term. In Azanir, you find a mate and bind your souls together. Sometimes finding a mate has nothing to do with love and all to do with the beast.

I get a solid side-eye that has me quickly add, 'just curious,' as if I have to reassure him that I haven't broken any more of our laws and fallen for some guy. I've never felt that way about anyone. It's only since being with these males that my beast seems to have woken up and paid attention to the opposite sex. Frankly, I thought something might have been wrong with me.

Now though, as I feel a great deal, and most of it towards a male I'm really confused about wanting in that way, I fear that my half breed status would be a deal breaker. I have no idea if any younglings I may have would have the same issues as me. The idea gives me a headache. What if my young couldn't shift? What if they are plagued with nightmares like I am?

'You were schooled in Azanir, Serafina. You should know.'

'Not really,' I shrug. 'I was taught the laws of our people. That our interaction with humans shall not cross any lines of intermingling.'

Alistair finishes another handful of chips before answering. 'It has been prohibited for longer than memory,' he says by way of an answer. 'I know that our ancestors lived in a world where humans and Azanites were equal in all things. They fell in love, as you say.' He throws me a look that has me grin. There's something about Alistair. He's always so calm, so sure of himself that being in his presence comforts me despite the fact that my entire fate is in his hands as the Prince of Azanir. He's way too big for the human sized car seat and his arm is very close to my thigh as it rests on the gear stick.

'They reproduced younglings and then the peace collapsed. An Azanite will always be a beast at heart and hold more power. Humans are said to have become jealous of that, and human men began to control and treat Azanite females badly even when they were bound as mates. Younglings were being born taking the traits of their human parent more and with tensions running high, males of both races fought. Battles were raged for decades. And the divide became a rift that was unfixable. Azanites took their position as the keepers of Azanir and my family began their rule of the lands. The humans that were not part of the fighting were offered a place for their families to stay in a position that benefited us both. The rest were sent away with no memory of our kind.' He pauses. 'Or at least that's what we're taught in our schooling.'

I consider what he's said while eating.

'I'm afraid that things might not be that way now after what has happened.' He continues after I throw him a questioning look, 'Human's stole something very valuable from us. While we've lived in peace and prosperity for many generations, I fear that tensions are beginning to build. My father was speaking of closing the Veil and stopping all humans from accessing our lands.'

That has me stop eating. 'Shit, that sounds serious. I'm sure the humans on Azanir don't like that.'

'No, they don't. Their council made that very clear before we left on this mission. They need new faces and new blood to keep their communities thriving.'

That has me thinking a great deal about my own situation. Definitely doesn't sound like a time to be a half breed in Azanir. Slowly freaking out, I open and close my mouth about four times wanting to ask him what is going to happen to me and flinch when he asks, 'what is it? Say what you want to say, Serafina.'

Exhaling loudly, I share the bag with him again and ask, 'what's going to happen to me?'

Alistair crunches away. He doesn't say a word for too long. 'You'll come back to Azanir with us and we will work it out.'

My eyes instantly fill with water and I turn to hide it by looking out the window. I gasp when a hand rests heavily on my knee. A little taken aback, I blink the tears quickly away and stare at the prince.

'Tell me why you left and I'll protect you, Serafina. When we get to Azanir you will not have to go back to your father's lair. You'll be under my protection. All of our protection. That means something considering the males in this vehicle,' he says it as if what he says is final. Like no one could possibly go against him or the others. Which may be true seeing as how he's royalty and Wilder and Viktor are...well, who they are. But even I know there are laws in Azanir. Laws that will force me back under the care and protection of my father or my brothers. I am a Lady. I don't have the freedom of getting an apprenticeship and living in the towns with the Thral or humans. Or picking where I want to live.

'Even though I broke the law and lived in the human realm or that I'm a traitor? Isn't that what you believe?' I ask softly, afraid of him hearing the fear in my tone.

Alistair makes a deep animalistic sound that has me shut my mouth. I don't know why I've annoyed his beast. 'I don't know what I believe anymore,' he says and he removes his hand to grab the wheel, leaving me confused and unsure what is going to happen.

CHAPTER THIRTY SIX

I HAVE NO IDEA what time it is when Alistair pulls over and yawns. He mumbles something about taking the time to sleep before closing his eyes. The rain has intensified and the temperature has dropped significantly.

Pulling my legs up on the seat, I try to keep my body temperature warm. I can't believe that I'm in a car full of Drengar, expected to sleep the remainder of the night in a minivan.

I need my bed. I need my pillows.

It goes against everything in my nature to not find a warm place to lay my head. I'm a half breed who didn't get any of the cool stuff like being able to shift and the power. No, what I got was the part of needing soft bedding and lots of blankets. Typical. The urge for our beast to be warm and comfortable at night is strong and is just as strong in me than it is in any other Azanite.

Females especially love to make our 'nests'. Van and the others never understood. In the beginning, I'd try and fight the instinct. However, it never worked. My beast would take over so I just decided to embrace my weirdness.

That's when I hear a voice in my head. *'Come here, Serafina. You're cold.'*

Turning to peek over the back of the seat, I glare at the male lounging at the very back of the car where I normally sit. With his damn eyes shut. The three seater doesn't look that big though. Not with the Medir sitting there.

Damn my beast! She really, really hates the cold. I swear Alistair is snoring already and with no real options, I unbuckle my belt and get off the seat with a few manoeuvres and walk up the middle of the minivan.

When I pass Felix, I swear I see him smile and scowl at him for no reason because his eyes are shut. It's really my beast who is moving my legs and I sit beside Wilder with a small huff.

'You need to stop giving me orders,' I whisper, hoping he can hear the bite in my tone. He cracks one of those black eyes open and shuts it without another word and I'm left with my thoughts.

I move around, trying to get comfortable and also fight with myself over what I'm doing. It's insane. Time after time, I keep trying to step into his presence. Try to be near him. My body feels weird. My skin is crawling and when I look down at my arm, I watch the movement underneath in confusion and a little horror. I've only ever seen my beast like this that one time at breakfast with Laney and the others. Instantly, I fear that something is wrong with me.

My heart begins to pound in my chest.

'You are fighting her, she is cold and wants you to sleep.'

Gaze snapping from my arm, I frown deeply up at the Drengar who is no longer pretending to be asleep.

Wilder sits up and goes to grab my arm. I pull it back on instinct and hold it against my chest. The Medir doesn't seem offended. He just stays where he is, too close, and with his hand out as if waiting for me to be comfortable.

'I will never harm you, Serafina DarkwoodsAzar.'

I believe him, which is shocking, and when the movement in my body borders on painful, I slowly and hesitantly lower my arm into his waiting palm. Wilder doesn't take his eyes off me. If I push aside my own fear of healers, I'm able to remind myself that Wilder isn't like the Medir of my childhood.

I have no idea what happens the moment our skin connects. All of my worries, fears and uncertainty disappear. The beast calms in my chest completely and all the discomfort and pain evaporates. My arm is no longer something out of a horror movie.

'You and her are one, Serafina.'

'What's that supposed to mean?' I mumble, focused on the hand he is rubbing slowly up and down my arm. I can feel every callous. Every groove. His rhythmic caress has my heartrate stabilise and my mind not so clouded by anxiety.

'It means that you have spent a great deal of your life believing that she is weak. If you tell someone that they are weak over and over again, then that is what you get. Weakness.'

Like a fool, I sit, unable to understand how I feel about what he has just said. What he's implying is both offensive and a little enlightening. From a young age, I was told something was wrong with me.

Annoyed at myself for letting Wilder get under my skin, I sit back when he drops my arm and try to fight against the burning need to press my body against his and feel his warmth while I sleep. We're already close enough though and I am lulled to sleep surrounded by the heat of the Medir and the four Drengar in the car.

Chapter Thirty Seven

I'm drowning. I can't breathe.

The pressure of the water is making my head pound.

Staring upward, I see flashing coming from above. It's storming and I'm drowning in darkness.

I kick but go nowhere. I try to swim upward and continue to sink.

I need to breathe.

I need to breathe.

I'm suffocating.

I'm suffocating.

I'm....

I wake up and grip my throat.

I can't breathe. I can't breathe.

Panic is an understatement. I can't see. It feels like something is sitting on my throat. Strangling me.

I lash out, unsure what is going on. A strong heavy body grips my shoulders softly yet firmly. I can feel the hard leather seat of the car under my back, however, I don't know where I am.

Then things start to focus and all I see is Wilder's deep frown, his face hovering over me. I try to communicate that I can't...I can't....my vision blurs and a ring of darkness around Wilder's face appears.

In that moment, I wish I had kissed him. Just once. I think he would've tasted nice.

I feel my body begin to drain. Like in my dreams, my limbs are weighted and my eyelids are heavy.

I'm dying.

I'm suffocating.

All of this happens while I stare into obsidian eyes, lost in their colour because as I stare they change. Starting from the outside of the iris, the red rim slowly drips into the darkness and in a heartbeat, I'm staring at Wilder's beast. My eyes burn, and a sharp pain shoots up my spin. I regret so much. My chest is on fire. There is so much noise. Voices bombard my senses. My skin stretches and I hear a whisper in my mind that makes no sense.

I'm dying. I can't breathe.

I'm dying until...

Lips of pure fire touch my own. Shocking me and releasing the pressure on my throat. I draw in a deep, shaky, excruciating breath. My mouth fills with the taste of ash and nature.

It takes my mind a long time to understand what is happening and how I have wrapped my arms around a muscular neck and am kissing Wilder back with as much enthusiasm as he's showing me.

I'm kissing Wilder BlazeAzar-Drengar-Medir.

And it's the most all-consuming thing I've ever done in my life. His breath is my breath. He forces me to stay here in the world with his touch.

Pulling back, now no longer suffocating, Wilder and I stare. Inches apart. I can taste him on my lips. On my tongue.

'What in the Sun Gods was that?' Felix's demand cuts through our moment and I have to stop myself from reaching out and frantically grabbing the Medir when he pulls away to give me space. I still have all of his attention though and he's the only thing I can see.

'Thank you,' I whisper to him, truly shocked at what just happened. Never has a dream bled so much into my reality and I know I would've died if Wilder hadn't brought me back.

'Are you going to tell me what that was?' he asks, his tone unreadable.

'I can't.'

'One day you will tell me what is happening. One day, you will tell me your secrets.'

'Are you sure you're feeling all right?'

'Yeah,' I reply softly. I'm not and haven't been since that kiss in the car. I feel off. Like I might lose control over my emotions at any minute. I'm hot and bothered.

The Drengar found the nearest town and we're now in a damn motel that is probably the worst of them all. It smells funny in here and the guy at the reception desk was really rude and smirked at me when I left the office space.

I can only imagine what he was thinking. A lone female, four very intimidating and attractive males. He's probably right now texting his friends about seeing a girl with four men wanting a one bed room. The memory of his sleezy grin has me shiver in disgust.

I'm lying on the bed while Felix finds the extra blankets and pillows in the tiny cupboard near the bathroom. He is stacking them around my body, giving my beast exactly what she wants and needs without me asking. It's the first time in ten years that someone has understood what I needed without me getting teased or embarrassed for it.

It's not that the teasing was made in a bad way. However, it did remind me that I was different when I tried so hard to fit in. It's weird to think that I feel less awkward and odd with a group of scary Drengar. I need comfort and without asking for it, Felix keeps stacking them until there is no more.

'You're freaking us out, Raff. All these dreams and now you waking up not breathing.'

'I'm sorry.' I feel weak and drained. I feel like I died in that car. I bite my wobbling lip that still feels bruised by Wilder's hot kiss. It can't pull me from my mind though. Deep down I think I know the truth. I think I witnessed my death.

In that moment my body tightens and I whimper. Felix is there instantly. His worried face is all scrunched as he touches my forehead and cusses softly under his breath.

'I'll get Wilder, just stay here.' He backs away and hurries from the room, leaving me silently weeping at the horrible feeling that has formed in my chest. I saw my own death and it has rocked me to the core.

Tears slip down my cheeks until I'm a pile of emotions and drama. That's how Wilder finds me. Wrapped in blankets and pillows, silently crying.

'*Serafina? Tell me,*' Wilder's voice sooths my mind and gives me a moment to pull myself from the well of despair. My beast feels as if she is pushing against my skin, making it impossible to breathe or think. I have no idea what she wants.

'I don't feel good,' I say and notice the others standing around the bed watching me.

'*Explain it to me, Astgeer,*' the Medir coaxes and I close my eyes like an idiot and relish in his touch when his fingers caress the side of my face.

'I feel uncomfortable. She's unhappy. Or maybe anxious. I feel like I need something but I can't tell you what. It kind of hurts.' I know I'm not making any sense and they're all fools to think that I don't see the look they all share.

'Wilder! We don't need this right now.' Viktor is not happy and I have no idea what he means or why Wilder is in the shit. Alistair doesn't look too impressed either and I cover most of my face, offended and ashamed for acting strangely.

Wilder draws his gaze from Viktor and settles it back on me. *'I'm sorry, Astgeer. I should have realised this would happen.'*

I have no idea what Wilder means and watch as the others nod to the Medir still sitting on the bed and leave the room.

Alone with Wilder, who tells me in his calming voice to move over, I do, and only because I'm not thinking straight. I latch onto him when he gets under the mountain of blankets and pulls me into his side. He makes a point of lifting the back of my shirt and resting his gigantic hand on my bare skin. The tension in my body evaporates and my beast calms.

'Better?' There's humour in his tone and I realise it's because I sighed in relief out loud.

'Yes,' I mumble. I'm so close to his body that half of it is buried underneath him. It feels amazing. 'You haven't used your healing power on me yet so I have no idea what you're doing, but I love it.'

'No, this is not my healing magic. This is all me.'

Cocky bastard makes me huff and smile to myself. 'You keep saving me,' I whisper, half asleep.

I think he says something like, *'it's you who saved me, Astgeer,'* but I'm already being pulled into sleep so I can't be sure.

Chapter Thirty Eight

THERE IS SOMETHING WRONG with me.

I haven't been able to stop staring at Wilder. There have been moments throughout the day that I find myself reaching over to touch him without consciously realising what I was doing, until I physically come in contact with whatever body part is closest.

He's pushing the trolley at the market and I've caught myself three times since entering the shop trying to reassure myself that he is close. I don't know if it was the scare from my dream and the breathing in the car or if my oddness has just amped up a thousand points, but I'm freaking myself out.

The other thing that's making the entire situation worse is how the others watch me do it and don't say a word. Actually, they're acting like I'm totally normal and that I'm not losing my mind. It's infuriating. I want them to tell me to stop.

I'm deeply shocked that Wilder hasn't told me to go away yet. He just lets me touch him like I'm not some kind of freak. He even runs his hand over my back and rests it there for a moment every so often like he's helping me to stay calm, which seems to quench this growing need within me to be close.

'Serafina?'

My name pulls me from my thoughts, 'hmmm?' I reply to the prince and register what I'm doing and snatch my hand back. I had twisted it into the side of Wilder's t-shirt. They're all staring now as if waiting for me to answer them. I didn't hear a question and stand, unsure what to do or say.

A wave of panic washes through my system and the way Wilder steps into my space, as if to comfort me, has me spin and hurry out of the small grocery store.

Drawing air in and out of my heaving lungs, I grip the brick wall and try to find my centre. I'm losing my mind. Something that is confirmed when I look up and notice a group of men across the road at the petrol station. I swear I've seen the group before but my mind is all muddled and I can't put my finger on what has upset my beast.

'You okay?' Spinning, I shake my head and rest my back along the wall. Felix mimics the action.

'I think I'm going crazy.'

He laughs lightly and shakes his head. 'You're not crazy, Raff. There's just a lot going on.'

'I *feel* like I'm going crazy. I've never felt my beast like this.' I wrap my arms around my middle and sigh.

'Is that a bad thing?'

I don't understand his tone and turn my head to study him. He's watching the people in the petrol station across the road and I follow his gaze and track the car I was studying before as it pulls out and onto the road. 'Everything okay?'

Felix seems to come back to the present and while his brows are knitted together, he reassures me that all is good. 'My beast just had a moment. He wasn't happy about something and I couldn't work out what.'

I don't believe him. I get the feeling he knows exactly what has his animal frowning so hard. Maybe it's the way he shuffles closer or the fact that I can feel his beast against my bare arm where we are now touching but worry floods my system.

'You're freaking me out a little,' I confess and eat my bottom lip.

'Why are you nervous?' Wilder asks as he steps from the store doors. His eyes scan the area, assessing any danger. *'What's going on?'*

There's a pause and I realise that Felix is communicating with him.

'Can you guys stop doing that? I hate when you leave me out of the conversation,' I huff and fold my arms over my chest.

'Sorry.' Felix throws me an apologetic look and explains that he was just telling Wilder that he thought he saw something strange and that his beast got a weird feeling. Which would explain why the massive Medir is now beside me like a guard, still monitoring the area.

'Do you think something is wrong?' I ask them.

'No. Let's get back to the car.' Wilder holds out his hand and I take it hesitantly and let him lead me back to the minivan.

We head straight to the motel with the sleezy man who watches us from the reception window.

I sit on the bed next to Wilder eating dinner that night and smile to my self when he stays close while I fall asleep. He said nothing about the way I clung to the front of his shirt. I put it down to being afraid of the drowning dream coming back even though I have no real answer for my behaviour.

Chapter Thirty Nine

THE NEXT DAY, I sit quietly at the back of the car and watch the forest fly by, contemplating my existence and the way I've been acting. I know I saw my death and it has shaken me on a level I can't explain.

I find myself thinking of Azanir again and what it would be like to go back. Sitting and listening to the Drengar speak of home and the fact that we are only a few days from Satmark, I know that if I let my beast grumble or make a noise, they wouldn't bat an eyelid. It has me wondering things I never thought I would. They wouldn't care if I ate the entire box of cookies Felix handed me just after we left the small town like my human family would.

I happily took the box after the sleezy guy winked at me when I was getting in the car and then went white as a ghost when Viktor turned around and growled deeply at him. I didn't see Viktor's eyes but I can imagine they were lined red.

It made me smile.

The others are talking about the humans who are part of the group who stole the book. It seems they have no idea why they did it. That's when I see a car pass us. The one from yesterday when I was at the market. It moves by and the man in the backseat slowly turns his head, he stares right at me and smiles.

My gasp is audible and I reach out for the hundredth time today to touch Wilder's shoulder on the seat in front of me. My beast completely in control of my hand every time. I get the attention of all four Drengar.

The car speeds off.

'All okay, Serafina?' Alistair asks.

Not sure if I was just seeing things, I tell them I'm all right. I haven't slept. It could be just my mind playing tricks. There is no chance that the guy from the bar, Joseph, would be in a car, passing us on this barely used road, heading to Satmark.

I snatch my hand back from Wilder's muscular shoulder and fight the need to pull my hair out in frustration at how I'm behaving.

I have no idea why we stopped or why I'm trudging through the forest with Felix in the lead. The sun is high but unable to reach us properly because of the canopy of the trees and I really want to go back in the car and sleep. I'm miserable. My future looks bleak and I don't know what I want. Not even the idea of heading home to Laney and Van makes me feel better. If I really consider my life, I don't belong there either. The Drengar have shown me that. Not that my place is with them. If they found out what I could do or how I'm only half Azanite, they'd leave me right here in this odd forest to deal with the wraiths.

'Where are we going?' I sound petulant and miserable. Which is on-point, that's how I feel right now.

'That's a question I would like to know too.' Looking over my shoulder at the three Drengar trudging along behind me, I realise with a frown that they too have no idea what we're doing.

Felix is carrying two bags and I don't have the care to ask what's in them.

'Not much longer,' Felix exclaims. He sounds so excited.

I'm about to tell him that I'm going back to the minivan when we finally break the tree line.

My mouth hangs open. The others step up beside me and seem to be just as stunned by the sight of a beautiful meadow. It's something out of a dream. Flowers and butterflies and soft grass.

'How did you know it was here?' I ask in wonder.

'I used the smart device I was given and listened to you about searching for things and this came up. It was on a list of top ten things to do while heading to Satmark.' Felix looks mighty impressed with himself, and frankly he's earned it. The sun is hot and strong and I close my eyes as the heat of it touches my skin. Knowing I'm being watched, I look up and smile at the mighty Medir who stands close to my left.

I can still feel his lips on mine. They still burn with a phantom heat. My hands curl so that I don't try and touch him again.

'Come, I packed lunch for us all. We all need the sun today before this damn weather changes and the snow starts closer to Satmark.' Felix hurries over to the middle of the meadow like a youngling, excited to show his parents the craft activity he's just created.

Wilder's large hand falls on my lower back and he gently urges me to follow, which I do. A newfound lightness to my step.

Laying on the grass beside Viktor and Wilder, I feel so much better. I think we all do because I've heard three rumbles of laughter in the space of ten minutes and that is testament enough. I removed my shoes and socks almost the moment I sat down and loved that I wasn't mocked for my 'weird' behaviour. I even lifted my shirt to sit just under my black bra so that I have optimum exposure to the power of the sun. Not one of them looked at me with a strange glance or mumbled under their breath that we're out in public and that someone could see. Something that happened once at a park with Brent and Scott. They covered me instantly that day. I got 'the talk' that night.

I've eaten my body weight in cheese and crackers and want a nap. The sky is clear and the crispest of blues. I can't believe that there is a storm set for later tonight and that snow could start any day now.

I feel good. Better than I have in a long time. Being in nature is so important to our beasts. We're constantly exposed to it. We walk with bare feet. We eat under the sun. Our lairs are built with sections for protection and different ones with open roofs to bask in the power of the Sun Gods.

It's the first time in ten years that I find myself missing my homelands.

CHAPTER FORTY

THE RAIN STARTED JUST after our picnic stopped and has been steady ever since. I feel light and calm. My skin is warm and the beast is content and happy. The picnic in the meadow was beautiful and exactly what I needed.

Night has fallen and I'm having a hard time fighting my heavy lids. It has been a good day. A day of thinking about my options. I'm afraid of how quickly my mind has changed. I'm frightened to go back home and yet, I'm considering it. These four Drengar have shown me something I haven't had in ten years. When I left, I left thinking that I had a better chance with humans. I never considered that I could be wrong.

I listen to the rain hitting the roof of the car and drift off to sleep.

The hum of the car is almost peaceful and I blink away to the darkness outside and the sound of heavy rain. Windscreen wipers scrape against the windscreen. The sound annoying and rhymical at the same time. It is hard to see and the concentration on Viktor's face is hard to miss.

Sitting up, I finger the jacket that has been thrown over my body as a makeshift blanket and quickly look over at Wilder. His bare, thick arms on display. He smells so good. Smells like a dream, one that had me crying when I woke.

My thoughts are all jumbled. I look around at the males in the car. Viktor driving. Alastair formulating plans. Felix eating chips from a packet and Wilder looking out the window as if he's ready for battle. The rain is relentless, almost torrential and the car slows to a steady pace. I can't see the forest anymore but know that it still surrounds us because it will until we reach the city that holds the golden book.

I ask Felix what time it is and why we haven't stopped for the night but he doesn't answer. It's as if I haven't said a thing. The clock on the dash flashes ten pm, giving me my answer.

Skin crawling, I hug my arms to my chest and look around, unsure what's happening and then the world explodes in noise and screeching and we spin.

Glass shatters and flies around us, cutting through random parts of my skin and I scream and cover my head when the car is jolted violently and then we are airborne.

The world slows.

I see Wilder rise from his seat, uncaring of the situation or the fact that we are rolling in the air. His black eyes are calm and almost soothing as he locks them with mine and says, 'come to me!' in a clear demand within my head that has the beast in my body wake and react. I push myself forward, grabbing the hand he holds out and before I can say anything, he pulls me as he turns, catching my body. He slams me against his chest and curls his frame over mine so that when the car hits the asphalt I am completely secure. His body absorbs the impact. His skin rippling and stretching, then hardening into scales against me. Heat surrounds me. His scent intensifies and I bury myself deeper into his secure embrace.

Everything stills and the silence is almost painful. All I can hear is the steady rhythm of Wilder's heart and the heaviness of my breathing. Until, the distance sound of wraiths has me scream in fright. The body above me tenses and then Wilder erupts in flame. The flames dance and lick against my skin. He roars a guttery sound and jumps up, his legs on either side of where I lay, ready for battle. Wraiths descend on us in waves. But all I see his him. All I feel is him and all I want...is him.

Heart in my throat, I grip my chest and blink awake. My entire body feels electrified and I slowly become aware of my surroundings. And stop dead. I touch the jacket on me and close my eyes and open them a few times to make sure that I'm awake. I look over at Wilder and his bare arms. Felix is chomping loudly on his packet of chips and when I slowly sit up, bile rises in my throat because Alistair is talking strategy and the rain is torrential and the clock flashes, nine fifty five pm.

'Stop,' I whisper, my voice shaking. 'Stop,' I say louder and then scream, 'stop.'

Viktor reacts like anyone would. The tires screech against the road as the car stutters and swerves slightly before he gets it under control and we come to a complete stop.

Four males swing around and glare at me.

'What's the matter?' Viktor shouts, I clearly took him off guard and he obviously didn't like it one bit. The images of my dream causing my stomach to churn and bile to rise into my throat.

'Wraiths,' I stammer. 'Wraiths are coming.' I pray my tone leaves no room for them to question me.

There's a heartbeat of silence before the males erupt into the Drengar that they are.

'Tell me.' Alistair is all Prince of Azanir in that moment, a Commander and leader.

'Five minutes.'

Viktor's eyes glow in the rear-view mirror as he stares at me. Alistair turns in his seat to look to Wilder before landing his gaze on my face. 'How do you know this?'

Heart pounding, I try to formulate some kind of lie. I didn't really think this through when I opened my mouth. All I could think about was how the car rolled and how I was wrapped up in all kind of male-ness. 'I can't tell you,' I say quietly. 'It's the truth. I promise.' At least I hope it is. It's hard to work out what is nightmare and what is...well, whatever the fuck I can do.

I'm afraid they won't believe me but then Alistair spins in his seat and barks at Viktor to turn around the way we came. The Drengar does, spinning the wheel. Tires screech and swerve and I'm thrown into the side of the car painfully. Viktor accelerates and I'm thrown backwards into the seat.

The clock is flashing nine fifty six.

'There is no time!' I shout. Driving at this speed, we are screwed. 'They smash into the car and we roll. We need to stop the car.'

Viktor doesn't slow. I jump forward in my chair and grip Wilder's bare arm.

Mind screaming that I shouldn't be thinking about how delicious he feels at this exact moment, I can't believe how calm he looks despite the situation we're in and it hits me that he probably thinks that I'm lying. Maybe I am. Maybe it was just a dream but everything is so similar and if it was real then Wilder will listen to me. I've learnt that about him.

'Wilder, I'm telling the truth. In...' I look over at the clock. 'Three minutes, we're going to crash and the car is going to spin and you...' I try to get control over my shaking voice. 'Please believe me.'

I have no idea what Wilder sees on my face or why he frowns before leaning forward. I gasp, our faces are inches apart and I taste his scent on my tongue. Feel his heat. The fact that we're about to all be under attack seems to not matter anymore.

'Tell me how you know,' he says, very calmly.

'Please,' I say. 'Just believe me.' I don't want to tell him. I'm so afraid of his reaction. It's as if I can feel time ticking down in my soul though, causing my anxiety to rise with each passing breath.

'Tell me,' he repeats, his black eyes locked on mine. He can see my hesitation and says, *'tell me, in your mind.'* He reaches out and tucks my hair over my left ear.

'I don't know how—'

'Speak in your mind,' Wilder coaxes, cutting me off. We're sharing the same breath, he searches my face and I can't help but shiver in need. *'Focus on my face. Focus on telling me.'*

I take a deep breath. Never breaking our locked gaze and say, *'I dreamt it,'* in my head and have no idea if he has heard me or not. *'I have these dreams and sometimes...they come true.'*

The car comes to a halt. I get thrown forward and would've collided with Wilder's face if he hadn't grabbed my arms and held me tightly. He drops his hold too soon though and I feel his absence in my chest.

There's a heartbeat of silence.

Then...

I jump when Felix shouts at me to, 'get down!'

I manage to cover my head just before something collides into the side of the car. The impact is jarring, but not as damaging as it could've been if the car was still moving. I squeal and fall on my ass between Felix and Wilder's seats.

Felix's blue eyes are wide and suspicious as they look down on me. 'How did you know they were coming?'

Blinking up at him, I have no time to respond because the windows in the car explode.

Instinctively, I throw my arms over my head once more and then peek through the gaps when all the light is blocked to gape up at the male who is using his body as a shield to protect me from the shards.

I watch, stunned as pieces fall and cut along Wilder's bear arms. His face is stoic and unaffected, his obsidian eyes are dark and full of determination.

Then he's gone. The Drengar jump from the vehicle, their fire burning bright and the shrieking of wraiths and the roar of beasts is deafening, even with me safely in the minivan.

Adrenaline pumping, I keep myself as small as I can on the floor while trying to see as much of the battle raging on the road. It's just one big clump of darkness and firelight.

The car is jerked violently and I swing around to the left when the door is peeled back with an ear-piercing screech that has me clap my hands over my ears and try to react in time to miss the razor sharp teeth that barrel towards me.

Chapter Forty One

I'm trapped.

Stuck between the two captain chairs in the minivan, I start jerking backwards to avoid the wraith trying to sink its teeth into my calf.

Kicking furiously, my foot keeps going through the demon who continually solidifies and then turns into smoke the moment I nearly land a blow.

It's impossible and frustrating and I scream when its razor sharp claws pull back and I barely dodge them in time.

My terror is choking. My body shakes violently and then it all disappears.

The world turns red.

My skin ripples, stretches and pulls and I have an overwhelming sense of vertigo. And then...I'm no longer fully in control of my own limbs. The beast under my skin roars inside my head. She comes to attention so fast that I don't really register what I've done until I'm kneeling between the seats, blinking at the back of the chairs in front of me in a daze. Their charred and burnt to a crisp. Completely incinerated like the wraith that was attacking me.

All I'm left with is a scratching throat and the taste of smoke in my mouth.

I twirl around when Felix whistles in approval and grins at me. He's at the door, looking at my handy work. 'Nice shot, Raff. That was a decent fire ball.' He doesn't sound affected by what I've just done and I have to remember that he's Drengar and not a human. If I did that in front of Van or the others, it would've been a different reaction all together. I don't know why my train of thought heads in that direction or why my mind starts going through all I have suppressed and held inside since coming to the human world. Yes, I felt more love here with them, but just like in Azanir, I never fully belonged.

'Come on,' he says, holding his hand out to me and cutting off my deep sense of loneliness. 'There's no time to admire your handy work, we need to leave.' He looks over his shoulder and when he swings his gaze back to me, the humour is long gone. 'Now!' he shouts and I take his hand and am pulled out of the car.

That's when I see it. The horde of demons is terrifying. Hundreds swarm the three males fighting like the warriors they are. They dance and twirl and set the night aflame.

With my hand in Felix's and my other now gripping his thick forearm in fear, I've pressed my body so close to his that I'm surprised he hasn't demanded I get off him. I don't think I could move if he did though. He doesn't seem to mind and keeps my hand firmly in his as he pushes me up against the side of the ruined car. With his body blocking mine, he monitors our surroundings and the battle that's raging only a few feet away.

'I've never done something like that before, Felix,' I whisper in shock and terror. I just used fire to kill a demon.

Felix shushes me. There's nowhere for us to hide and while these males are fierce and amazing, even I know that we don't stand a chance against this attack. Night is heavy around us. My stomach churns under the demanding pull in my soul to find Wilder. It almost hurts.

'I understand that you haven't used your fire like that. Right now though, you have to focus. You have to leave, Lady Serafina.'

My heart drops. He's back to calling me by my title so the situation must be as bad as I fear. He takes a deep breath and looks down at me, his blue eyes full of the beast. A ring of red encircles the beautiful crisp colour and I know he's barely keeping himself contained. To not be able to shift into their beast form must be so difficult, especially in these circumstances.

'The map of this area shows that there are dwellings...um, cabins,' he tries to remember the human word and I nod, indicating that I understand. 'I don't know the name but it's a place people can go to visit but not live. Lots of cabins and flat land.' Felix is desperately trying to communicate this information and I can see the frustration on his face at not knowing the correct names.

'Like a campsite,' I offer and watch as his features light up with understanding.

'Yes, that's the word. There's a campsite about three to four hundred metres, that way.' He points towards the forest and I swallow my terror.

'Okayyyyy,' I drag out the word, not sure what he's telling me but also trying to keep up.

'You need to run. That way. We will be right behind you.' I can't believe my ears. I can't go into the forest...I need to stay with them. I need Wilder. These absurd, overbearing males have grown on me. How can I leave them? I should help, shouldn't I?

The other thing is, I feel that he's lying somehow, like he isn't sure if he'll actually be right behind me.

I just hold him harder which seems to communicate my fear in some way. Felix rests those blue eyes on me, his hand comes up to push my—what I can presume to be— very messy hair behind my shoulders.

'We will be right behind you, Raff. You need to run and not look back. Do you understand?'

Nodding frantically, I know my time is up when he makes a frightening sound in the back of his throat and I gape at the male who is no longer looking at me. Whatever is on the other side of the car, has his full attention.

'Now,' he snaps out and when I hear Wilder's smooth voice in my head telling me to go. I spring into action and disappear as fast as I can into the trees.

CHAPTER FORTY TWO

TEARS AND RAIN MINGLE on my face making it hard to see as I run through the unknown forest. Imagination on overdrive, I feel as if my body can't contain my energy as I squeal and push harder with every shadow or movement I think that I see.

My beast isn't making it any easier. Her display back in the car seems to have given her more control over my instincts and I don't feel the ground under my feet as I sprint toward the direction Felix told me. I have no idea what I'll find when I get to this 'campsite' and hurl arse as quickly as I can. The fear of being mauled and energy sucked by a fucking wraith helps a great deal.

The forest floor is littered with branches and leaves and the trees are so firmly packed together in some sections that I have to contort my body at points to fit through the gaps.

Breathing heavily and realising with panicked realisation that I'm ridiculously unfit for this sort of exertion, I trip over something sharp. I feel the object slice through my jeans and my shin just as I stumble and fall to the ground. Water and mud splashes up into my face as I hit the floor, hands first.

'Fuck,' I cuss loudly, afraid to look behind me and then gasp when I finally look up. A flat clearing welcomes me and it's a sight that has more tears stream down my face. I eye the cabin and a lake further in the darkness. I can kinda see a few more buildings in the far distance and pray to every Sun God that might be listening that this is where Felix wanted me to go.

Spying what appears to be a gravel road heading back the way I just came, only a few feet to my left, I get to my feet and mumble a curse to the universe. The fact that there was a road I could've run on instead of taking the dangerous way through the forest has me almost growl.

This damn rain is making it hard to truly see anything so I move forward in trepidation. I should be running to the cabin and the safety it offers but instead, I'm even more nervous about what could be waiting for me than what's in the forest. All I can think is that this is a perfect backdrop to one of those horror-slasher films that Brent likes to watch.

With each squelching step on the muddy floor, my heart rate spikes. My beast is on high alert and as I take the first stair to the wrap-around decked porch, I get a good view of the wooden dwelling.

It's very run down and looks like no one has inhabited the place for quite some time and I wonder for the hundredth time how old that freakin' map is that the Drengar use.

There's an overgrown garden on either side of the stair rails, it's really old by my guess.

Heart pumping, I'm bracing myself for some masked, axe murderer to jump out of the bushes and chop me up into a million pieces. I use all my senses to assess the place. I can't smell or hear another living being in the vicinity. Even the animals in the area have taken cover from the storm. Thunder rolls overhead.

Cautiously, I make my way to the windows along the right side and peer in to see absolutely nothing. Investigating a few more windows, I try the door and force it open with the strength of my beast.

The lock comes loose pretty easily and I wait a few heartbeats for an alarm or for someone to start shooting, but nothing happens.

I enter with a sneeze as I kick up the layer of dust on the hard wood floor. It's a single dwelling. I see a decent sized bed along the back wall, tucked nicely in the left corner. There is a dead fireplace to my right with a patchwork lounge and old looking rug that would be an allergy-sufferers nightmare.

A kitchen takes up the rest of the back wall and an old table that looks like it belongs in one of the many motels we've been staying at is near it.

Despite the state of the place, it is free of axe wielding murderers and safe from the storm that shakes the foundations with the next rumble of thunder. But that isn't the sound that has me squeal in fright. I swear mingled with the booming thunder, I heard the distinct shriek of a wraith.

Anxious, alone and frightened, I jump at the sound and spring toward the door and slam it shut. Locking myself in the darkness.

Chapter Forty Three

I FOUND A WHOLE bunch of candles and have spent the last hour trying really hard to coax my beast to help me start them.

She has been zero help.

They're now scattered around the floor and flat surface in the cabin, just sitting there while I'm curled up in the corner of the lounge, watching the door, feeling miserable and inept. The rain is still hammering outside and there are about five leaks in the roof dripping water onto the hardwood floors.

I'm cold and soaked through.

With my head on my knees, I sniffle and wipe at the tears falling down my face. I have no idea if I'm crying because I fear what is out in the forest or that the Drengar who have wormed their way into my damn heart could be dead, or if it's because I don't know what I'm going to do if they die. Or, the most frightening one, because I need Wilder. I need him with a soul crushing urgency that is making me hyperventilate.

I have no money. I have no transport and I'm stuck in a forest in some horror movie cabin on my own.

My situation is bleak to say the least and isn't made any better when I think I hear a noise that has me uncurl myself from the scratchy lounge.

Completely frozen, I come to attention and listen. I listen so hard that I fear my ears will pop.

There is nothing. I barely breath in case I miss something.

Then there's a distinct bang and heavy boots on the steps outside and I back up until I'm against the wall and watch, wide eyed and praying that it's one of the Drengar and then jump out of my skin when the door flies open.

Heavy wind brings in rain and I don't move for a moment as I process what I'm seeing. Wilder takes up the entire door frame. He's carrying Felix over his shoulder like a hunter bringing home a kill and I spring into action when my brain catches up.

'Wilder!' I half shout, rushing to the door. I panic at what I see.

Felix doesn't look good. There's water everywhere and the expression on Wilder's face is enough to have me stop and give him room.

The cabin no longer feels so big with the male in the space. He runs his gaze over the place, assessing our surroundings instantly and when those black depths land on me, I gulp down my fear. They're ringed in red and the sight does some weird and strange things to my body.

'You're hurt!' he states, his tone unimpressed.

I look down at myself and register the vertical cut up my shin. 'Shit,' I mumble, it's as if his mentioning it has made it start throbbing.

Wilder looks at me like I've done something wrong by allowing myself to get hurt. Grumbling a deep sound in his throat, the large male strides through the space and gently lowers Felix onto the rug in front of the dead fireplace. I see the gaping wound on Felix's side and the one on his neck and nearly scream in fright.

'Fuck, is he going to be okay?' I shriek and fall to my knees beside the unconscious male. I don't know what to do. I'm stunned that his uniform has been cut through. It looks bad. It looks life threatening.

'It's freezing in here,' Wilder grumbles from somewhere behind me.

His words have me almost break down. 'I couldn't get her to light the candles or the fireplace. I'm useless.'

Wilder growls in my head and I look over my shoulder when the energy in the cabin changes. He walks around the room, candle wicks igniting as he brushes his hand over them and when he stops back where Felix and I are, I watch in awe of his power when he breathes out a small, deep breath between his o shaped lips. The fireplace erupts in flame instantly and I wipe away my tears feeling worse about myself.

'Stop it,' his voice states in my head and I try, I really do, but I can't get the tears to stop. Then he is there, crouched down beside me. His hands on my face, brushing away the water and I blink up at this stoic face.

'You made it here on your own. You led the way and through your scent I knew where to go. You are not useless.'

I lean into his touch, completely at the mercy of my emotions. 'I was so scared. I needed you so bad and I was really worried. And I...I couldn't light the candles,' I whisper.

'You are exhausted and you used a great deal of your fire to protect yourself in the car. It is not that your beast is useless, she is just spent and untrained, Astgeer.'

His words hit me in the chest. I have no idea how he knew that I used my fire with the wraith. Sniffling, I nod, accepting what he has just said and marvel at the small smile on his face and the feeling of his calloused fingers as they push the hair plastered to my wet face.

Eyes locked, we sit for few heartbeats, just staring and I realise how afraid I was of losing him. 'I was so scared. I couldn't think of anything but you and the others.' The damn tears are back and Wilder gets to work wiping them off my skin.

'I'm sorry, Astgeer,' he says and I shake my head. He's nothing I ever thought a male Azanite could be and yet everything I want and need right now.

Searching my face, Wilder leans forward, bridging the gap between us and just before his lips touch mine, he waits. Letting me decide if I will allow this to happen.

My mind screams to hurry and feel his lips on mine again. My heart sits confused in my chest and yet wanting this all the way in my soul.

His breath mingles with mine and I raise my arms to grip his wrists as his massive hands hold both sides of my face and lean forward.

I kiss him. This time, I'm fully aware of what I'm doing. This time, I feel as if my entire world tilts on its axis.

Chapter Forty Four

H IS LIPS ARE ROUGH and demanding. His kiss turning more and more hungry as we stay locked together. It's everything I remember from the car and more.

He licks my bottom lip and I shiver and open my mouth wider for him. I feel his invasion in my toes.

Our tongues dance.

My beast purrs in the back of my throat and I sit up on my knees so that I can get closer. So that I can lean into his body and feel his heat. A heat that wipes away all the fear and the drama from before to replace it with a fire of my own. One that sits in my core and has me completely overheated.

I want him.

I want everything and when one of his hands slips from my face to wrap around my back and rest between my shoulder blades so that he can pull me closer, I feel like I'm being sucked into a vortex of feeling and emotions.

Connecting my chest to his, he holds me with such care and strength, I gasp, allowing him more access to my mouth. Our breathing becomes one and it tastes like ash and power and flame.

With each passing second, I feel the tension in my body rising. His hands begin to move and caress and grab until I am panting and moaning and wishing my damn clothes would disappear.

Completely lost in him, I almost jump in fright when a deep, pain-filled groan breaks through the haze shrouding my mind with lust.

I sit back a little and am momentarily spellbound by the hunger looking back at me as I stare and stare at the male and his red rimmed obsidian eyes.

Sun Gods! I have an overwhelming desire to jump him but the noise happens again, drawing both our attentions slowly from each other to the poor male bleeding out on the fucking floor.

'Oh shit! Wilder!' I rebuke like he's the one to blame for our getting distracted and totally forgetting about the wounded Drengar.

Wilder's chuckle fills my mind and has me shiver and clench my thighs together. That sound will be the death of me, I'm sure of it.

'He is fine, Astgeer.'

'How can you say that?' I demand, watching as he moves to Felix's other side and kneels down beside him. I frown and make all sorts of sounds and demands that he be careful. 'Watch this', 'watch that', 'gently'—I can't help it.

I watch the Medir move his patient around so that he's lying flat and comfortable on the floor. Wilder keeps throwing little amused looks my way like I'm the funniest thing he's ever seen.

'Felix SkyfallDrengar is a strong and powerful young male who has had much worse in our short time working in this cohort together.' Wilder speaks as he works. Ripping the uniform around Felix's wound, he touches certain spots and observes the way Felix groans again.

I can see the wound better now and am afraid I might lose the contents of my stomach. It's like he has been... 'Fucking hell, has he been munched on by a wraith?' I'm appalled. Disgusted. Mortified.

'How do you think a wraith sucks the life from an Azanite?' Wilder asks, but he sounds distracted and I look up to double check that he isn't teasing me or something. He is serious. Or at least his face is.

Wilder's eyes are closed and he's leaning over the younger male. His hands hovering over Felix's wound.

While Wilder does his mysterious Medir thing, I sit on my knees trying to process what I've just heard. Wraiths literally suck our energy from us! It's the most disturbing thing I've ever heard in my life and find I'm not able to form a coherent thought for a few minutes as my brain screams and screams thinking of how many Azanites have been killed by a wraith eating them alive.

'I think I'm going to be sick,' I mumble, hand flying to my throat. I feel an intense warmth wrap around my body. The feeling lingers before it soaks into my skin and settles inside my chest. It's unlike any power I've ever felt before. As a youngling, this is not how it felt to be healed or inspected by a Medir. Butterflies erupt in my stomach. My core clenches.

My jaw hits my lap and I stare at Wilder in shock. I can feel him inside me and it is so sensual and a little weird. The heat of his healing power moves and begins to search for what is making me feel ill. That's when I finally look properly at the wound on Felix's side and watch as it begins to close.

Blackish blood oozes from the gash as if something is pushing it out and then I squeal a sharp sound and spin to land on my butt when the warmth in my body moves and pools on my shin. The heat of it borders on painful and I bite my lip and watch in awe as the cut along my leg knits back together.

Chapter Forty Five

Resting on the lounge, watching the rise and fall of Felix's chest, I try to process everything that has happened in the past hour. I was sitting here crying because I was frightened and alone, then I was kissing Wilder, a male who possesses power and strength like nothing I've ever experienced before, and then I was healed by that power in a soul claiming way that I'm still tingling from.

That's when it hits me.

I told him my secret in the car.

Heart rate spiking, I track the way Wilder moves around the large space, checking that every window and door is secure. He has been at one particular window across the cabin for a while now.

'Will Alistair and Viktor be here soon, do you think?' I sound concerned, which is warranted. Not only is my anxiety peaking because the others aren't here yet but also because of what I said before the wraith attack. I told him...I told Wilder about the dream.

'They should be.' His answer pulls me from my thoughts.

Maybe he has forgotten. Maybe he won't ask. 'Did you see them in the fight?'

He doesn't respond for a few minutes and my imagination runs wild.

'They will be here. I took Felix and came for you. Viktor and Alistair stayed behind to handle the wraiths. They would've lured them in a different direction.'

I swallow my panic. 'What if they're hurt or if they didn't get away?'

'Astgeer, I have grown up with these males and they are perfectly capable of handling themselves. We just have to wait for them to find us and then we can proceed on our mission.'

'So we just sit around and wait?' I frown, considering what that means. There is no food here in the cabin. No electricity. No nothing.

Wilder moves over to the couch and sits heavily beside me. I feel him watching me, and because I'm a grown up, I proceed to look anywhere but at him.

'So, you dreamt the wraith attack?'

Wide eyed, I try to understand his tone. Sun Gods, the male is attractive, for a moment I forget that he has asked me a very serious question and just stare at the size of him. He takes up most of the three seater lounge. His black leathers fit him like a second skin and I have an overwhelming need to reach over and run my hands through his shoulder length, black hair.

'Serafina?'

'Hmmm?' I reply, completely distracted and smile when he laughs sensually in my mind. My beast is awake and there are parts of me clenching that I didn't know could clench. I want to touch him so bad...

'Focus, Astgeer. Your dreams. Tell me about your dreams.'

His tone this time is easy to decipher. Unable to not answer, I sigh and say, 'this is very uncomfortable for me to discuss with you. I grew up with my father and the Medir in his lair telling me to keep this secret.'

'That would explain why he kept you separate from your court.'

Nodding, I lift my legs and turn so that my body is facing him. Legs up against my chest, I lean my head on the back of the lounge. Wilder grabs my feet and rests them on his lap. His hands get to work massaging the soles. I groan, loving the feeling.

He stops and I shoot him a glare. *'You speak and I will continue.'*

'That's mean,' I mumble, unable to resist. 'I've never spoken about my dreams with anyone before,' I whisper and get lost in his eyes. They hold me captive.

'Then you don't have to,' he replies, our gazes still locked. I see the sincerity in what he's saying and know that he means it.

Sitting in a cabin, listening to the rain hammer aginst the roof, enjoying the peaceful firelight, silence, and his hands on my body, I find myself wanting to tell him. To unload this burden.

'You might think...' I start and can't find the words until he leans over and caresses the side of my face.

'There is nothing that you can say that will make me think any differently of you.'

Sun Gods! I'm in trouble. I think I'm falling, no, I think I have fallen for a damn Medir and after everything that has happened in my past, I'd never could've imagined that this would be my life.

'I've always had nightmares,' I begin and have to draw in a shaky breath before I can keep going. 'Since I can remember, I've always hated going to sleep. It wasn't until I was about five that I woke up to my father and a Medir standing over my bed.' I shuffle and Wilder's brow furrows as if he's preparing himself for where this story could be going. 'My father had parchment and a quill writing something down and when I asked what was happening, he told me that I was talking in my dreams and that what I was saying was something he'd liked hearing. He told me to go back to sleep. When I refused and cried, he had the Medir...' I bite my lip to keep it from wobbling.

Wilder makes a sound and I have no idea if I heard it in my head or if it was audible. He rises from the lounge and stomps over to the same window he was looking out of earlier. I watch as he clenches and unclenches his fists. His features are set in that very Wilder stone-like way. I know he's upset and I know he's realising now why I've been so afraid of him.

'I will end them all,' he declares.

My heart skips and flutters and I probably shouldn't love that he said that, but I do. I really, really do. I don't know what that says about me.

'Sorry,' he says, obviously taking my silence the wrong way. *'Tell me more.'* I don't answer until he says, *'please. I'd like to know. I would like to know you better.'*

How can I resist? 'It got worse after that. The Medir I grew up with wasn't as powerful as you. He'd inject something into my skin to make it happen.'

'A sleep serum is a common medicine. Any fool Medir could make one. We learn it in our first week of the academy.' He doesn't sound too impressed. *'No Medir worth his weight would ever force anyone into sleep for no medical reason.'*

'You did it to me and to my family.' I don't mean to say it, it slips out.

Wilder looks over his shoulder and studies me. *'You were in danger. Your beast was sending out waves of pain that I couldn't go against. You were frightened and untrusting and I did what I'm obligated to do.'*

I nod. What he says is true, even if it still rubs me the wrong way.

'If I had known Astgeer,' he voice is full of remorse and I quickly tell him that it's fine and mean it.

He goes back to looking outside. I take that as an invitation to keep speaking. 'I didn't realise what the nightmares were. I'd wake screaming, covered in a cold sweat to my maid cradling me most often than not on the nights my father wasn't there recording what I had said.'

I hug myself and close my eyes against the onslaught of emotions and keep going. 'When I was eight, I watched a human servant fall to his death in the grand hall of my father's lair and I just stood there. My shoes and dress covered in blood, shocked because I had seen it happen. For two nights, I watched the accident in my nightmares and then it was reality. I couldn't eat. I refused to sleep, which made everything harder with my father and the Medir. I learnt to be quiet and shut my mouth and as I got older, I had them believe that it didn't happen anymore. I grew up in such isolation. My mother hated me and my brothers barely interacted with me. The only ones who showed me any kindness were the humans in the lair.'

I take a deep breath and watch as Wilder moves from the window and crouches down beside me. He's still imposing and big, even though he's on the floor. His presence helps me to keep going. He rests his hand on my knee and I grip it with both hands.

Offering him a small smile, I continue softly, choosing my words carefully. This part of the story I'll never tell anyone. This part of the story would definitely change his mind about me and put me in danger. Humans and Azanites are forbidden to procreate. One of the many laws of our people. I am an abomination.

'I couldn't stay there. I turned fourteen and knew that my life was not what I wanted it to be. My father was already talking about my future and I heard some other things that spurred me to leave. I dreamt about a family waiting for me. I saw them without really seeing them and I wanted it. I wanted that dream. A dream that wasn't a nightmare. So, I went looking for it.'

Wilder's fingers brush at my face. 'I found them too. Laney, Van, Brent and Scott. While I always felt odd and different, they love me and I love them.'

'I understand now why you left. You were raised by the humans in your lair. They're the ones that showed you happiness and kindness as a youngling. It was only natural that you believed the human realm would be where you would get what was lacking. Family. Love. Protection.'

My entire body stills. I never thought of it like that.

'However, I think you are keeping more from me but I will not push you further tonight,' Wilder says softly and I hope that he realises how grateful I am when I thank him for listening.

'You dreamt the book and the location, didn't you?'

'Yeah,' I sigh. 'That's why I couldn't really give you much information and why I didn't know the name of the city until I saw the picture. It's hard to remember details.'

A heartbeat of silence passes while I stare and he stares, and we both just stare. I can practically see his mind ticking and fear for what is to come. He is studying my face with such intensity that I don't think I'm breathing properly.

Wilder's hand returns to my face and I sit in stunned awe as he says, *'you are a remarkable gift, Serafina DarkwoodsAzar. I hate that the beasts you grew up with didn't treat you as such. You're a rare treasure.'*

Twenty four years of pain comes up and I sniffle, 'really? That's all you have to say. You aren't thinking about how you can use me? Or that keeping me asleep so that you can use my dreams would be the best option?'

Wilder looks bewildered by my words and then smiles a smile that cuts through my bone aching sadness. *'If you were asleep all the time, I'd never get to kiss you again, and Astgeer, now that I've tasted you, I fear that I'm addicted to your flavour. You have turned me into an addict and I never, ever want to live a day not in your presence.'*

I bridge the small gap between us instantly and slam my lips onto his. Our kiss is consuming. It's rough and passionate and healing and I find myself agreeing because now that I have sampled the lips of the AzarDrengar-Medir, I am hooked for life.

CHAPTER FORTY SIX

I spend the remainder of the night on the couch, curled up into Wilder's side for both warmth and comfort. I get minimal sleep and only stirred when the sun bathed the room with light and Wilder told me he was going to go for a perimeter walk of the premises to ensure everything was safe. Like me, I feel that he finds this entire campsite a little odd and I have a sneaking suspicion that he believed that Viktor and Alistair would find the place by now. I think that is why he broke off the kiss before and stopped it going any further—well, at least I thought it was. That was a while ago now.

I only get off the couch when Felix stirs and I fall to my knees beside him and try to understand what he's mumbling about. His eyes are closed and his face is all scrunched up like he's in pain and I contemplate if I should call out for Wilder.

'Felix? Are you okay?' I ask, afraid to touch him in case I make it worse. He mumbles again, so I move to hover my ear over his mouth to better hear him. 'What was that? Do you need Wilder? He's outside but I can go get him. What was that?' I ask again, unsure if I understood what he just said.

I lean in closer and hear, 'food. I need food.'

Huffing my annoyance, I slap his shoulder and watch him open his eyes with a smile. I don't care if I hurt him so I slap him again. 'You idiot, I thought you were in pain or something.'

Winking one of those stunning blue eyes, the smart arse laughs and then groans in pain. Genuine pain this time. I help him to sit up and can see how much he's hating the fact that he needs my help.

Stupid, proud male.

'What in the underworld happened?' he asks, looking around with a frown. 'Where are we? This place smells like the book room in the sacred temples in the Riverways.'

Looking around at the abandoned and very run down cabin, I can't help but agree. 'Yeah, this place has seen better days.'

'Damn, I feel like I was chewed on by a wraith,' Felix jokes and I swear I could slap him again because he laughs at whatever he sees on my face—which I'm sure is a look of total horror.

'It's not funny. You know, I had no idea that's what they did? How did I live so long without knowing that they ate us. Like ate us, Felix!' I exclaim, feeling a little stupid.

His laughter is a little strained this time and my annoyance turns into concern instantly. 'That's okay, Raff. It's not something that is taught to the females of our kind often.'

'Well, it freakin' should be!'

'You said Wilder is here?' he asks, he's pale and again I fear that he might need the healer.

'He went to check outside. Do you need me to run and get him?' I'm kinda being selfish because I've been fighting the urge to run out and find him to ease the ache in my body at his absence.

'Nah, just glad you weren't here on your own is all.'

'Lier,' I growl and jump up.

Smiling, Felix has a dopey look on his face and I glare. I don't know why he's annoying me so much. Maybe it's because he looks like he's on deaths door and yet he's making jokes.

Shuffling, unsure what I should do, I'm fidgeting and he smiles wider. 'I'm okay, Raff.'

I bite my stupid wobbling lip. 'You nearly died,' I say, realising how anxious I was about him.

'I'm sorry for worrying you, Lady Serafina.' He's teasing me. I stand in silence, just staring. My mind works through all the emotions that've been bombarding me since I woke up. He says sweetly, 'help me up, Lady. I'd love to go outside and find the sun.'

That has me spring into action. I bend down and give him my shoulder to lean on and wrap my arms around his thick middle. I have no idea if I'm actually helping when he pulls himself up though.

He weighs a ton and we shuffle slowly towards the door. Each step seems to take a great deal of effort.

'Nearly there,' I exclaim, bucking a little under his heavy muscle. I struggle to open the door and with a few curses and a couple of stops so that we can both get our laughter out of our system, we get out on the landing and then stare at the dreaded stairs.

'How badly do you want the sun?' I ask, unsure how we're actually going to do this.

'Not this bad, let's go back inside,' he teases.

I swear colourfully as we make our way slowly down the stairs, nearly both tumbling down the uneven, bent wood twice, and I'm almost crushed under his heaviness when he slips at one point and I have to use all my strength to keep us upright.

'Fucking hell,' I groan and letting go, I drop Felix when he says to dump him on a patch of grass a few feet from the damn steps.

He lands on the soggy, wet floor with a thud and I'm right next to him in the mud on my knees, helping him to move to his side and then open the ruined uniform so that it's exposed properly to the warmth and power of the sun. For such a crap day yesterday, this morning is clear and fresh, with not a cloud in the sky.

Panting from the exertion of getting him out here, I sit down beside Felix and lift my face to the extraordinary healing properties the sun offers. I feel every ray hit my skin, each one soaking into my body, much like Wilder's power last night. It's invigorating and magical.

All my exhaustion is chased away and I know Felix is feeling the effects because he makes a very male, very sensual sound beside me. I laugh and ignore the flirtatious grin he throws and keep doing what I'm doing.

'You smell like Wilder,' Felix says out of the blue and I turn to him in shock.

'What did you just say?' I stutter.

Felix is laying with his eyes shut, completely casual. 'I hope you two didn't do anything in the cabin while I was on my deathbed. While I knew this was leading to you figuring it out, I really don't want to be in the same space when your beasts take over.'

Jaw dropping, I try and fail to come up with a decent response. I have no idea what he means and don't have the chance to clarify because Wilder strides from the trees to our left, Alistair and Viktor beside him.

CHAPTER FORTY SEVEN

'**S**O, YOU HAVE DREAMS that tell you the future?'

Clearing my throat, I stupidly look to Wilder before forcing my focus back to the prince. Alistair seems deep in thought after I nod to Felix's question. Viktor hasn't said much but he looks concerned or unconvinced, I don't know which to be honest.

'Wow, Raff that's so cool and totally bad ass!' Felix whoops and I flinch at the outburst.

I've been shitting myself since the moment Alistair said we all needed to talk. I practically word vomited all over the place when it was my turn to explain what happened in the car, like I couldn't keep the secret anymore.

'Is this why your father kept you separated?' Viktor asks. He's sitting at the bench against the wall near the front entrance. He definitely doesn't sound impressed.

I just nod and watch his face harden.

'It seems the Lord of the Darkwoods and his Medir would force Serafina to sleep so that they could record her dreams.'

The temperature rises with each word Wilder projects into all of our minds. I fidget more with the pillow on my lap. Felix is no longer finding this situation so 'cool'. In fact, he looks like he could give his beast full rein and go on a hunting trip in the Darkwoods. They all do.

Alistair rises from his chair and runs his hand through his hair. 'You were afraid of Wilder and I didn't understand why. We put you in so many situations that are unforgivable.'

Not sure if I'm understanding him correctly, I quickly add, 'how could you have known?'

'You ran away for a reason, Serafina. I should've realised.' I have no idea what to say to that. Alistair looks just as angry as Felix. He curses in Zaric for a good minute and I finally look over to Viktor and catch him staring. Those honey lined eyes are full of too many emotions.

'I watched you from afar. I watched you laugh with your maids and the elite Drengar your father used as your protection. They always spoke of you as a friendly and quiet female who'd leave artwork for them at their posts outside your rooms. Did they know what was happening to you?'

Images flash in my mind and the scariest sound comes from Wilder. It bounces around my mind.

'I will kill them all!' Viktor rages, he too is on his feet and sweat beads and pools along my body under the heat in the room. 'I should have seen it and helped. I was there when this happened.'

Closing my eyes, I suck my bottom lip into my mouth to keep from saying something stupid or start crying like a moronic female. These males barely know me. I barely know them, and yet I'm making out with one last night and crying over the idea that they care enough to be so enraged that I was hurt ten years ago.

It really is too much to handle and I open my eyes and blink at the black depths looking down on me. I didn't even hear or feel Wilder moving towards where I sit on the lounge, tucked in the corner like I was last night when he and I were talking.

'No more secrets Astgeer. Tell us now. Is there anything else that we need to know about you? That will help us to learn who you are and help us to protect and keep you safe. You saved our lives. You are one of ours now and we look after what is ours.'

The offer is made with sincerity, loyalty and devotion. A declaration of who I could be to him and to the others. My beast comes awake and sits staring back at the male asking me to bare my soul completely and allow these four males to judge and make their own assumptions. He's asking me to trust them fully and be vulnerable when all my life I've learnt not to trust and to build barriers around my heart.

What they're offering is everything I've ever wanted. A place amongst them fully. A chance to maybe fit in and find out who I really am.

I hesitate. The words of my parentage sits on my tongue. All I have to say is my mother is a human and I am an abomination. Tell them that my birth breaks multiple laws of our people and pray to the Sun Gods they don't execute me instantly.

'No.' Damn me, but I can't. 'That's all,' I whisper and watch and wait for Wilders reaction. For a moment, I don't know if he believes me and I fear that he can read my mind because he frowns slightly before it disappears and he nods. Bending, he plants a kiss on my head and I stupidly close my eyes and suck in his scent.

The others watch our exchange and I feel my cheeks go red. Felix cackles when he gets a good look at them and I throw him the middle finger which he just shrugs at and I remember that they aren't from around here.

'Trust me, it isn't a very good gesture,' I say a little petulantly and get a very Felix grin.

After a few moments of small talk, the males seem to calm down and then Alistair is talking again about the mission. 'I fear that we are being hunted by this swarm of wraiths and not the other way around. They're acting strangely.'

'Strangely? How?' I ask, eating my bottom lip.

'Well,' Alistair hesitates and looks to Wilder for the briefest of moments before he finally says, 'they were not there for us, Serafina. I think they were after you.'

That has every hair on my body stand on end. 'Me?' I stammer. Sitting up, I don't know where to look or what to do. For some reason, I can feel the four males speaking to each other and that I'm being left out of the conversation. I turn on Wilder. 'What? What are you all saying?'

That gets his attention back on me. The male looks confused for a moment and suspicious. *'You knew that we were talking?'* he asks, a little intrigued.

'I'm guessing, but it doesn't take a genius to observe how you all look at one another and the room goes silent. Don't leave me out of things. I don't like it.' Jeez, my tone sounds like my father and I shut my mouth on that thought.

'We were just discussing if it's possible that they're actually after you and not the book,' Viktor explains.

I feel the colour drain from my face. 'Because of my blood after the stabbing?'

'We cannot know for certain, Lady. It is just a theory.'

'But you all sound convinced.' I have an overwhelming need to run away.

'They seemed to want to get to the car where you were last night.' Alistair has his diplomatic voice on and I swing around to focus on Felix when he says, 'but that could be because they sensed you and a wraith is always going to go for a female Azanir before a male Drengar. We know this.'

'Why?' I snap. Fucking sexist demons.

Felix stumbles over his words as he goes to explain like he's picking his words carefully.

'Because a female's life force and energy is stronger than a males. They are vessels of the Sun Gods. You give and nurture life,' Wilder says, saving the younger male from trying to not offend me or every female of our kind.

'Yeah,' Felix declares eagerly. 'What he said.'

Wilder shoots Felix a very stern look that has him shut up instantly.

'So, what does this mean?' I ask no one in particular.

'It means that we have to be extra careful. We travel during the day and at night we find shelter and we stay low. Firstly, two of us will go find the car and bring it back and we can fix it up and keep on our mission. We will stay here another night. There are provisions in the vehicle.' Viktor seems quite confident that is all it will take. Me, I can't help but notice the look between Wilder and Alistair. 'Then, I want you to tell us everything you saw in the dream about the book. Every detail so we can start to figure out where in the city it could be located.'

We are so fucked.

CHAPTER FORTY EIGHT

S TANDING AT THE WINDOW near the door, I watch the four males as they have their little 'boys only' meeting.

They've been out there for a while now, while I've been inside writing down every detail of my dream about the book, including the office building. At first they lied and said that they were going to inspect the car that Viktor retrieved, now they're just blatantly standing outside in the light rain chatting.

Furious, and a little hurt at being left out, I manage to crack the window open a little and find a position close enough so that I can hear without being seen.

'These setbacks are ruining the timeline. We need to be on that ship to Azanir or we have to find another way to get home. That means making our way to Satmark and then back to Grisham and on that ship in a matter of days.' Viktor doesn't sound upset even though his voice is raised. I've clearly missed the first part of the conversation that annoyed him.

'We have to consider Serafina,' Felix states, I can't see his face from where I stand or understand his tone.

'That's the problem. We have a female with us.' There's a distinct, guttery growl that I recognise as Wilder's beast and it takes me a moment to understand.

'I'm not meaning any offense, Wilder. I care for her deeply. She's a remarkable female who needs our protection and she will be coming back with us to Azanir. However, I suggest we leave her here.'

My face falls.

'How can you say that?' At least Felix seems to be on my team.

'Obviously, we don't leave her on her own. We could have Felix stay here and—'

'Hey!' Felix exclaims, interrupting Viktor's speech and is completely ignored.

'*And,*' Viktor emphasises the word while looking to the younger male in warning. 'We quickly travel to Satmark, it's only a day away. Keep in the forest, use our beasts if we have to and then come back and get them both.'

There's a pause and I swear my ears are hot, I'm so annoyed. They're the ones that took me from my life and made me come on this mission and now they're acting like I'm some kind of burden.

'I don't know. We need to think about this. We can't risk her life.' Pause. 'I know Wilder, no one wants that and we understand the strain you have been under. To find your female in this situation is difficult,' Alistair says. Questions explode in my mind. I have no idea what that means and quickly move from the window when Wilder looks over at the cabin.

Found his female?

'She is invaluable. She has helped us so many times. She saved my life. I think it is wrong to leave her behind. And I'm not just saying that because you want to leave me here with her.' Felix is pissed. I've never heard him speak so aggressively or challenge the older males.

'Wilder cannot leave her. His beast will go crazy if he does, especially now that the mating dance has started. We have all seen the way she has been acting with Wilder. They can't be separated for too long. Their beasts will go mad.' I don't know if Alistair sounds annoyed or not, and frankly I don't care, because THE MATING DANCE!

The voices in my head scream and shout and my beast rolls her eyes at my reaction. I can't be in a mating dance with Wilder! Can I? I don't want a mate. I'm afraid of binding my soul to another…right? Isn't that what I was so worried about?

However, now that he's here and I feel the craving growing in my chest to go out there and touch him, I don't know if that is actually how I feel. I thought I was being silly or losing my mind. I never considered that my beast is trying to finish the binding of our souls.

'Can they go mad if they haven't…even if…you know…they haven't…' Felix makes an inappropriate motion with his hand and I scrunch up my face and then swallow the trepidation that lodges in my throat.

'Sun Gods, Felix, do you have a death wish?' Viktor snaps just as Alistair steps in front of an advancing Wilder who looks ready to kill the younger male.

Throwing his hands up, Felix doesn't appear to be very remorseful when he apologises. Damn, if Wilder had that expression directed at me, I'd be shitting myself. 'It's a fair question. You haven't finished the dance. I know that the ceremony and parties are really just pomp and procedure. But the sex, that has to happen to become one.'

I have no idea if Felix is seeking clarification on his knowledge and I would really like to know the answer because this is all news to me. I have minimal knowledge of a mating dance between two Azanites.

'Yes, coupling intimately will finish the dance,' Viktor answers, throwing him a very stern look. 'You need to go back to your studies.'

Felix clearly didn't like that. He wraps his tree-trunk arms over his chest and pouts.

There's a pause and I wish I could hear Wilder right now. I need to hear his response. Did he know we were in the mating dance? Of course he did! I'm such an idiot and yet, I'm physically fighting with myself to not go out there and wrap my arms around his middle and ask him to touch me.

'I agree with Wilder,' Alistair states. 'This is not the time or circumstance for them to seal the bond and bind themselves together. However, we can't separate them. They wouldn't survive the distance and our top priority is Serafina's safety. It is a duty to our kind to protect her and it's a duty as Drengar who care for her.'

I've heard enough.

Storming through the cabin, I slip out the back door needing air to clear my mind.

Chapter Forty Nine

I stomp a safe distance away from the cabin and tilt my head up to the sky. This is a mess. I'm a mess.

I'm outraged that they all stood outside, discussing my fate without me. So typical of an Azanite male. Yet, here I was thinking that they were different. Clearly not!

They can all go fuck themselves if they think that they can force me to bind myself to anyone. Which isn't all together true because it wouldn't be forcing me to do anything. I want Wilder. I want him with a need that hurts to breath.

Is that bad? I left Azanir to start a new life and fate has put my future back on a course that includes beasts and danger and wraiths.

I've seen my death. How could I bind myself to Wilder when I know that it's coming, and soon. I can feel my end looming. If a mated female dies, her male dies with her. They slip into the afterlife together, no matter what. A female would only stay around, a shell of herself if there are youngling. To only go into death once her young are old enough and safe enough to look after themselves. It's messed up and beautiful and tragic.

I hear leaves crunching under a light footstep and believe it to be Felix or one of the others as I can still feel the distance between Wilder and myself. Turning to tell them that I just need a moment, I gasp and open my mouth to scream. I stop dead when something pricks my neck painfully. I look down to see the dart poking out the side of my skin.

The world goes completely dark.

My lids are heavy and I try to open them. I can hear voices and see shadows looming over me but can't move. Darkness pulls me back into its embrace.

Everything is too bright when I wake next. There are men talking and I can smell humans. After speaking Zaric for this long, it takes my mind a moment to understand them but nothing makes sense and I fall back asleep.

I'm jolted into awareness by something that causes pain to radiate through my body. I'm being dragged by the arms. There's a man on either side of me, pulling me through a long hallway with grey carpet and as the world spins, I feel like I've been here before. We pass three elevator doors to the left and I try to focus to see the strange black logo on the right wall. My brain is so fuzzy and everything hurts. I have no idea what's happening.

I see lots of black, closed doors and realise that I'm in an office building. Lifting my heavy head, I stare at the opened one that we seem to be heading towards. I try to resist and get sworn at by the guy to my right who bends my left wrist back so hard, I fear he has broken it. My scream vibrates off the walls.

Feet scraping along the carpet, we make it into the darkened room and it all comes back to me. The office we are now in is like any other and isn't what has my attention. It's the floor to ceiling windows and the city scape below.

I'm pulled and dumped into a chair roughly and my teeth clink together painfully.

I'm not aware of the time but it's dark outside. My eyes take too long to open between blinks and I'm unable to fight against the men who restrain me in the chair.

I don't see their faces.

'Where am I?' I ask groggily, the effect of whatever they darted me with is strong. My beast is completely gone and as I become more and more aware of my surroundings, I begin to long for the effects of the drugs. I know that I'm in danger.

There is a dull, throbbing pain in my chest.

I suck in a breath and finally have enough of my senses to start testing the ropes.

'What are you doing?' No reply from the two that finish and step behind me without a word. 'What is going on? Let me go?' I shout. The bindings cut into my skin.

I stop when a familiar voice filters through the space and I look up to see the guy from the bar walking in through the door. 'Raff, what a pleasure to have you here with us.'

I try to remember his name and swallow my fear when a large group of men come in behind him. I become instantly aware of my situation.

Joseph.

'What the fuck do you think you're doing?' I snap, unable to control my rage. 'Let me go.'

'I'm sorry, we can't do that. You see, we need you.'

Frantically monitoring all the activity in the room, I bite out, 'what does that mean?'

There are men standing around the room, some watching me eerily while others head to the oDce desk that takes up so much of the space.

I watch Joseph take a position on the opposite side of it. My beast stirs. She is miserable and hurting and I bite down on the immense sadness that overtakes me now that she is awake. I feel like my heart is going to split in two and I try to get her to go back to sleep.

She quietens though when Joseph lifts a book that has me gasp. Colour explodes in the room and the most intoxicating warmth fills my body. I don't know if the humans can feel what I can. They all seem unaffected as they stare at the thick, oversized text now back on the tabletop.

My heart begins to pound in my chest and I try to work out a way to get myself out of this situation.

'You see Raff.' Joseph speaks to the book. 'We believe we need an Azanite to open this thing. We need your blood.'

CHAPTER FIFTY

'WELL, YOU AREN'T GETTING it,' I growl and try to test the restraints. All that gets me is rope burn. New tactic. 'I can't help you. I have no idea what you're talking about. I've never heard of an Azanite before.'

Joseph and a few of the men at the table chuckle and I hate the sound. It grates on my nerves. They're all wearing the same pants and button up shirts. 'Oh, we know who and what you are. You see, we have been tracking you for quite some time.' Joseph steps from the table, his gaze fixed on me. It's slimy and gross.

'It's illegal to kidnap someone and tie them up,' I spit out. I'm raging. No way are these fuckers getting my blood.

His head tilts to the side. He's smiling like I'm funny. 'Yeah, if you were human then maybe. But you're not.'

'You're a fucking freak. You all are. Of course I'm human!' I shout. I am in so much trouble. Stall. I need to stall them. Wilder will come for me. The Drengar will come for me. They have to. I want to cry because I have no idea if they can. I left the cabin. They might think I ran away.

'No,' he shakes his head like I'm daft. 'You aren't. I told you we have been watching you.' He is standing way too close now. I can smell the cheap cologne and the lemon citrus on his skin and hair. It's enough to

270

have me almost gag. My beast is curled up crying in my gut. She is broken. Unable to help. I follow his gaze when he looks towards the door and my entire world stops moving.

I can't process. My mind is so blank that I believe I'm hallucinating. 'Miles?' I manage to whisper.

Someone that looks like my friend Miles strides into the space. The others move aside as he goes by, giving him room. 'Hey Raff,' he says but it is not my Miles. It can't be. Then I smell him and my world comes crashing down.

'You...what is this?' I have no idea how I'm able to speak over the lump of bile in my throat.

He's only a few steps away. I don't believe what I'm seeing. Miles is my friend. 'Help me Miles. These guys kidnapped me and tied me up,' I beg, not sure why he isn't doing anything but standing there observing me. 'Miles?' I cry out. This can't be happening.

'For years, I've followed you around. Tried to get you to come home with me so that I could somehow test your blood. For years, I had to befriend a monster and you just never cooperated. I put up with your brothers being massive dicks and still, nothing.' This is not my Miles.

'What?' My lip is wobbling and I hate it. I look for someone, anyone in the room who might look like they could be on my side, but they're all just as emotionless as the next. Some look angry. Others are so fixated on the book that this entire building could collapse and they wouldn't stop looking at it.

'Once we got the book, we had to gather up proof, so we had you attacked in that alley.' Joseph takes the last three steps so that he's directly in front of me and I turn my head quickly away when he bends to place

271

his lips against my ear. I nearly vomit at the smell of him. I see the white tattoo on his wrist and the entire situation comes to mind. The kid in the alley had a tattoo just like him. I swing my gaze to Miles, knowing exactly where I've seen one like it before. Miles has a tattoo. A white one. On his forearm. 'Do you know what happened, Raff?'

I try to move my face further from Joseph. 'You didn't die,' he whispers in my ear and my entire body stills. He pulls back and I can breathe again. My gaze instantly goes to Miles. 'You recovered quickly actually. Too quickly.' He projects his voice like he is talking to a conference room full of people. 'It was the proof that we needed. It's just a shame that Miles here couldn't get you to go with him to his apartment. We waited months and months there with a team to snatch you when you did.'

My attention is on Miles though. I try to communicate with my eyes, I'm practically screaming at him to help me. He just stands there, unaffected. Uncaring. It breaks my heart.

'Why?' I don't know what I'm asking in particular, frankly, I just want to keep him talking. Talking means I'm not being murdered by these psychos.

'As I said we need the blood of an Azanite to open the book and well,' Joseph shrugs, 'who wouldn't want a beast as a pet?'

My beast lifts her head on that and growls low. That just seems to excite the crazy man even more. Joseph's eyes widen in joy, like he has just found the most precious of treasures.

'Oh, it is going to be so much fun playing with you.'

I go back to fighting against my bonds. The chair squeaks. That's when one of the men behind me steps up and slaps me across the face, so hard that I see stars.

I taste blood. Heaving and too busy trying to focus on drawing enough air into my lungs, I have no idea what the humans are doing. They're all moving around the table, discussing the book.

'What do you want with it?' I mumble, my head is fuzzy from the slap and I cough. Blood drips from the side of my mouth.

Joseph has his hand hovered over the cover. 'It holds the secrets to the Azanite power. To the power to shift from one form to the other. There are stories amongst the humans of Azanir that there is a way for us to become like you. To become an Azanite and have our own beasts.'

I'm not sure if I'm hearing correctly. My brain is throbbing or at least that's how it feels. My left eye is closing and my lip is already swollen. I'm going to kill that guy first. 'You're insane,' I snap, the fire in my tone is causing ash to fill my mouth. My beast is trying to pull out of the intense grief she is dealing with and I can't even process what is wrong with her. I think I know and it starts with 'W' and ends in 'ilder' and the fact he is not here with me. It just confirms what I heard about the mating dance back at the cabin. I talk to help me stay present. 'An Azanite is born not—'

'You're a fool,' Joseph cuts me off. 'You believe everything you're taught but we humans have kept our knowledge from the days that humans and Azanite ruled together. We know the truth. You can make an Azanite and this book is the answer.'

I bite my tongue. There is no point arguing. These guys are insane and when one of them pulls a large knife from a draw at the desk, I feel the colour drain from my face.

'What is that for?' I shout. Joseph is smiling wide and grabs the weapon and I know what they're about to do.

Gaze flying to Miles, I try again to implore him to help. 'Please, Miles. Don't let him do this to me.'

'You'll survive,' he says, unemotionally and I feel my already wounded heart break completely. I can't comprehend the disloyalty and betrayal. It's so foreign to me.

'I should have listened to my brothers,' I snarl. 'You're a creep! They were right!'

He turns his back and I know that I'm screwed.

Or...that's when images flash through my mind. Images that have my skin crawl and my mind clear.

I dreamt this and I know how it ends. It's my time to use my dreams as a tool and not a curse, even if it's dangerous.

CHAPTER FIFTY ONE

I FIGHT AGAINST THE restraints as hard as I can. I twist and pull and relish in the pain radiating through my hands and arms. The chair creaks and cracks. I can hear the men shouting at me to stop and I can feel two grabbing at my shoulders, trying to keep me still.

Someone shouts, 'what is she doing?'

While someone yells, 'she is a fucking animal. Tranquilise her again.'

I get slapped again by Joseph who's now standing over me. My head is flung to the side and I laugh. Turning to glare up at him, I collect the blood in my mouth and spit. Every drop matters.

He is shouting at me to stop. My life is threatened over and over.

Nothing matters though. I pull and pull and then smile when I scent the blood. It's dripping in thick drops from my wrists now and I just keep going. These arseholes are scrambling. The one with the knife is in my peripherals. He has stopped moving and is looking out the glass windows at something I can't see. It's Miles who has my full attention.

Eyes locked, I snarl and refuse to look away. The arsehole slowly backs up towards the door. His brow is creased like he knows I'm up to something and I give him a half smirk that I hope promises the death that is coming his way.

The humans are arguing, disturbed by my behaviour. Joseph yells for two of the men to run and get the tranquiliser gun they left somewhere. It's pandemonium. Funny even, despite everything.

Until...

The entire floor stops moving at the screeching sound that fills the space and while I'm shitting myself, I'm fully aware that this is my only chance of escape. Wraiths don't just eat Azanites, they can suck the life from humans too and I have hopefully served up a feast for them tonight.

There's a heartbeat as everyone stills before the world explodes. Wraiths smash through the floor to ceiling windows and storm the room.

The screaming starts and amplifies as my attackers pull weapons and start shooting. Their useless toys mean nothing to the demons of darkness and one after the other, men are pulled off their feet and devoured by hungry wraiths, looking for a fix of energy. More and more stream through the windows and while they are distracted, I put all my energy into getting out of the chair and after a few good tugs, the chair falls.

My entire left side slams onto hard carpet. My poor body can't take much more of this and I eventually get my hands free of the bindings. My blood is everywhere and yet I still make quick work of getting to the rope around my legs. These bastards know how to tie a fucking knot.

The screaming and shouting and shooting is making my head all scrambled. The wraiths are taking down humans—one by one. More of the arseholes are coming into the office, trying to fight back, which I can mildly respect. They even have fire, which is impressive.

When I get untied, I crawl to the corner of the room and sit heavily against the wall. The drugs are still in my system, making the room spin and my stomach churn. At least it helps with the bone deep sadness weighing heavily on my soul. I don't look at the carnage around me. The sound alone is something out of one of my nightmares. I quickly take off my tee, leaving me with a sports bra and my jeans and tear it in two. Wrapping one around each wrist to curb the bleeding, I finally get it under control enough to know that I'm not a beacon for hungry demons any longer.

They haven't seemed to notice me yet. I think the influx of humans are keeping them distracted and I watch as one man is lifted off his feet. His leather shoes scrap the floor as a wraith holds him by the throat and with his mouth open at an incredible, grotesque amount, the man's screams are lost when the demon inhales him whole. Leaving a skeleton behind.

It's the worst thing I've ever seen and I have dreamt some pretty messed up shit.

I know my luck is going to end soon and I'll be swarmed with demons. Time is ticking and I can feel it.

Scanning the room, there doesn't seem like a way out though. The doors are blocked with men trying to run or fight. Demons stream through the broken glass and while I thought my ending would be completely different to dying in this damn office from a wraith munching on me alive, I find my options are zero. I wasn't really thinking this far into the plan when I used my blood to get the wraiths here.

Granted, I didn't actually think it would work. The Drengar said the wraiths are drawn to me. Who would've thought that they'd actually be right.

Heart rate accelerating, I look over to the forgotten book on the table and know what I have to do. Even if I really...really don't want to. All I can focus on is the massive, now glass-less, windows behind the desk I need to go towards. There is nothing between us in the room and a long fall to our deaths. Which is exactly what happens when one man is picked up by a demon, bitten and then discarded. The voices in my head scream at me to run the other way, not to crawl towards certain death. I ignore them though and it takes everything in me.

With my limbs barely working, I begin to army crawl to the table. I feel sick and try to keep from vomiting in fear. Sticking to the perimeter of the one-sided battle, I dodge a body that comes out of nowhere and panic for a moment before starting my slow movements again.

Finally getting to the desk, I use the minimal energy left in my body to lift myself up. Crying out with the exertion, I manage to get one hand onto the book before pulling it down with me as I fall back on my arse facing the city. The book slams on my legs, shocking me.

Breathing hard, the world spins and I stare out into the night, unsure now what I should do. The wind coming in from the glass-less window is violent. My hair flies around my face and I scoot backwards on my butt to fit myself in the chair hole of the desk.

Cradling the book to my chest, the oddest sensation covers my body, like a thousand spiders crawling over my skin. The feeling intensifies as I pull the book back and rest it in my lap. It's exactly like I dreamt. It's solid gold, however not as heavy as I thought it'd be and as the noises of the dying fade out of focus, I trace my finger over the inky, black wings on the cover. The pattern is intricate and seems to bleed over the hard surface.

I stare, transfixed by a book that doesn't open. It hums with a life that radiates a warmth that I can feel against my fingers. That heat seems to call to me. Knowing that it is useless, I slowly move my hand and try to lift the cover and sit in shock when it peels back with minimal effort.

The force of the vision has me slammed back against the side of the hard inner table and I suck in a breath as a vortex of darkness sweeps me into a waking dream of words and images. I see faces of human women. So many faces and none of it makes sense. I see Azanite males and then...

I'm in Azanir, but it looks different, like I've been sent back in time.

Standing on the top of a hill, a hill that is familiar, yet not, I watch as beasts and humans interact in the town down below. I see human women kissing their Azanite males and I watch as younglings play and laugh through the busy streets of the market.

Movement catches my eye and I look to my right to see a little girl hurrying down the hill to my right towards a woman and a male in beast form. The human lady crouches down and just as the youngling leaps into her arms and shifts. The mother cradles her beast youngling before placing her down on the ground. I fall to my knees, unsure of what I'm seeing as the lady kisses the mighty head of her male as he lowers it to rub against her body in an affectionate move that has tears fall down my face. The youngling bounces around the pair, clearly excited to be in her beast and then as the parents finish with whatever moment they're having, the woman stands and before my eyes does something that has me grip my chest and weep.

I come to my senses crying, and squeal and curl into a ball when the table flies away, leaving me exposed.

Weeping at what I've just seen in my vision, I begin to crawl to the corner of the room, away from the drop and from the battle. Leaning my back against the wall, I grip the sacred text, feeling completely beaten and bruised. I know I have just witnessed something momentous. Something from the past. Azanir like it used to be.

I have no idea what to do. There's no escaping the carnage before me. That's when two wraiths eye me from across the room. Again and again, I try to use my limbs with no success.

The demons float towards me. It's fucking creepy.

Cursing my useless body, I try one last time and fail. The demons are closer now and more and more of them seemed to have gotten hold of my scent. The room darkens as the wraiths come together as one big blob of misty black-ness. All I see is teeth and claws that go in and out of transparency. Maybe calling the demons wasn't the best idea. I probably had a better chance with the humans.

Looking at the faces of my pending death, I find myself no longer weighed down by the crushing emotions eating at my beast. My shoulders feel like a massive weight has lifted off them and I take a deep, steady breath, totally confused. I have no idea what has changed and when two wraiths fly at me, I find I no longer have any fear.

Chapter Fifty Two

S TEADY AND SURE, I sit watching teeth near my face, unable to scream and then watch as they disintegrate like someone has blown out a candle. That's when I see him. Wilder.

He stands like the Sun God he is, handsome and furious and dangerous. The damn beast under my skin has my right arm come up and reach towards him before I realise what I'm doing and snatch it back.

The Drengar's sword swings to cut down a row of demons as he steps closer, his focus is the wraiths, his body now before me and I stare up at his back, wondering how it would feel to run my tongue over the muscles I can see contracting and moving under his fighting leathers. Something I really shouldn't be thinking or focusing on right this very moment with the whole stuck, unable to move with all these wraiths trying to eat me alive thing goin' on.

With the appearance of the Drengar, the world has seemed to have gotten louder. The shouting and screaming intensifies and the thunderous roar of Azanite males raging out adds to the volume. I think my ears are bleeding.

Felix appears from nowhere with a swift move of his body. He dances and sways and cuts down demons effortlessly. It's a sight to behold. Wilder, on the other hand, moves like a seasoned warrior. He only moves his body when needed as if he has fought battles where energy conservation has been important. As if he has seen everything and knows what he's doing. It turns me on so hard, that I forget once more about the life threatening situation. I have to physically shake my head to focus.

There's a confidence to them both that's so different. Felix fights like he's enraged. Like killing as many wraiths as fast as he can is the goal and he is good at it. Such youthful arrogance.

Head resting on the wall, my arms around the book, I can only watch as he expertly takes care of the soulless monsters and before he crouches down beside me, he turns abruptly and opens his mouth. Fire shoots from his lips, completely taking care of the four demons that were getting too close.

Blue eyes assess me quickly, I watch as the crease between his brow deepens. 'Raff, are you all right?'

'I am now,' I mutter through a dry throat. I need water. I can't remember the last time I ate or drank anything. I have no understanding of how much time has passed and how long I was drugged out for. 'I was ambushed.'

'We figured that,' Felix chuckles. He wipes the hair from my face with a small growl. 'Is that the book?' He sounds shocked and a little in awe.

'Yeah,' I mutter.

Felix blinks at me like he has seen a ghost and then he smiles wide as if he's finally composed himself. 'I think the humans of this realm should be lucky that we found your scent so quickly. We used the information you gave about your book dream and then your blood was a great idea, helped Wilder to find you quicker. Wilder was ready to set this world on fire looking for you.'

A little stunned, I look up at the male using his body as a solid wall of pure muscle between me and the room. 'He would've?' My voice cracks.

'Of course I would, Astgeer.'

I can't help but smile to myself when Wilder's voice fills my mind and I feel the tension in my body evaporate.

Closing my eyes for a moment, I fight the exhaustion.

'You're safe now,' he says and it's the most beautiful sentence I've ever heard.

Alistair appears at my left, his eyes fixed on my face before falling to the sacred text. 'Serafina...' his words trail off and then he clears his throat and says, 'give me the book.'

I don't and he seems to understand. His eyes soften and I swear there is a moment of newfound respect that passes between us. 'I know, you risked your life. Give it to me to carry while we save yours, Lady.'

Nodding, I let the prince take it and feel an emptiness at the loss of its warmth. The vision is still bouncing around in my skull and I try to get up when Felix tells me that we have to go.

When they realise that I'm unable to stand on my own, things happen pretty fast. There are still so many wraiths and surprisingly a number of humans.

Felix and Alistair disappear from my side and I now have a three male wall blocking me from the room so that when Wilder turns around and scoops me up into his arms, I don't fight it or feel in danger. Actually, I lean into him and suck in his scent. He smells so good and I feel instantly safe.

Swiftly and without much effort, the Drengar cut down wraiths and humans as we move through the office to the wall that used to be floor to ceiling windows.

I have no idea what the four have planned until we are standing on the threshold of office building and air.

'Can you wrap your arms and legs around me, Astgeer?' Wilder's tone is loving and full of emotion. His dark, red eyes blaze down at me, his beast is raging. I can feel him against my body, hammering against Wilder's skin, demanding to be let out. The pain these Drengar must feel while they're in the human realm is hard to comprehend. It makes me more in awe of their greatness and I never, ever thought I'd be saying that. A few weeks ago, the idea of seeing a Drengar sent me into a cold sweat.

I haven't got the energy to nod or reply, not when I use the last of it to fold my legs and arms over his neck and torso like a monkey. His solid grip means that Wilder is keep me against his body more than I am.

Head resting on his shoulder, I finally get a good look at the carnage in the room. It's a mess of limp bodies and shrieking wraiths. Most of them are too busy eating the humans, I'm guessing because they're the easier targets. The ones that come close to us are taken care of by Viktor who stands between Wilder and Alistair. His fire doing the job nicely. It feels magical against my skin.

We're in a line. Felix is on our other side looking over the ledge. I notice the book strapped to Alistair's chest, much like I am on Wilder's. The wind is dramatic and biting cold against my back. The heat radiating off the Medir is keeping me from totally freezing to death. We are high up. Like fourteen storeys high. The rush of not being able to see the darkness and the city below is invigorating. I can feel only air as Wilder takes another step. The males are communicating and I can hear their words in my mind but can't focus on it.

I find myself looking for someone and am not sure what I feel when I don't see Miles amongst the dead. I should probably feel terrible for walking away from this mess and I don't know what it says about me at the fact that I don't.

'We land along this side. It's a back alley. It seems everyone in this city is at that damn festival that made it hard for us to get here quickly. Felix, do you see anyone?' Alistair asks, his hand is on Viktor's shoulder as he is the only one facing the office, keeping the enemy at bay.

Felix's voice comes next, informing him that there are no humans in sight.

'Let's get out of here. Is everyone ready?'

Their voices confirm and Wilder's arms tighten further. *'I have you now,'* he says to me. *'You're safe.'*

'I know,' is my simple response and I rest my cheek on his broad shoulder, completely at ease.

Then he steps off the ledge.

CHAPTER FIFTY THREE

WE FALL AND I haven't felt this alive in ten years.

I see a handful of wraiths following and I watch as they are taken care of by the Drengar who hold a tight formation with me at the centre. These males are capable of taking flight and I'm astounded that even in the human form they command the skies without their wings to help. But we aren't flying, we are falling. Falling in a controlled way, led by Drengar who've trained most of their lives for these situations.

With my chest pressed tightly against Wilder's, I feel his steady heartbeat. It never once falters or shows concern about what we're doing. Frankly, I feel like his beast is happy. This is his domain. His territory.

I can only imagine what we must look like if someone was watching. Lucky for us, humans rarely look up. They don't care what's happening in the sky.

In Azanir, it's the complete opposite. An Azanite lives in the air and while my beast is unable to take over completely, it's still something I crave. Something that I forgot I needed in the ten years I've been here.

The pain of not being able to get airborne was hard to manage when I was younger.

My hair whips against my body and my stomach is in my throat in the most exhilarating way. I feel so true to myself in this moment that tears stream down my face and get collected by the wind.

Wilder's hold never wavers. One of his hands comes up and rests on the back of my head, keeping me in place and with the buildings no longer below us, but on all sides, I know we're about to land.

Wilder's feet hit the floor and he bends his knees, absorbing the impact in his massive frame, leaving me completely unaffected by the power of the fall.

Breathing hard and allowing myself a moment to collect my thoughts, I hug Wilder like it's the last time I'll ever touch him.

His hand starts playing with my hair in a petting motion as if he too doesn't want to let me go just yet. The conversation I overheard at the cabin comes to mind and I try to remember if the idea of us being in a mating dance infuriates or excites me.

Pulling back, the entire world slips away and it's just me and the male I'm wrapped around. Wilder searches my face, his gaze hard and all-seeing.

'You were going to burn the world down for me?' I whisper. Our lips are ridiculously close and having him with me has eased the ache in my heart that I have been feeling for days. I was right, my beast was mourning the distance between us.

'*Always,*' he answers and Sun Gods save me, I believe him. After a life of running away and trying and failing to belong, I finally found it in an Azar-Drengar-Medir, an Azanite who possesses the power of all the magic of our people. '*No one is allowed to harm you.*'

'Because we're in a mating dance?' I speak softly knowing full well that the others can hear me.

I don't know if he'll deny it. He doesn't. He just says, *'yes.'*

Smiling, even though for the last few days I never thought I'd smile again, I thank him from the bottom of my heart for saving me and not just from the humans and the wraiths, but for saving me from myself.

He has given me something I never thought I could ever have. After the strange vision of the past, I have no idea what is in my future.

I see the moment Wilder feels the shift in my body as tension creeps in at the manic thoughts now bouncing around the inside of my skull about who I really am. His brow is furrowed and I want to reach out and soothe the creases now forming between them. *'What's wrong? Are you in pain?'* That voice. It's full of fire and authority and it turns me on so hard, I shiver.

'No, I'm just tired and thirsty,' I manage to say and while he nods like he accepts what I've just said, I get the feeling that he doesn't believe me.

'We need to move out,' Viktor states and with Wilder not wanting to put me down, and me not wanting him to, they take me towards a very run down SUV they've parked along a side road near the alley.

I'm whisked into the back seat, only removing myself from Wilder when he peels me off. However, in moments, I'm in his lap, curled up against his chest and listening to the words he utters in my mind. Words that comfort me.

We speed away from the city, Viktor driving and muttering to himself about traffic and cursing the humans that kidnapped me.

'Thank you, Raff.'

I'm so tired that all I'm capable of is moving my eyes to stare at the Prince of Azanir. He called me Raff. He has never called me Raff, and in that moment I feel a shift in the air. Like my soul, my beast and human side, have finally felt a sense of acceptance. No matter what happened the last few weeks, it is this moment that changes everything for me.

Turned in his seat, his complete attention is on me, Alistair says again, 'thank you for helping us to recover this,' he taps the text still attached to his chest. 'With the information about where the book was located and the description of the building, we could pinpoint where the humans had taken you and where the book was because of everything you gave us. We are honoured to have met you, Serafina DarkwoodsAzar and your name will be revered in Azanir.'

I fall asleep on those words, with Wilders power moving through my blood. My dreams are filled with visions of the past and fears of my future.

Chapter Fifty Four

'*ID YOU RUN FROM us? Is that why you were out in the forest?*'

Spinning, I was so lost in thought that I didn't even sense Wilder coming up behind me. 'I didn't run,' I confess and slowly turn back to the bathroom sink to wash my face. 'I needed some air and I went for a walk. That's when those bastards tranquilised me.' My rage hasn't died down. It has been two days. Two days of me sleeping in a lumpy motel room bed while the Drengar keep watch. I woke up this morning to the room completely empty and needed to clear my mind.

My body aches from misuse. I don't think I moved the in two days. Wilder steps up behind me and I close my eyes and feel his presence. He has the most amazing smell. Like fire and ash and forest. It's deep and I want to bath in it. I want to wake up with that scent in my nose and on my skin. I want to have access to it for the rest of my life.

His hand comes up to touch my hair and a wave of his power fills my body. Heating me from the inside out, calming and soothing every muscle ache and pain. It's amazing that in such a short amount of time, I have gone from pure terror at being in the same room as him, to missing his touch.

'*You heard our conversation?*' It isn't an accusation but it has me open my eyes and stare at him through the small, cracked mirror in the bathroom to understand his tone better.

'Yeah, I did. After hearing that you're in a mating dance with a male you've only just met requires a walk and some air.' I don't know why I sound so childish. Maybe its because I still hate that they were all discussing something that's really personal without me. That I wasn't included or Wilder didn't think to come to me.

Wilder's expression stays neutral and I get lost in those obsidian depths.

'Are we in a mating dance?' I whisper, afraid of the answer. I can't mate with someone like him. And it has nothing to do with him and everything to do with me.

He's a BlazeAzar. His family are famous and strong and hold just as much power in Azanir as the royal family. And what am I? A fucking half breed freak who has nightmares every second night of destruction and death. Who opened a sacred text that hasn't been opened in thousands of years and gave me a vision that has confused me even more.

The thought is enough to have me grip the edge of the porcelain and fight back tears.

'You're not happy to hear that we are?' he asks so softly that I have to process before shaking my head. *'Then explain your sadness.'*

Damn, powerful Drengar can read my emotions. 'I'm sad because I am me and you are…well, look at you! You're a freakin' AzarDrengar-Medir. Who am I to claim a mate binding with a beast like you?' The words slip from my mouth. I'm not one to lay my feelings and emotions out for someone to see. Nor am I a female who doubts my own worth. I have lived the past ten years independently and taking care of myself. The more I think about my absurd behaviour, I feel the tension in my body rise. I wish like anything to be able to suck my words back into my stupid mouth and swallow them.

Wilder smirks as if he heard the entire conversation I've just had with myself in my head and then it dawns on me, if we are in a mating dance that is probably exactly what has happened.

Glaring suspiciously, I'm still staring through the mirror. 'Are you sure you can't read my mind?'

His chuckle fills the space in my mind that my harsh self-loathing words had just damaged. Every time he speaks or touches me or stares, I feel calm. I feel healed. *'No Astgeer, but as I said to you, your beast communicates with your body. Through your scent. You are sad, I will know. You are angry and I will feel it. If we are mated then yes, we will share our thoughts, to an extent, but until then it's just the power of our beasts.'*

I want to shout, 'not mine, I don't feel you like that,' but keep my mouth shut for a change.

Feeling left out, I turn and stare up at him. His body takes up most of the space. I can't even see the door past his wide frame. 'How come I can't feel what you're feeling?' I ask and regretting it instantly. Could it be because I'm half human? Did I just confess to not being fully Azanite?

'My answer might upset you,' Wilder tells me, raising a hand to brush some of my hair behind my ears. I lean into his touch, feeling it in my soul.

'Say it.' I hold my breath at what it could be.

He frowns slightly before he states, *'it's because you don't listen to your beast. I think you have supressed her for the majority of your life. Especially in your formative years. Your education was disrupted. You have lived amongst humans too long and you've forgotten how to be one with her. It has affected the connection you have with the other half of your soul. She is probably very angry with you.'*

I swear my heart hits the floor, I have no idea how to respond and don't think I have the capacity to, even if I wanted.

My emotions jump around dramatically, from one to the other, and I push past him to storm into the motel room just so that I can get some space. I'm no fool and know that if Wilder wanted to stop me, he would've easily.

Stepping toward the bed, I try to focus on my breathing. Try to focus on something other than the overwhelming emotions threatening to choke me.

'You're angry with me.' I don't have to turn around to know that he's standing at the bathroom door.

'No,' I sigh. 'Yes...I don't know, Wilder. I just...I just don't know what I'm doing anymore. I have no idea who I am and what I want and I'm so confused.' The words that I believe what he has just said sticks to my tongue and refuse to be spoken.

I find myself lost in my own mind and what a horrible place to be in at the moment. From the moment the Drengar entered my life, I have been forced to reconsider my entire life. Ten years of trying to establish myself and now this...what he has just said to me makes so much sense and breaks me at the same time.

I don't know who I am. Human or Azanite or both. I don't know how to be anything. I know deep in my soul that I have to go with them back to Azanir to find the answers, even if it terrifies me.

'Are you going to come back to Azanir with us?'

'Yes,' I say without hesitation. 'I didn't know I had a choice.'

'You always have choice. I will never let anyone take that from you.'

I know his words mean more than just my decision to go back to Azanir. He means with this mating bond. 'I just need some time,' I tell him and hope he gets it.

The beautiful male just nods as if understanding what I'm saying. *'And you will have it. There's no pressure here for you to accept this bond, Serafina. We are fated to be mates and it's inevitable that we will bind our souls, but that doesn't mean we have to make decisions now. I will be waiting for you though. I will wait for you and be here when you're ready.'*

'I don't know who I am,' I whisper.

'I know, and I will always be here for you, Astgeer. Anything you need, it is yours.'

'And what does that mean for...us,' I say, unused to the idea of that word. 'Like with the mating bond?'

'It might be uncomfortable, especially with both our beasts wanting to finish the bond but we will manage.'

'Do you mean the way I always want to touch you and be near you isn't going to go away?' I don't want to sound panicked but it's hard.

Wilder just nods apologetically. *'Our beasts want us to be together, Serafina. They will be like this even if we consummate our mating.'*

'Great,' I mumble, unsure if I will ever get used to acting like this forever. 'I'm sorry for making you wait.'

'I will be here whenever you are ready. I'm not going anywhere, Serafina. If we are bound together officially or not.'

I don't say anything else. Words are unnecessary. I stride towards him and throw my arms around his middle and breathe a sigh of relief when his tree trunk arms wrap around my body.

CHAPTER FIFTY FIVE

THE NEXT FEW DAYS go by in a blur. We travelled, at speed, back to Grisham. Crappy motel rooms blended together. We were up with the sun and only slept when the moon was at its highest. Alistair, with the book strapped to his chest, was so focused on getting home to Azanir that his tunnel vision meant that we all fell into our beds at night in exhausted heaps, unable to do anything but eat and sleep. Some nights with Wilder beside me, some nights with one of the others. Everything has changed since I realised that Wilder is my mate, and while we haven't made it official, the others treat me a lot differently. Like one of their own. No more conversations with their eyes. No more leaving me out of important decisions.

Felix and I are cross legged on the motel bed sharing a massive bag of hot chips and chicken nuggets. The others are sitting on the table near the window discussing the book that's laid out reverently between them. Alistair never lets it go. He even sleeps with it.

When the prince tried to open it before, I held my breath, keeping still and quiet and blew it out through my nose when it stayed glued shut.

'What do you think it says?' Felix asks with a mouthful of food. 'Like on the pages?'

'No idea,' Alistair replies, he's lost in thought, studying the wings on the front and I don't blame him. They are odd. The way the ink drips hints to the image melting or something, which is totally strange.

'They say that the wings weren't like this originally. They say the ink began to melt a few generations ago.'

Viktor's words have me choking on the chip I just tied to swallow. Nodding my thanks to Felix as he pounds on my back, I find my breath and wave him away. 'You good?'

'Yeah,' I cough and throw Wilder a quick, reassuring grin when his voice asks me the same question in my mind.

'So why would the image be melting? It doesn't look like a good omen,' Felix asks, focusing back on eating.

'The book is said to be given to us by the Sun Gods themselves.' Wilder's words make me shiver and Felix seems to have the same kind of reaction, he looks more concerned than I am.

'That can't be good then,' he utters.

'No. It's not. It's said this book was the key to our existence. It held stories of our magic and purpose and why Azanites were given the power of our beasts by the Sun Gods.' Alistair sounds sad.

'The humans thought it held the key to them getting the power of a beast. That Joseph arsehole thought the Azanites needed to share our power.'

There is a round of comments that let me know what the Drengar think of that. Mostly that the humans are stupid.

'Could the answers to why our race is slowly dying out be in there too? Like why our birth-rates are dropping rapidly and why even less females are being born?' Felix's words hang in the air. My heart-rate spikes and I sit up straighter. I have been dreaming about the book and what it showed me over and over again, not sure of what it all meant and now...

'Who knows,' Viktor shrugs. 'Not that it would matter. It doesn't open, so we never will.'

Shit. Shit. Shit. Fuck... 'It did.' I stutter and freeze when all four males stare at me in a mixture of confusion and shock.

'Astgeer?'

I don't know why I'm so afraid. 'It opened for me.'

They erupt. Males stand abruptly and chairs hit floors hard. They speak at once, demanding me to explain myself 'now'.

'Stop!' Wilder is mad, very mad, and I have no idea if it's directed at me or the ones yelling. It doesn't matter because they all stop and I'm grateful.

Wilder strides to the bed and kneels down before me. His focus is on me and only me. *'Explain for us, Astgeer. We need to know what happened.'*

I'm powerless to his words and taking a deep breath, I tell them about the male and his family. I tell them how happy they were, a human and an Azanite. I go to tell them about what happened at the end, with the female human and what she did, but stop myself for some reason though.

It's quiet. Too quiet and I can't stop fiddling with the blanket under me as I watch Alistair and Viktor pace back and forth, each going the opposite way and staring at each other as they pass.

I feel like I'm in trouble and the only thing keeping me from losing my mind is the fact that Wilder is beside me on the side of the bed, with his big arm curled around my back. They all listened while I explained what happened in the office.

'You have to complete the mating bond,' Viktor says out of nowhere and the quiet is interrupted again by the newest argument for the evening.

Wilder makes it very clear that we aren't going to be forced to complete the bond out of some kind of fear.

'Should I be afraid?' I whisper up at the male sitting next to me but Viktor answers before Wilder can.

'Yes! You should be and don't growl at me Wilder! She has to know.' The pair share a glare while I try to process.

Alistair, ever the diplomate, stops pacing and takes the bed across from me. I have his undivided attention. 'Raff, you have done something that no one has been able to do in thousands of years. You have seen something that's both confusing and confronting and I'm not sure how to interpret it.'

Sun Gods, how they have reacted if I told them what happened with the human woman at the end of the vision?

'I do,' Felix says from the window. He keeps looking out at the carpark like he is worried about something. We all wait and wait until Viktor snaps at him to share with the group. It's pretty funny and only because I know Felix has only stopped for dramatic effect. Something he confirms when he winks at me. 'It means that we were never meant to live as masters over humans. That we have lost something by changing the relationship.'

That doesn't go down well. While they all bicker and argue, I sit wondering why I should be afraid of learning this information.

'How do you think the Azar in Azanir will react to this? Do you think the leaders will accept that humans could be the answer to our problems? We're bringing back a female that ran from our world, that lived amongst humans, which is forbidden, who has dreams of the future, and we have to try and keep her safe. I'll not be the one to announce that the most sacred of our texts opened for her and only her. That it gave her a vision.' Alistair's words hit me hard.

'Raff is in danger,' Felix states like he has just worked it out.

'Of course she is.' Damn, Alistair sounds super mad.

Wilder's calm response has the energy in the room ease. *'Then we will protect her.'*

'I don't need protection!' I snap.

Wilder's hand comes down to stroke my face. *'I know Astgeer, but we will protect you anyway. You are ours.'*

Chapter Fifty Six

W E MANAGED TO GET back to Grisham just as the sun rises on the day Viktor said we needed to be at the docks for our ship to cross the Veil. It's a massive boat, *Unnasti*—Lover. The name made me smile, even though my heart was pounding erratically in my chest and has been since the moment we got here and the human captain and his crew greeted us.

It was confronting to say the least. The four males, who I think I sometimes forget are all powerful Drengar as I sleep next to them each night, slipped back into their high-ranking persona. Gone was their kindness and charm to be replaced with cold-hard efficiency and command.

I didn't miss the small glances I received from the crew at there being a female Azanite in the group, which I'm sure they weren't expecting. I was met with unease and a little fear. Can't blame them really, especially when they saw Wilder step up to my side and place a possessive hand to my lower back. That had them all look away quickly and keep their gaze on their captain.

The *Unnasti* looks like something that you'd see on a human pirate movie but with more luxury and less wood-legged looters, well, not that

I can see anyway. The crew are actually very well dressed and appear scurvy-free in their navy and white uniforms.

The docks aren't busy at this time of the morning. There are a few men unloading a ship a few yards away, keeping to themselves, and there's a cluster of about a hundred or so humans by the gangway, all ready to board the *Unnasti* to Azanir. They show their paperwork to a line of ship workers, each human who works on the ship is a high ranking officer. The migration to Azanir is a tricky one and can only be achieved through sponsorship by a human already in Azanir.

The Drengar left me here so that they could organise whatever it is they need to organise on the boat.

Standing at the edge of the dock, I watch the colours of the rising sun play across the sky and reflect onto the dark ocean that we will cross to get back to a place I haven't seen in ten years. In all my time here with Laney and Van, I never once came down here in fear of the memories and emotions that it would conjure. Now, I find myself conflicted. On one hand, I'm scared and sad to leave, in fear of never seeing my found family again, and on the other, I believe that the answers to who I truly am and how I can better learn about myself are back in Azanir.

Not to mention, I don't think I could be separated from Wilder. Our bond is only growing and I find myself constantly reaching to touch him, to ease the relentless ache in my chest at our absence. At least now I have answers as to why I'm acting so weird. We haven't completed the bond but I'm slowly working out that it doesn't matter if we're physical in that way or not, he and I, our beasts, we are already bound. Through the events of the last few weeks and triggering the dance with our kiss, Wilder is my destiny whether I find myself or not in Azanir, or if I believe myself worthy of his love and devotion.

Lost in thought, and absorbing the beauty and warmth of the growing sun, I don't hear the commotion happening near the ship until its almost too late.

The group of humans shout and scream a name that really just sounds like a jumble of words. One man's voice, or in particular the fear in it, is what has me turn. I see a young child running after a small bouncy ball. A mass of orange curls surround her face. They bounce around as she blindly follows it. Its trajectory is clear.

I react without thought, my beast roaring in my chest at the sight of a child in danger. The fall alone might not kill her but Sun Gods only knows what hunts under the docks or if she can even swim.

With my beast in full control, I get to the innocent girl just before she follows the ball right off the edge of the dock. I catch her and lift her in my arms as she cries out in shock and we both look down at the ball as it splashes into the water below.

Brown eyes fly to mine and I hide my smile at the open mouth gape she has on her pretty, round face. She's probably about six or seven. She smells like cherries and pastries and a splatter of freckles dust her nose and cheeks. With the mane of orange, tight curls, she looks like a doll.

'I lost my ball,' she says and I watch as her little lip wobbles as she tries to compose herself.

'I know,' I reply and place her down on her feet. We both look over the edge. 'That could've been you.' I point to the ball that is now bobbing away from us, out into the ocean.

'Daddy is going to be mad at me now,' she sighs heavily, a little too mature for her age, and I turn when the man I'm assuming is her father comes hurrying over and lifts her off her feet to hug her close to his chest.

I wait, watching the exchange with interest. The open affection is not my experience with dads. Not that this guy looks anything like a typical father, certainly not mine. His blonde hair is well maintained and sits in a stylish curve at the top of his head. His brown eyes match the girl's and his arms are defined and strong as he holds his daughter securely in them. He is tall, young and lean, and I get the mildest scent of mint and cinnamon.

'Roxy! My gods, what were you thinking, baby?' he exhales. He is handsome with a warm energy that my beast seems to like. She has been watching the exchange between the pair as if ready to jump in and defend the girl if her dad was like mine or something.

'Sorry, Daddy,' Roxy replies and looks up with the cutest doe eyes when her dad frowns down at her. I know he's trying to be stern but that doesn't last very long with that look and I think I could learn a thing or two from this kid because her dad just tells her that she has to be careful. 'But she saved me so I'm okay.' A little finger points in my direction.

That's when the guy finally looks at me and I watch as he tries to work out what to say as he rises to his full height. I don't blame the way he grabs Roxy's hand and pulls her to his side.

'Thank you, My Lady.' He bows deeply and I bristle at the action which seems to shock him. I have no control over the noise of annoyance I make in the back of my throat. 'I'm sorry if I've offended you, Lady. I was told that we should bow to the Azanite. Also, that I shouldn't be talking to you. Also, that you won't understand the human tongue,' he says, still slightly bent. Poor guy seems lost. 'So why am I still talking? Shit, I've never been good with directions. Sorry, Lady.' His eyes widen and throws the child a remorseful look like he didn't mean to cuss in front of her, but she isn't listening, she is taking out a small doll from his pocket and is now fixing the doll's hair.

'What does that mean?' I ask, really confused. 'Who told you that you can't speak to me?'

'Uhhh...the others. They said you wouldn't understand me. It was also part of the list of rules we were given when our migration papers were accepted.' He motions to a paper sticking out of his other pocket and I ask if I can see it. He hesitates before handing it over. 'I've never met an Azanite before. I hope I didn't do something wrong.'

'You did nothing wrong.'

'I am indebted to you, Lady. I've never seen anyone move the way you did,' he says while I read the stupid list that the humans were given. They include things like areas in Azanir that they're forbidden to go near. The way to identify an Azar, Drengar, Thal, and the long list of things humans in Azanir can't do, including speak to a female Azanite.

The entire thing leaves a terrible taste in my mouth. I don't know what he sees on my face but he has an odd expression as he takes the paper that I offer him back.

'You seem like you've never seen that list before,' he chuckles and I scowl.

'I haven't, and frankly, it's a bit repulsive.'

He laughs a very attractive sound that has me finally realise that I don't know his name.

'Raff,' I say, holding out my hand and wait as he stares at it like he's trying to decide if he should or not.

I admire the way he does though, it tells me what kind of man he is. 'James McCloud and this here is Roxy McCloud.' The little girl smiles up at me when her dad tells her to say hello.

'It's nice to meet you both,' I reply, meaning it and am cut off from asking more questions about why they're heading to Azanir because Wilder appears at my side scaring the human off with his presence alone and I'm whisked onto the ship before I'm able to process what's happening.

Chapter Fifty Seven

'This is a bit ridiculous, don't you think?' I scoff, totally baffled as to why we're all sharing this massive cabin on the top floor of the ship.

There's a typical Azanir bed, meaning it is beyond huge, in the centre of the space. I instantly fall on the mattress and moan my pleasure. I have missed the beds and the pillows and the warm furs that Azanites use. I spend ten minutes puffing and smacking pillows trying to get them all comfortable and tell the males watching me that they better not be assuming that they're staying in here with me.

They ignore me. I was delusional to think that these males wouldn't be by my side the entire trip. The room holds a few amenities and has a small private bathroom but still smaller than any motel room we've been in for the last few weeks.

Wilder and Alistair dump their bags and let us know that their heading out to speak with the Captain and the Chief Mate. Wilder strides to the bed and kisses my head after telling me to stay close to Felix and leaves.

'We'll be on deck most nights, Serafina, so you'll have the room mostly to yourself. So, you will have the bed to yourself.'

Grinning, I let Viktor's words sink in. I feel good, until he explains why they'll be on deck at night. 'What?'

'Wraith attacks will be one of the biggest dangers on this trip. That and storms. The closer we get to the Veil, the likelihood of us meeting a storm is very high.'

I have no control over the way I shiver. I remember crossing the Veil. Ten years ago. There was one particular storm that raged during the day. It wasn't pretty and I was below in the human quarters but we never saw wraiths.

'You will stay close to us all while we're on this ship. Things are different now. We aren't in the human realm any longer. Things are different in Azanir.'

'Yeah. Yeah.' I sigh. I've been hearing this speech for days now. I have to act like an Azanite female, even if I don't want to.

'Come, Raff. Let's go get some lunch. I'm starving.' Felix is beside me in a heartbeat, hand extended, waiting for me to take his offer.

I jump at the idea of food.

Hand firmly in his, Felix and I laugh and joke all the way down to the mess deck.

The noise when Felix opens the doors to the designated eating and dining floor of the ship is invigorating and soul warming. Well, until the mass of humans eating and socialising stop talking at our appearance. There is a long line at the buffet along the wall to the left, where ship workers serve food, cafeteria style, and I try my best to not be self-conscious or fix my hair or something with all these people looking at me.

Felix still has my hand in his and drags me over to the food line and the humans must understand the look he throws the room because they all go back to doing whatever they were doing.

Felix nods when I thank him, that's when I see the difference of his features. He doesn't look like my Felix. His features are too hard. Too deadly. I hate the way the humans in line step aside for us to go right ahead to the front. Felix doesn't seem to have a problem cutting-in. He grabs trays for us both and gets to work moving in front of the people who've stepped back to give us access.

I lose my appetite instantly.

'What's wrong Astgeer?'

Shrugging, I go back to looking at the view. I haven't felt good about the situation at lunch all day and I shuffle over and let Wilder take a seat beside me on the narrow bow which I have now claimed as my own. 'I'm just thinking of what is going to happen when I get back to Azanir.'

I lean into his side when his arm comes around me, hugging me close. *'You will stay with us, Serafina. We will be heading to my home. To the Drengar Academy in the lands of the BlazeAzar. You will be safe with me. If that is still what you want?'*

'I don't know what I want,' I whisper. I feel him tense. Pushing off him, I make sure that I can see his face when I say, 'but I know that I want you, Wilder. I'm just scared,' I confess. 'I ran away for a reason.'

'I know you're scared but you are not the same youngling that felt you had to run. You're strong and intelligent and you're ready to find who you are. And I will be there right beside you, every step of the way.'

His words make me smile and I sit up and brush my lips over his. *'Thank you, Wilder. I don't think I could do this without you.'*

I get a very un-Wilder like grin that brightens his entire face in a way that has me gaping at the beauty of it. He is magical. *'Will you help me learn how to connect with my beast?'* I ask him.

'*Of course,*' he says and when our lips brush again it turns into a passionate kiss that has my toes curl.

Chapter Fifty Eight

THE SUN IS AMAZING and I find myself loving every minute of this trip which is weird seeing as how we are heading towards Azanir.

The seas are calm. The sky is always blue and I've carved out my own little section right at the bow where I have sat for the past three days feeding the beast the energy she craves. At night, I curl up in the massive bed, waiting for Wilder to come down and slip under the covers behind me.

Today, I managed to get away from another one of their meetings around how we're going to handle the announcement of where I've been and how we found the book. They don't necessarily want to lie to anyone but they genuinely care about me, which is still shocking after everything that has happened. It feels like a lifetime ago that I was fighting with them in Laney's living room, defending Van.

My Van.

I miss my family so much it aches. I feel terrible about leaving without saying goodbye but there's no way I could have visited them. I would've refused to go back to Azanir and I know that my future and happiness lies with me finding answers to who I am and why I have these dreams.

'Hello.'

Startled out of my endless thoughts, I notice Roxy for the first time. She is lodged between two crates to my left. 'How long have you been there for?' I ask, really confused by the fact that I didn't scent her.

'You have been staring for a long time and didn't see me,' she giggles.

There are a few humans on deck working and getting some air but I can't see her dad which worries me. 'What are you doing out here alone?'

Her little face falls and I bite my lip to keep from grinning, she is so cute. 'I ran from Daddy because he asked Ethal to do my hair and I hate when people touch my hair. They make it hurt.' She pouts and I hum as I think about how to respond. There's a part of me that wants to go find this Ethal and rip her hair out.

'Who is Ethal?' I ask instead, maybe if I get a description, I'll be able to find her and tell her off.

'She's one of the older ladies that helped Daddy get onto the boat. I think she knew my mummy.' Roxy is brushing her dolls hair, completely unaware of how much she has grabbed my attention. She can't possibly be comfortable crammed in where she is and I'm a little surprised that she listens when I ask her to come and sit next to me.

'And where is your mummy?' I really shouldn't pry but the damn beast is curious.

'She went to the gods because she was sick. Daddy said if I look into the stars I'll be able to talk to my mummy, so I'm going to stay up here all the time.'

Her sad voice makes my heart break and I study the top of her head in shame of asking her to relive that for me. 'Would you like me to do your hair? I promise I won't hurt you,' I say instead and pull her into my lap after asking permission so that I can start untangling the tight ringlets framing her face.

We chat and laugh for hours and when Felix came over to give me a tray of lunch, he didn't say anything at the fact that I have a little human shadow chatting away beside me. He raised an eyebrow, walked back into the stairwell to go back below deck and came back fifteen minutes later with a tray for my new best friend. Roxy was shy at first at being around the Drengar but she slowly got over it.

'Roxy! Rox...' Jason's voice trails off when he gets close and realises that his daughter is having an in depth conversation with an Azanite Drengar as she learns all about the ship. Felix is holding Roxy on the taffrail, pointing at different things.

'She's perfectly safe,' I hurriedly tell him which he seems to hear because he slows his steps and releases a deep breath as if his entire body wasn't functioning while he was looking for his daughter.

'Thank you, Lady.' I stop him quickly before he can bow. 'Sorry,' he chuckles.

We both just end up staring at the pair who are totally oblivious to the fact we're watching them.

'She's a cute kid,' I say and giggle when he tells me how much of a handful she is.

'She's like her mother.' The pain in his tone is sad to hear.

'Roxy told me she was sick and passed away.'

He nods sadly and I pat the space beside me on the deck. I reassure him that he's allowed to sit with me, which earns me another chuckle.

We sit watching Roxy and Felix for a little while.

'Is that why you're headed to Azanir?' I ask him.

'In part. I found out about some distant relatives that lived in a secret place. It was a story in my family and when my wife died and my grandmother told me that it was a family secret and not a story, I started doing my research. It eventually led me to a great aunt and the application to migrate to Azanir. At first I didn't believe it, a magical world where men and women turn to beasts, it sounded like a fantasy movie.'

I can't help but giggle at the idea of learning about Azanir. It would sound like fiction for sure.

'You aren't like any female Azanites they speak about below deck,' James says, shocking me a little.

'What are they saying?' I enquire, only the Sun Gods know what they'd say about me.

'That you don't seem like the others.' He smiles at the eyebrow I have raised in his direction. 'For example, apparently most Azanites don't speak the language of humans, where you seem very at ease around the humans on board.'

I don't reply. I don't know what to say really. They're right, I'm not like other Azanite females.

'The crew didn't expect you either. You weren't on the list. Everyone is really curious about you being here with the Drengar.'

Again, I stay quiet, and I appreciate that James seems to understand that I'm not going to give any information.

I'm happy. I'm on a boat heading to Azanir. A place I never thought I'd ever see again, and I'm happy.

I spend the next few days with Felix and Roxy on the deck playing games and making music with some instrument Felix found us below deck. Even some of the other children on board have joined us. Roxy is always on the deck, even at night, which the Drengar don't like. She is always sent back to her rooms by someone and she always sneaks back up.

James is also a regular source of company and I've enjoyed getting to know him. He reminds me a little of Scott and Brent, and when I'm around him I don't hurt as much from the loss of them.

Wilder and I have spent a great deal of time together too. Most mornings I wake with him curled around me or with our limbs tangled up together under the mountain of blankets I like to sleep with. We even had a moment last night were I thought we'd maybe take the next step in our relationship, but after the lust wore off, we both backed away, readjusted our clothes and took a breath. It was fucking hard. He's gorgeous and talented and powerful and his body...Sun Gods, that body of his is so lickable. Which was part of the reason we got a little too heated last night.

I'm in love with him and it's scary and messy and a little fast. I crave his touch. I crave his mouth and I'm so hot for him, it's hard to breathe.

CHAPTER FIFTY NINE

HUNGRY AND DRIVEN BY my need for food, I decide to not listen to the males who told me to wait for them to finish with their important meeting with the ship's captain and make my way down below deck to the mess.

I walk slowly through the lower levels of the ship, nodding hello to the crew and the handful of humans I pass, who look at me like I'm in my beast form and hurry away. It hurts my feelings and makes me deeply uncomfortable so that when I get to the large doors on the noisy level of the big dining and eating area, I have to give myself a solid pep-talk before pushing my way into the space.

Instantly, the noise dies just like it did the last time I was here with Felix. I refused to come down after that first time. Having made a decision though, I steel my spine and head to the line of humans and ship workers waiting for their dinner.

There are long tables lined up in a row to the right that can easily seat a hundred people and a small section further at the back of the level that is clear of tables like it could be used for more social gatherings.

The left wall is the cafeteria-style buffet and there are a handful of crew spooning from the trays to the waiting passengers. It isn't until I head to the line and pick up a tray from the pile that the place begins to fill will noise. The two humans ahead of me in the line have a hushed conversation and the poor lady looks totally freaked out as the guy next to her passes her their child. I try not to eavesdrop but it's hard when they start to debate what they should do. I stand, waiting, trying to not look bothered or appear intimidating. Yes, I'm taller than every woman on the ship, and nearly half the men, but I can make sure that my energy is positive.

A ship worker comes from nowhere and appears in front of me, a good, safe distance though. He's wearing the uniform that all the crew wear, the difference is the badge on his blazer indicating that he's a high ranking officer. His aging face is covered in sweat and the poor guy looks a bit grey, and I worry for a moment if he might need Wilder's help. The thought evaporates when he opens his mouth and says, 'My Lady, please go to the front of the line and help yourself.' He speaks in Zaric and bows. He blanches at whatever he sees on my face.

I try really, really hard to keep the frustration out of my voice but fail when I say, 'there's no need. I can wait like everyone else.' I speak the human tongue I'm so accustomed to and hear the murmur of whispers around me. I guess I need to get used to the whispers, I'm sure I'll be surrounded by it in Azanir.

I look around and notice the many eyes watching the exchange and contemplate if I should leave.

'Are you sure, Lady? I can make you a plate if you'd like to go back to your room.'

My anger boils and spills over. I have to take a deep steadying breath to keep it in check. 'I'm fine here, unless you're telling me that I should leave.'

'No, My Lady. We just want you to be comfortable.' The guy is dripping in fear and I feel instantly bad.

'Please, I'm fine.' I hope my smile is enough to get him to understand and leave me alone. Which he does after bowing one more time. I can see the apprehension still on his face though and noticed the way his brow rose when I said please.

Fiddling with the tray, I follow the slowly moving line, feeling heartbroken and self-conscious. This entire situation is so triggering.

I just want to fit in.

Spiralling into the pit of pity forming in my chest, I smile to myself when a smooth voice enters my head. *'Astgeer, you are sad.'*

'I'm just thinking.' Speaking to Wilder with my beast is becoming easier by the day. Another example of our growing bond and I wonder for the hundredth time what else will change when we are fully mated.

'I will be done with this meeting soon and then I'll get you food. I can feel your beasts hunger, she is very upset with me.'

I laugh out loud and snap my mouth shut when some of the humans throw apprehensive looks. I don't need them to be thinking that I'm any more of a freak than what I am. My soul doesn't feel so heavy after hearing Wilder's voice. My beast isn't happy with him now that I really focus on it. I did ask for him to come with me to get something to eat before he went to the meeting but Viktor said he needed Wilder for some important reason. I think he didn't want Wilder to go anywhere with me because yesterday we both went to eat lunch on deck when Viktor and Alistair wanted to organise some training exercise. Wilder and I ended up making out for hours and he missed the session. Viktor wasn't too pleased.

I don't get a chance to reply to Wilder because a small body collides with my legs and I look down to see Roxy hugging me. My spirit rises again until I don't feel so bad for myself anymore. 'Hi Raffy!' she squeals, she heard Felix call me that and has picked it up for herself.

'Hey, Rox.' I bend down and give her a proper hug. The collective gasps around us is actually pretty funny and I feel my mood lift further. 'You hungry?' I ask and stand. She worms her little hand into mine and I grasp it firmly. Roxy and I have become good friends and if any of these humans ventured up to the deck they'd know that. Only a handful actually do. I have no idea if it's in fear of the Drengar or the sea or if they've been told they aren't allowed, it's a shame.

'I have dinner with Daddy.' She points toward all the tables and I follow the general direction and catch James watching us. So are a good chunk of other tables, but I ignore them and wave. James throws me a small one back and then he's the centre of attention for a moment. The elderly woman beside him begins to whisper frantically in his ear and I watch as his face falls slightly.

'You have to come sit with us,' Roxy exclaims.

'Okay,' I agree, not wanting to hurt her feelings. She is a ball of excited energy and no one will make me feel bad for being here.

Roxy helps me pick the best food and carries a bottle of water for me as I follow her past watching tables.

'Daddy! Daddy! Raffy is going to eat with me.' Roxy's voice bounces off every wall of the mess deck. I try not to look at everyone as I walk down the aisle of long benches to where her dad sits.

Roxy is so excited that she nearly falls when she sits on the vacant spot in front of her dinner. I catch her easily and nod when James thanks me. He was half off his seat as if ready to catch her.

'May I join you both?' I ask and smile wide when James invites me to sit.

I hesitate with my tray though and there is a moment of pause as the humans sitting around Roxy look to each other and then move down on the long bench seat. My thanks is met with awkward glances.

James doesn't sit back down until I do and I appreciate the smile he gifts me when I finally get comfortable. Roxy helps. She talks and talks and tries to share her meal with me.

Eventually everyone around me begins chatting again and I finally relax enough to enjoy my meal with James chatting away. He is hilarious. I laugh loudly when he tells me what happened last night when Roxy was found on the deck again. Felix apparently walked her back to their sleeping cabin and scared pretty much every person on the ship. Well, all except Roxy who idolises the Drengar.

CHAPTER SIXTY

I WAKE SCREAMING AND sit up in the bed holding my chest, afraid that my heart is about to explode. The dream was terrible. There was a horrible, violent storm, and Roxy...Tears still stream down my face at memory of watching her little body disappear over the edge of the ship into the darkness.

Confused, my sleep muddled mind takes too long to process why I don't feel right and I blink at the walls of the cabin and watch as the room tilts dramatically from one side to the other, bending forward and back. I almost crack my head on the backboard of the bed in the next dip the ship does and I finally become aware of the siren blaring through the loudspeaker attached to the far wall. I fell asleep on my own and none of the Drengar are here in the room with me.

I hear the crack of lightning and the entire ship vibrates with the booming thunder that shakes my bones, and then it hits me...it's storming.

'No,' I shout and jump out of bed. Yanking the door to the cabin open, I run down the short corridor that links to the main deck. My shorts and singlet are not nearly enough clothing for the onslaught of rain and wind that hits me when I open it.

I have to close my eyes at the intensity of the rain that slams into my body. It hits with such force that it hurts.

The madness is what I see first. The absolute chaos of crewmates running this way and that, trying to secure the sails and items down. I hear shouting and shrieking and almost lose my dinner at the creaking-crack the boat makes as it rocks violently under the force of the waves. Waves that rise up in front of us like a wall of darkness, takes our ship and flings it around. I hurry out onto the deck, slipping and stumbling as I go.

Frantically looking for the Drengar in the darkness of the night, I see nothing but panicking humans. The captain is screaming instructions that get eaten up by the wind. The siren is blaring through the night and with my heart in my throat, I feel everything slip away when I recognise the scene before me. I have dreamt this and I realise that I've witness this all before. Many times. In many dreams. I've just only seen the ending. It's a realisation that has me shaking.

A sailor slips and slams into a stack of boxes. My stomach drops. Another sailor nearly collides into me before he rolls and gets to his feet and hurries off to do his job, I feel the colour drain from my face.

All the same order. All the same madness and chaos. I don't feel the storm anymore. My body is numb to the reality of my situation. I'm very aware of how this will end for me. I slowly turn, my breathing the only noise I can hear, and look over at the bow of the ship and see the mass of orange curls.

Brown, scared eyes slam into mine and I react too slowly. My scream is drowned out and I take off running, but I'm too late. I scream and shriek and shout for Roxy to stay where she is. She can't hear.

Roxy stands from her hiding spot and the moment she does the ship takes a huge hit from the right, sending me flying into the rails with a crack.

My body explodes in pain but none of that matters as I watch Roxy topple over the side of the ship and into the dark, violent waters below.

I take off after her. My name erupts into the night and in my head, causing it to ache. I can't see the Drengar, but I hear them. I hear Wilder demanding that I stop. With one final glance over my shoulder, I see the male who has stolen my heart standing up on the captain's deck and I commit his face to memory. *'I'm sorry, I love you,'* I say in my mind and then jump overboard.

The water is freezing and the shock of it has me nearly taking a breath underwater. I have no time to consider the damage or what I'm doing. I see Roxy bobbing up and down not too far away and I swim with every last bit of energy that I have.

The ocean is unforgiving and relentless. I lose her three times before I find her sinking and only get to her in time to lift her up into my arms because my beast is helping.

Crushing Roxy to my chest, I try to focus enough to work out if she is breathing but it's too hard. Keeping us both above water is impossible.

My head slips under the surface multiple times and I pray to every Sun God to help me. To save Roxy. I know what my fate is. I have dreamt this before, but not the little, sweet girl that makes me laugh.

I can't see the ship. I can't see anything. No one will be able to find us in this storm. I try to shout in my mind. To connect with Wilder but I'm so panicked that I can't focus enough.

'Please,' I splutter, afraid that the water will take Roxy away. I cough and spit liquid from my mouth. Roxy is so heavy. A complete dead weight. 'Please,' I say to no one, completely lost, frightened and alone.

That's when I feel her. When the voice in my head whispers to me that she has us, if only I let her take control. It's a voice I've heard my entire life.

'*I don't know how to,*' I reply. Completely sure that I've lost my mind but the voice tells me to just give her permission. '*I give permission,*' I say and scream when my body burns up, a fire deep inside me erupts and I throw my head back and make a noise that I didn't know I was capable of. The thunderous roar fills the night, vibrating within my body as energy flows through me, giving me what I need to stay afloat and fight the relentless wave.

The darkness isn't so dark and I weep when I hear the answering call of multiple beasts. One particular booming roar seems to respond and I know that the Drengar are coming. That Wilder is close, that he heard my call for help.

The beast under my skin isn't strong enough to keep us both above water for long and I end up making a decision that'll save Roxy, and I find myself okay with it.

Sinking, I use the last of my energy to lift the small girl up, keeping her free of the deadly water and pray that the males hurry. As darkness pushes in around my body and I feel myself losing the battle to take a breath, I hold onto life as long as I can, only aware of the weight of the child being taken off me in the back of my mind because I have no more fight left.

I sink. Suspended in darkness and know that this is it. There's a peace in dying.

I know that I've made some poor decisions and that my biggest regret is not telling my family that I love them more and not giving myself to Wilder fully. Though, none of that seems to matter.

I sink further into the deep, knowing that I've died saving a life, and I'm okay with that.

I'm okay...limbs heavy and darkness thickening, I see a flash of lightning come from above and watch as a mighty mass covers the sky. It has my attention as my thoughts drift.

My eyes close and then fly open when I feel it.

I feel the claws wrap around my body, the heat of it shocking me into consciousness, and I suck in breath and cough and spatter when I'm pulled roughly from the ocean's embrace.

'Breathe, Astgeer. That's it. Take a breath.'

'Wilder?' I whimper, my body rejecting the water filling my lungs violently onto his paw.

'You're safe.'

The wind is hard against my cold body as we fly through the night sky. High enough so that the waves are safely below us.

I begin to shiver and hold my breath when Wilders beast moves the paw I'm sitting on up towards his chest and keeps me close to his magnificent body. I'm surrounded by his heat instantly. It chases the cold from my veins, giving me enough brain power to really register what's happening.

Taking in my surroundings, I look to my left and see the row of beasts. Mighty animals of the sky. Alistair. Viktor and Felix. Their colouring is magnificent. Their wings beat with power. It's Felix who has the small child clutched in his mighty paw against his chest and I breathe a sigh of relief.

'You saved her. And you will never, ever, do that to me again!' Wilder demands and I smile to myself and snuggle in closer to his body. *'I'm being serious.'* I can hear the beast in his tone, he's definitely not happy. However,

I can also feel his relief and the healing energy he's sending through my body.

'I know,' I say, placating him, and he knows it, because his entire body vibrates against me as he growls. It makes me chuckle. 'You saved me. Thank you. I was supposed to die. I dreamt that was how I died and you saved me.'

The underside of his beast is thick, smooth black skin and I look up when he cranes his long neck so that I can see him fully.

'If you die, I die. A dragon cannot live without his mate and you are mine, Serafina DarkwoodsAzar. My wings will never work without you.'

Lost in eyes of red fire, I take in the black, shiny scales that reflect the light flashing below us with the storm. The massive snout and rows of teeth. I watch his nostrils flare and I pull in his scent at the same time he does it to me. Those eyes are locked on my face and while I can't see his wings from here, I can feel the power of them as he flies us to safety.

He is beautiful. Absolutely breathtaking.

The dragon shifter and the male.

I know that no matter what is going to happen when we reach Azanir, I am going to learn more about who I am. I'm going to find the answers to the visions the sacred text showed me about our race, help save my people and I'm going to complete the bond with my mate.

I'm no longer the lost Lady of the Darkwoods.

I am Serafina DarkwoodsAzar, a human and an Azanite. The beast under my skin is a dragon and I will discover and claim my own power once I reach Azanir.

BOOK TWO OF THE

SHIFTERS OF AZANIR SERIES

COMING SOON

ABOUT THE AUTHOR

A L Rojo is an author, educator, wife and mother who lives in Sydney, Australia. From a young age, she understood the power of getting lost in a good book. After giving herself permission to explore her creativity, she found that she loved writing novels that focus on strong female characters, love, spice, and the wonderful complexities of life. Her goal is to simply create worlds where anyone can escape into, for however long they may need. She says that along this journey she has left behind a piece of herself in every character she creates.

To get the latest updates, follow A L Rojo on:

Website: www.alrojo.com.au
Facebook: A L Rojo
Instagram: alrojo_writer